BLEEDING THE SUN

A WWII NOVEL

CHRIS GLATTE

CONTENTS

Prologue   1
Chapter 1   9
Chapter 2   22
Chapter 3   39
Chapter 4   51
Chapter 5   61
Chapter 6   73
Chapter 7   83
Chapter 8   89
Chapter 9   96
Chapter 10   106
Chapter 11   113
Chapter 12   121
Chapter 13   132
Chapter 14   143
Chapter 15   150
Chapter 16   160
Chapter 17   166
Chapter 18   182
Chapter 19   197
Chapter 20   214
Chapter 21   227
Chapter 22   234

Afterword   243
Also by Chris Glatte   245

PROLOGUE

Sam Santos woke to the sounds of his Grandmother, Lola stoking the cooking fire in the middle of the room. It was dark, the sunrise hours away. Sam flung the thin sheet off his body and swung his bare feet to the hard, dirt packed floor. He rubbed his eyes and stared into the gloom. He could hear the soft snores of his older brother, Berto. Sam reached across the short distance and slapped his brother's shoulder. The snoring stopped but Berto rolled away and groaned.

Sam heard his younger sister, Yelina stirring. "Good morning, Yelina."

A small voice spoke from the darkness. "Good morning, Sammy."

The sound of their grandmother shutting the clay door of the stove reminded Sam of his morning chores. He smacked his brother again, pulled back the thin sheet that acted as a wall, and saw his grandmother's face glowing in the firelight filtering through the stove slats. Her face was old and wrinkled, but when she saw her grandson she smiled and the wrinkles turned to deep smile lines. "Good morning my lazy grandson."

It was the same greeting every morning. No matter how early he woke, his grandmother was always awake before him. "Good morning, Lola." He stepped forward and held his hands out to the glowing stove. "It's cold this morning."

She waved as if it was nothing. "Work will warm you. We need more wood. I need it hot for the water."

He nodded and extended his hands for one more warming. He pushed the rickety wooden door open and it creaked and moaned on rusty hinges. He'd found the hinges amongst the rubble of a burned down house a few months before. He'd only found a few screws, but it was enough to provide a working door.

The family that owned the burned house hadn't been seen since the night of the fire. Everyone knew their probable fate. They'd been a part of the Filipino resistance and the Japanese weren't known for their mercy.

Sam took in the night smells. Theirs wasn't the only cooking fire. It was dark outside and he waited for his eyes to adjust. The Japanese had strict rules about light discipline. He wondered if he'd ever see Cebu City lit up again.

The Japanese occupation began three years ago, but it seemed like a lifetime. He could barely remember how the city looked under the lights, but remembered it was beautiful.

An hour later the Santos family huddled around the stove eating dismal portions of rice and fish from steel bowls. It didn't take long before the food was gone. Sam scraped the bowl and tilted it to his mouth, coaxing every last morsel.

"Don't be crude," Berto said. He scooped his remaining crumbs. "We're lucky we have as much food as we do." Sam rolled his eyes. Berto flushed. "You're ungrateful. My job allows our family more food. You should be thanking me, not rolling your eyes."

Sam looked at Grandmother Lola who was staring into the flickering flames, then back to Berto. Sam said, "You're going to get us killed. People talk about our family as if we're *all* collaborators."

Berto put his bowl on the floor and stood. He pointed at his brother. "You watch your mouth. Who's threatened us? I'll make them pay. Give me a name. The Japanese will reward us for rooting out resistance fighters."

Sam stood. He came to Berto's chin. "That's the kind of thing that'll get us killed. Can't you see the Japanese are losing? What happens when they're gone? What happens to us, our family? They won't only punish you, but all of us."

Berto gritted his teeth and spoke through them. "You watch your mouth. The Japanese will win, and once they do, they'll reward us with a good piece of land, just like they promised."

Sam shook his head and was about to continue when Grandmother Lola's soft voice pierced the tense air. "Stop this talk. Both of you." The arguing stopped and the only sound was the crackle and popping of the fire. "This war will end." She remained squatting in front of the fire. She opened the clay door and poked the fire with a metal poker. She nodded. "All wars end."

ONCE THE CHORES WERE DONE, Sam watched Berto getting ready to leave. He was putting on a fresh shirt. Everyone working with the Japanese were required to wear the beige button-down shirts.

When Berto first donned it, he'd been nervous about his decision to collaborate. Now, three years later he wore it like a shiny medal. He liked the fear his presence evoked when he entered a room. The shirt marked him as someone of power and influence.

He lifted his chin and saw Sam watching him. "It's time you joined. You're old enough. You can do what you want. You don't need to be led by the nose by Grandmother."

Sam shook his head. "I'll never join the Makapili." His face flushed as soon as he'd uttered the derogatory term.

Berto's jaw clenched and he reared back and hit Sam. "Don't you dare use that term. We're patriots."

Sam deflected the blow, but pretended the punch hurt him. He whimpered and cowered. "Sorry, it slipped out."

Berto leaned close. "I'm going to recommend you to the Kempei Tei. They're always looking for new recruits. They'll come by today for your indoctrination." Without a glance back, Berto strode from the shack. The door slammed and nearly broke from the hinges.

Sam stood and saw his sister watching from the corner. In her soft, song-like voice she asked, "Why did you let him hit you?"

Sam shrugged. "It's easier. He's stronger and won't stop until he thinks he's hurt me."

"Do you think he'll be coming back with the Kempei Tei?" She had trouble pronouncing the words.

Sam thought about it for a second then shook his head. "I think he was trying to scare me. He wouldn't do that."

"What if he does?"

Sam laughed. "They'll have to deal with Grandmother first. I fear for the Japanese if they tried to do anything against her will." Yelina smiled and laughed. Sam put his arm around his sister's small shoulders. "Don't worry, little one."

THE JAPANESE CAME JUST before lunch. Sam had returned from the jungle near the sea with a bag of snails. The Japanese didn't allow Filipinos to fish for themselves, so he'd taken to foraging through the jungle in search of edibles. He'd found a good stash of snails that day and was looking forward to showing them to Grandmother Lola.

He'd just plopped the bag in front of his grandmother when there was a loud knock, and in broken Tagalog, "Open the door."

Sam's knees felt weak as he realized his brother hadn't been trying to scare him. He'd sent the Japanese.

Grandmother Lola stared at the door. There was another loud knock and Sam moved to open it, but she held out her hand. "Stay put. I'll deal with them."

She shuffled to the door and mumbled, "Coming." She opened the door and stood facing a squat Japanese soldier. He was young and his scowl made him look cruel. He stepped away from the door and took up position beside it, like a guard. The Japanese behind him was dressed in the black of the hated Kempei Tei secret police. He was taller and older.

He stepped forward and gave a slight bow. Grandmother Lola returned the courtesy but didn't move from the doorway. In near perfect Tagalog he said, "Good afternoon. I'm here to speak with your youngest son, Sam."

Grandmother Lola shook her head. "I know why you're here and I won't allow you to take him. You already have one grandson. You don't need both. I am old and need his help."

Sam held his breath wondering where his grandmother got the courage to deny a Kempei Tei officer. There was a long pause. Grandmother Lola kept her gaze slightly down, but her strong stance didn't falter.

The officer chuckled. The sound made Sam nauseous. The officer continued. "I have heard good things about your son. I'm in need of his skills. We'll increase your rations and give you an even larger piece of land once this war's over. Your family will be considered heroes." He smiled and gestured into the shack. "And you still have your lovely daughter to help around the house."

The mention of Yelina made Sam pull her behind his back. He'd heard what the Japanese did to young Filipino girls, turning them into comfort women for their troops. Everyone knew it meant a life of rape and an early death.

Keeping her gaze lowered, Grandmother Lola gave a slight shake of her head. "You've already taken their parents. We have heard nothing of them these long years. I was put in charge of the children; my grandchildren. You won't have more from us."

The smile disappeared from the officer's face. His hard eyes turned to black, stony orbs; bottomless and full of hatred. "You dare say no to me?" His gaze drilled into her. "You're wasting my time. There will be no more discussion. Either he comes willingly or we drag him. Either way, he's coming with us."

Sam looked to his grandmother. She hadn't wavered, her feet still firmly planted as if she'd grown roots. Sam had no choice, he stepped forward and put his hand on his grandmother's shoulder. "It's okay. I'll go." He felt her shoulder tremble, but she didn't move. She shook her head.

The Kempei Tei officer reached out and pushed her aside. She fell to the floor and Sam reached out, exposing his sister. The Kempei Tei stepped over them and reached for Yelina. He grasped her thin arm and shook. She screamed and tried to break away, but his grip was too strong. He leered and leaned close. Yelina's nose crinkled in disgust. "Aren't you a pretty thing? Your brother, Berto didn't mention you."

Sam stood, turned to the officer and without thinking pushed him away from Yelina. "Take your hands off her," he yelled.

Sam was immediately grabbed from behind by the accompanying soldiers. He was dragged toward the door, but he pulled away and went back for the officer. He threw himself at the officer. He heard his grandmother yell, 'no,' but he was committed. The thought of this disgusting man touching his sweet Yelina, sent him into a rage. He smashed into the officer and they both went to the ground. Sam was no stranger to violence; the city streets were filled with it. He punched the officer and blood spurted from his lip where his fist mashed it into his teeth.

He only got one punch in before the soldier recovered and yanked him off the officer by his hair. Sam reached back for the new threat, but the soldier was strong and lifted his light frame off the ground. Sam kicked and grunted but was soon thrown outside in the dirt.

He heard his grandmother yelling. He glimpsed her through the dim light. She was hitting the officer with ineffective fists. As if in slow motion, he watched as the officer pushed her away, unholstered his sidearm and aimed. Sam sprang up but fell back with the blast of the pistol.

All sound ceased as he watched his grandmother sway, then fall as if her puppet strings were cut. The world focused down to her face. Her staring eyes, normally full of laughter and depth were suddenly masked with a thin film of milky-white. She was gone.

Yelina's scream jolted him back. She lunged onto Grandmother Lola's body and prodded her as if trying to wake her from a deep sleep. The sight broke his heart. He felt all joy and light leave his world as if the entire cast of a play suddenly walked out in the middle of a masterful performance. He was numb and confused.

Yelina was lifted off the body by her hair. The grinning officer held her as she kicked and screamed. The officer's teeth were stained with his own blood, making his visage even more sinister. He threw Yelina out the door and Sam reached out and caught her. He held her tight, trying to squeeze the ugly memories from her soul. She sobbed into his shoulder. He whispered into her ear, "Be strong, little one. Be strong."

The words calmed her, she relaxed slightly in his embrace, but the moment passed when she was ripped from his arms by the officer. Sam reached for her but she was thrust toward the soldiers. She struggled but they held her tight.

The officer crouched in front of Sam and pulled out a white hand-kerchief. He wiped his pistol and the kerchief came away red. He folded it and used the clean side to dab his lip. He looked at the blood then back to Sam. "Your Lola will rot and your sister will please many soldiers." He leered, "I will break her in myself. Teach her how to be a good whore."

Sam lunged for his throat, but the nearest soldier restrained him with an iron grip. The officer smiled, but it didn't travel to his eyes. "You are strong willed. We can use your strength on the work crews. You can follow in your parents' footsteps." He paused as Sam focused. It was the first he'd heard anything about his parents.

"Hopefully you'll last longer than they did."

1

May 20, 1944

～

PLATOON SERGEANT CARVER shook himself awake. He looked around the dark room trying to figure out where he was. He wiped the beads of sweat from his brow and felt for his Thompson submachine gun, but it wasn't there. He searched everywhere in the darkness, his panic rising in his gut like a cancer.

He heard the wind racing through palm boughs. He smelled the rot of nearby jungle, mixed with the antiseptic stench of a hospital. It raced back to him. He took a deep breath, feeling the ache in his left leg. He remembered. He was in a rear area hospital far away from the front lines. He was safe, but he yearned for his weapon, like a drunk yearns for his wine. But like a recovering drunk, he knew it wasn't allowed. Against hospital rules.

He leaned back on his sweat soaked pillow and stared up at the thatch roof. He couldn't see it, but he knew there was a lazily spinning fan above him, shifting the fetid air. He closed his eyes, trying to remember the dream. It was combat, shooting, screaming, dying, but what seemed so real was now a faded memory he couldn't bring into focus.

He knew sleep wouldn't return and the thought of another nightmare, even one unremembered, made him want to stay awake. He swung his legs off the cot and placed his bare feet on the floor. He winced as the blood flowed to his injured left leg. The doctor said he got most of the shrapnel out, but there was nerve damage and he'd probably always feel some degree of pain. The trick now was to heal the muscle. To become strong enough to return to his unit.

He reached for the bedside light and pulled the short chain. The soft glow illuminated the area around him. He could see other nearby cots. There were soft snores mixed with moans and thrashing from other dreamers. No matter how far behind friendly lines, these men were never free from their memories and dreams.

Carver's dreams had gotten worse the more time he spent in the hospital. On the line, dreams were a luxury. Sleep never truly came when death lurked only feet away.

He rubbed his leg, massaging more blood into it. He leaned forward, took a deep breath and stood. Fresh sweat broke out on his forehead as the pain raced through his body. He kept most of his weight on his right leg, slowly transferring more and more to his left.

Once the pain equalized, He tried to take a step with his left leg, but it was too much too fast and he collapsed with an involuntary yell. The crash of his body hitting the floor brought the nurse, Lieutenant Lilly James running from her metal desk near the front door.

She got there in time to see Platoon Sergeant Carver pulling himself back onto his cot. She took in the scene and put her hands on her hips and glared. Her dark curls had escaped her bun and fell around her face and shoulders. She blew out the side of her mouth sending the nearest curl blowing. "Sergeant Carver, what on earth are you trying to prove?" He squinted up at her and she continued, "When are you going to remember to use your cane?"

In his gruff voice he answered. "I'm not a damned cripple. I have to push or I won't heal. You've said so yourself, ma'am."

She crossed her arms over her full breasts. "Not if it means hurting yourself worse. There's a difference between pushing yourself and killing yourself. You need to be realistic. Your injuries need time to heal." She shook her head. "How many times have we been over this?"

He nodded. "Plenty. I couldn't sleep."

Her hard glare turned soft. "Nightmares?" He rubbed his eyes and nodded. She reached out and put a hand on his bare shoulder. "You're certainly not alone in that."

The feel of her bare hand on his skin sent heat through his body. He tried to ignore it. He looked into her hazel eyes and nodded. "I know. That's why I need to get out of here. To end the nightmares. They don't happen on the front."

She shook her head. "I'm no doctor, but that's the stupidest logic I've ever heard." She took her hand off his shoulder and he felt suddenly empty. She handed him his cane and he swiped at it but held it. "Let's go on a walk."

He leaned on the cane and stood, feeling the pain lance through him again. He didn't wince in front of Nurse Lilly. Instead, he flexed and did a short knee bend. "I think it's getting better. When's the doc coming to evaluate my progress, ma'am?"

"Captain Shane will be here this morning, and for the tenth time, call me Lilly." She stood straighter when she spoke Captain Shane's name and Carver wondered if she had a thing for him. Anger coursed through him at the thought. The anger confused him. *Have to stay focused on the mission. I don't have time for this horseshit.*

"That means I'll need to be up working till he gets here. I'm stiff in the morning, but I'll pass today."

She shook her head, "You just fell over. You'd be a liability to those GIs you're always talking about." She put her hand on her right hip and extended it, giving him a pouty look. "You trying to get away from me Sergeant?"

He grinned. "You're not a very good actress, Nurse Lilly."

She smiled, but her face hardened. He thought she looked beautiful. "You see right through me, soldier boy."

He smiled liking the way she talked. "Let's get this show on the road."

~

PLATOON SERGEANT CARVER FELT GOOD. HE' been walking all morning
using his cane. After lunch, he tried walking around without the cane
and was happy with the results. He hoped he'd pass his weekly evaluation and be sent back to his unit.

He pored over every piece of news he could find about the war. He
hadn't heard the 'Americal' Division mentioned in any news which
didn't necessarily mean anything. He'd gotten a letter from now
Sergeant O'Connor, which had miraculously found him amongst the
hundreds of wounded. The 164th Regiment had moved off
Bougainville Island, but O'Connor didn't have a clue as to their next
mission. Even if he had, the censors wouldn't have allowed him to
relay the information if he'd been dumb enough to try. All Carver
knew was his men weren't in combat operations as of two months ago.

When he'd first been carted off Bougainville, he'd spent a week on
a hospital ship, then been offloaded to New Britain Island. His leg
wound kept him from walking during the boat ride, but he knew they
were moving north. It felt odd to be steaming closer to the enemy, but
not as a combatant.

Once on the island, he'd toured the grounds of the mobile hospital
extensively. First via wheelchair, pushed by other convalescing GIs,
then on his own two feet with the help of his cane.

He'd seen his share of islands and this one didn't seem better or
worse. The Japanese had been pushed off, but it still smelled of death
and rot. He doubted the smells would ever leave his senses.

Soon it was evening and Carver anxiously awaited the doctor's
visit. His first doctor, a good natured, but overworked, Major had
rotated home. At first, the major hadn't been optimistic about Carver's
idea of going back to his unit.

The leg wound was infected and it took the entire first month to
beat it. After many fever-ridden days and nights, he'd gotten through
the worst of it, but he was left weak. He'd pushed himself, making
gains even the major was impressed with.

Now he'd deal with the major's replacement, Captain Shane. He'd
seen the tall, athletic captain making rounds the day before. He'd stood

in front of Carver's gurney and barely looked at him. Instead the captain concentrated on the clipboard with the chart attached and snuck glances at Nurse Lilly's ample cleavage. He'd barely given Carver the time of day. He hoped today he'd give him a clean bill of health and send him back to Able Company.

While Carver waited, he sat on the bed extending and flexing his legs until they ached. Sweat rolled off his forehead as if he'd run a marathon.

Finally, he saw the captain throw back the thatch door and enter the ward. His frame was well over six feet tall and he had to duck as he entered. He stopped, letting his eyes adjust to the light. Nurse Lilly sprang from her desk, fixed her skirt and saluted. Pleasantries were exchanged and Carver strained to hear what was said. He couldn't help feeling a wave of anger sweep over him as he watched them talk. He shook his head, trying to stay focused on the task at hand.

Carver saw Lilly hand Captain Shane a chart and she pointed at Carver. Carver brushed the sweat from his face with a nearby rag and stood. He could feel his leg aching, but overall, it felt good today.

Carver snapped off a crisp salute as the captain approached and he returned it with a touch of his brow. Shane looked at the chart then back at Carver. "Hello, Platoon Sergeant. How you feeling?"

"I'm feeling fine, sir. Ready to return to my unit."

The captain nodded and looked at the chart, seeming to study it intently. He pointed at Carver's leg. "Your leg was busted up pretty bad and you suffered a long infection. You're lucky you didn't lose it." Carver nodded but didn't reply. Captain Shane continued. "Nurse Lilly tells me you've been working hard…sometimes too hard."

Carver glanced at Lilly and she dropped her eyes slightly. "I'm motivated to get back to my unit before they deploy again."

Captain Shane shook his head. "There's no guarantee you'll return to your unit, especially if they've already deployed. You know that, right?"

Carver nodded. "That's why I want to get back now, before they deploy, sir." He tapped his leg. "I'm good to go, sir."

Captain Shane shook his head. "As you well know, combat requires every ounce a man can give. You're making great progress, but you're not ready. Not yet. I'm recommending another month of rehabilitation." Carver's jaw flexed as he gritted his teeth. Captain Shane continued. "I know you're disappointed, but my word's final."

Shane turned to leave, but Carver raised his voice. "I'm ready now, sir. You've gotta let me outta here. My men need me."

Shane handed the clipboard to Nurse Lilly. She gave Carver a slight shake of her head. Carver ignored it and was about to press the issue when Captain Shane pointed down the aisle leading to the exit. "Combat requires sprinting. You think you can sprint to the exit?"

By now the rest of the wounded GIs were paying attention. Those that could, stood or propped themselves to see better. Someone called, "You can do it Sarge."

Carver estimated the distance at thirty yards. Sweat beaded on his forehead as he thought of the pounding his leg would take.

Without another thought he moved to the aisle and took a deep breath, willing strength into his limbs. Lilly reached out to stop him, but he evaded her touch and took off. He made it ten yards before the pain lancing through his body caused him to step wrong and his left leg collapsed, sending him sprawling into the row of beds. The cheering GIs went silent as they watched Carver pick himself off the floor.

Nurse Lilly ran to his side and reached down to help him. He tried to push her away, but she only gripped harder. He felt her iron grip on his bicep and he couldn't help flexing. *Who am I trying to impress?*

She helped him get steady as Captain Shane approached. "Another month, Sergeant." He slapped the chart into Nurse Lilly's free hand and said. "I'd like to see you at your desk, nurse."

Lilly nodded, and watched him pass. She leaned into Carver's ear. He could feel her soft, hot breath. It sent shivers up his spine. She said, "I'm proud of you, Sergeant." He looked into her hazel eyes and for an instant, time stopped. Captain Shane called and broke the trance. She released her grip and pulled away. Carver felt empty as her presence faded. He watched her go, taking in her shapely butt and her tapered waist. The Army uniform couldn't contain her shapeliness. Just before she got to Captain Shane she looked back and saw him staring. She smiled and quickly turned away.

THE NEXT DAY, Carver lay on his bed thinking about his failure. His leg ached more than usual. He knew the captain was correct in his assessment, but Carver couldn't help feeling resentment. He'd purposely humiliated him in front of the other wounded men and in front of Nurse Lilly.

The day was like every other day on the island, sunny and hot. He seethed as he thought about the smug look on the captain's face.

He was lost in thought when he noticed Nurse Lilly standing beside him. He pulled himself from his self-pity and sat up. "What? Did you say something?"

She smiled and her eyes lit up. "I was wondering why you weren't up working out. It's not like you to lay in bed all day."

He took a deep breath and let it out. "Just remembering my failure yesterday."

She shook her head and her eyes went cold. "Never took you for a quitter."

He sat up in bed and narrowed his eyes. "Never said anything about quitting."

She reached her hand out. "Then take my hand and let's get after it, Sergeant." He gripped her hand and stood. The blood surging to his leg made his head swim, but he ignored it and took a step. He wobbled and she handed him his cane. He shook his head. "I'll go without it for awhile if it's all the same to you."

Nurse Lilly took his rehab as a personal mission, pushing him to do more every day. Soon the work started to show. He no longer needed a cane and his limp was getting less and less noticeable.

After one grueling day of work, Lilly sat on the cot beside him and asked, "Why haven't you asked me out on a date, Sergeant?" Carver nearly fell over. He stared at her until she finally looked away. She continued, "Am I too forward?" He stammered but couldn't respond. Her hazel eyes burned into him. "I can't wait any longer so I'm taking matters into my own hands. I've seen the way you look at me." His face turned red and he looked at his feet. She leaned forward and whispered, "I like it."

She reached for his face and stroked it as he looked into her eyes. Most of the other men were in the chow hall. The only wounded in the room, too badly damaged to notice their interlude. He was lost in her gaze. He reached for her face and her skin was smooth and warm.

She broke the trance. She pulled away and gave him a radiant smile. "There's a movie playing at the outdoor theater. I'll meet you there." He only nodded.

CARVER GOT to the outdoor movie theater forty-minutes early. He'd shaved, borrowed some aftershave and worn his least faded uniform. He wore his hat at an angle and paced. He felt nervous pinpricks of sweat threatening to ruin his undershirt.

He'd spent a lot of time with Nurse Lilly, but only in a professional setting. She'd pushed him and helped him achieve his rehabilitation goals. Of course, he'd noticed her shapely body and flowing, thick dark hair, but he'd tried to push his growing feelings away. He was a soldier fighting a bloody war he'd likely not survive. The last thing he needed was a romance...or was it? He could be sent to the front tomorrow and killed. Wasn't it better to live for today?

He didn't ponder the question too long. The feelings that coursed through his body when she'd touched his face was all he could think about. Her smell, feminine but tainted with a tinge of sweat made his head spin. She wasn't the most petite or pretty nurse on base, but to him she was the most beautiful woman he'd ever seen, and somehow, she was interested in him.

She arrived ten minutes early and Carver marveled at her beauty. He'd never seen her with makeup, and her hair was normally tied up in a tight bun. Now it flowed over her shoulders like a chocolate waterfall. He couldn't help staring.

She looked him in the eye and smiled. "Well, you gonna spend the whole night gawking, or are we going to the movie?"

He reached out and she took his hand. There were other movie-goers streaming past them, but Carver stood like a rock in a fast river. "You're the most beautiful woman I've ever seen."

At first, she looked at her shoes, then deep into his eyes. "I didn't really wanna watch the movie anyway." She pulled him off to the side and he pulled her into his arms. He bent forward and tasted her thick lips. His body was on fire and the next thing he knew she was dragging him back to her tent. They stopped to kiss multiple times. Each interlude pushing his lust higher and higher until he thought he'd burst.

As she pulled back the tent flap, she looked for any roommates. It was empty. In a husky voice full of passion, she said, "We've got a few hours till the girls get back." They collapsed onto her cot and the next few hours were the most memorable of their lives.

THE NEXT THREE weeks were the happiest of Platoon Sergeant Carver's life. Every morning they woke up early and left their love nest. They couldn't sleep together in Lilly's tent, nor on Carver's cot, so they'd borrowed a hammock and strung it in the jungle far enough away so no one would hear their passionate lovemaking.

Every morning, before light they'd stumble into their respective sleeping quarters and pretend nothing out of the ordinary was happening. Of course, they weren't fooling anyone, and there was good-natured ribbing from the other nurses and GIs.

Carver was still committed to his goal of returning to combat, but his motivation had waned since meeting Lilly. He devoured any war news he could get his hands on. As far as he could tell the allied advance toward Japan moved steadily forward. He hadn't heard from Sergeant O'Connor, or anyone else from his unit, nor had he heard the Americal Division being mentioned in any stories.

His leg improved every day. Soon he was able to jog and even run. He felt like a new man.

A month after becoming romantically involved with Lilly he returned to his bunk and saw Captain Shane waiting for him. Carver braced and saluted. Shane returned the salute. "It's time for your next evaluation, Sergeant. I've been noticing your progress and want to get you back to your unit as quickly as possible." When Carver didn't react, Captain Shane said, "I thought you'd be happy. I'm getting you back to your unit early"

Carver nodded. "Yes sir. I appreciate that very much. It's just a surprise is all. Kind of getting used to things around here." He saw Nurse Lilly doing her rounds. She threw a worried glance his way.

Captain Shane noticed the exchange. He flushed and cleared his throat. "You know relationships between enlisted men and officers are strictly forbidden."

Carver tore his eyes away from Nurse Lilly. "Yes sir, of course."

Shane leaned in close, "I'll be back tomorrow morning." He leered. "Don't worry, I'll take good care of Lieutenant James."

Carver turned beet red and his eyes went to slits. He balled his fists and was about to strike when Lilly appeared beside him and put her hand on his tense shoulder. With steady pressure she pushed him back until he was against his cot. She stood between Captain Shane and the Platoon Sergeant.

Shane looked surprised at her sudden appearance. "Lieutenant James, I was just reminding the sergeant of the strict penalties for becoming romantically involved with an officer." He looked her up and down, like he was sizing up a piece of choice meat. "Of course, there's no regulation between two officers."

Lilly could feel Carver's entire body tensing. With her back still to him, she held him steady, pushing back with her arms. "I'm sure we're all well aware of the regulations, Captain." She gave him a slight smile. "I'm sure I'd be happy to discuss your unwanted advances to General Shumacher."

It was Shane's turn to turn beet red. "Why you little whore," he spit.

There was no stopping Carver, he lunged past Lilly and tackled Shane to the ground. He ended up straddling the bigger man. He punched him and Captain Shane's nose spurted blood as it smashed flat against his face. He saw stars and his vision dimmed. Carver was about to land another punch when he was tackled from the side by two GIs.

Some of the men in the ward hobbled from their cots and blocked the entrance, while the rest clustered around the bleeding Captain

Shane. There was a ruckus from the front where guards were trying to force their way past the GIs.

Lieutenant James knew she had to act fast to save Carver from spending the remainder of the war in Leavenworth Prison. Captain Shane was spluttering and holding his nose. "You'll pay. You'll pay, you son-of-a-bitch."

Lilly straddled Shane and grabbed his bloody chin, forcing him to look her in the eyes. She leaned close. "You listen to me Captain. Not one of these men will corroborate your story." She let her words sink in. "Including me. It'll be your word against every GI in here. You fell and hit your nose. Understand?" She didn't wait for him to nod. She hesitated for a moment then continued. "You'll pass Platoon Sergeant Carver for combat duty tomorrow and you'll never see him again."

Captain Shane shook his head, but she leaned in closer. "If you don't do as I say, I'll tell the General you tried to rape me."

He shook his head. "That's a lie." His voice had a distinctive nasal tone.

"You're always grabbing nurse's asses around here. You're a known pervert. It won't be a stretch. Even if I can't prove it, it'll be enough to end your career."

He went silent. She got off his chest and started making a fuss over him as if he'd fallen. The GIs parted and they let the guards through. They went to the captain's aid.

Carver was shuffled away and given a towel to wrap his bleeding knuckles.

∼

THE NEXT DAY Platoon Sergeant Carver passed his physical assessment with flying colors. Captain Shane sent a junior officer in his stead. The officer, Lieutenant Smeed wasn't a doctor, but the test was only a formality. Even if Carver had failed miserably, he'd still be shipped out. As Lt. Smeed said, "He wants you off the books."

Lilly wasn't in attendance either. In fact, Carver hadn't seen her since the incident the day before. He knew she'd saved him from a certain court-martial. He'd asked the attending nurse where she was but couldn't get any information out of her. The nurse avoided him and wouldn't make eye contact when he tried to question her.

Later that day he went to the hammock where they'd spent so much quality time. He found a note inside. Before opening it, he sniffed it smelling her scent. He couldn't help smiling. He opened it and read. 'Meet me at 2000 in my quarters.' She signed her name and there was a messy lipstick imprint beneath it. He looked around and pressed his lips to the paper. He folded the note and put it in his pants pocket. He shook his head, *if the men could see me now, they'd puke.*

At exactly 2000 hours he knocked on the wooden door to her tent. The sun had been down for a half hour, but the last bit of evening glow was still hanging on. The side flaps were down keeping him from seeing inside. When there was no answer he opened the door. "Lilly?"

There was a soft glow in the center of the room and Lilly sat at a rickety table. The light from the candle danced across her tan face. She smiled when she saw him and waved him forward. He removed his hat and looked around the quarters. She was the only one inside. "Come here and sit down. I've found a bottle of wine."

He went to the table and reached out his hand. She took it and he stared at her. She looked him in the eye. "What are you staring at, soldier?"

"The most beautiful woman I've ever met." Without thinking he continued. "My future wife."

Her jaw dropped open and for an instant showed pure joy, but then her eyes dropped and she shook her head. "Don't say that."

He felt the room spin and stammered, "What? I had no intention of saying that, it just came out, but now that I've said it." He squeezed her hand. "I feel it's the most righteous thing I've ever said." He shook his head. "I didn't plan this, I don't have a ring."

He was about to continue but she interrupted him. "No." She reached for him, clutching his shoulders. She pulled him into her, wrapped her arms around him. She felt his strong arms tensing. "Doug, I love you. You know I do with all my heart. But we can't marry. We're not even supposed to be together. We'd be kicked out of the service. They might even send you to Leavenworth." He nodded and looked into her hazel eyes. "Once this war's over, then we'll marry."

She ran her hands through his short-cropped hair. It felt coarse and soft at the same time. He wrapped his arms around her and pulled her close. "You're right. Of course, you're right."

They drank the bottle of wine then made love on her cot. They lay beside one another panting. With the flaps down, the tent was like a steam bath. Their sweat mingled and pooled. Lilly leaned up on one elbow and played with the dark hair on his chest. She poked him and looked serious. "You have to live. You just have to get through the next few months. This war's coming to an end."

He looked at the ceiling and let out a long breath. Images of combat flashed through his mind. Faces of men he'd watched die played out like a movie; crystal clear, then fading. "Now I've got something to live for," he said.

2

Sam Santos didn't have time to mourn the passing of his grandmother and the kidnapping of his sister. He'd been beaten until he fell unconscious, then woke up chained to other prisoners. They were sprawled out around him, trying to sleep. He tried to get his bearings. He was in large room. He thought it might be a gymnasium, but he didn't recognize it. The chains led to a single metal manacle that dug into his narrow foot. The chain continued through a stout ring screwed into the floor, then connected the rest of the prisoners.

He sat up and felt his head throb. He closed his eyes, the pain like the worst headache of his life. The sound of the chains clanking sounded like deafening gongs. Someone touched his shoulder and he started and pulled away in fear, but the chains held him in place. "Sit easy, boy. Rest or you'll be too tired to work."

Sam opened his eyes to slits and peered at the small man beside him. He didn't recognize him. "Where am I? What is happening?" The sound of his own voice sounded unfamiliar. He tried to clear his throat but even that hurt.

"You're on a work crew for the Japanese. They threw you in here two hours ago. You've been unconscious."

Sam closed his eyes. The scene of his grandmother's head smashing to the ground while it pumped out streams of blood filled his mind, and he retched. Nothing came up, but the man shied away and shushed him. "You'll attract the guards. Quiet."

Sam looked where he was pointing and saw an armed Japanese soldier standing at the doorway. He was looking away. Sam whispered, "What work?"

The man laid down on the filthy floor and muttered, "You'll find out soon enough."

WHAT SEEMED like only minutes later, there was a harsh barking voice and the heavy shaking of chains. Sam opened his crusted over eyelids. His cheeks were swollen, making it seem he was viewing things from the inside of a cave. The man next to him sat up and shook his shoulder. "Time for work."

There were four shouting Japanese soldiers in the room. They kicked at nearby Filipinos and unlocked the chains from the floor. The Filipino nudged Sam and said, "Hold your foot like this, quickly." Sam was slow to respond.

The chain started moving through the ring on his ankle; being pulled by the farthest soldier. The sound of metal running across metal, filled the room and Sam thought his aching head would explode. The end of the chain whipped through the line. Sam realized too late why the Filipino held his foot the way he did, when the end came through the ring on his ankle. His foot was tucked near his butt and the end of the chain whipped his backside, sending a shock through his entire body. He yelped as he felt the skin break.

The prisoner beside him shook his head. "You need to listen if you wish to survive."

The pain in his flank shook the grogginess from his mind. He touched the area and felt the stickiness of fresh blood. He nodded to the man. "My name's Sam Santos."

The man nodded. "Felipe. Don't talk unless you're sure they can't hear you," he whispered. "Keep your head down and do as they say."

Sam nodded. The nearest Japanese soldier yelled something and Felipe and the rest of the men got to their feet. Sam staggered as he stood. He felt dizzy and thought he might pass out but concentrated and steadied himself. More shouting and the prisoners shuffled into a single-file line. Sam stayed behind Felipe.

Another order and they shuffled out the door. The heavy manacle on his ankle bit into his skin with every step. He looked at Felipe's ankle and saw discolored scarring and heavy callous. He realized how much pain he'd need to endure before his own body built up the callous.

It was still dark outside, but the growing light to the east told Sam they were heading north. They were near the outskirts of Cebu City. He knew the city well and recognized the area they shuffled through. They were headed out of the city.

Soon they were on a well-worn path in the jungle. Sam figured they'd walked a quarter mile before the column stopped and more harsh Japanese orders were shouted. Sam followed close behind Felipe.

The sun was peeking over the horizon, lighting the day. Sam saw a large area of cleared out jungle. At first it looked as though it was being cleared for agriculture, but upon closer inspection he noticed low structures built into the ground. They were made of fresh concrete and had firing slits. He knew he was looking at bunkers.

The line moved steadily forward until Sam was at the front. A young Japanese soldier handed him a shovel. Sam gripped it and he had a brief urge to swing it at the soldier's head. It passed quickly when he realized he could barely lift it in his weakened state. The soldier pushed Sam along muttering something he couldn't understand.

Felipe looked back and motioned him to follow. Sam followed.

EVERY DAY WAS THE SAME. Up before the dawn, walk to the worksite, backbreaking work, measly lunch of weevil filled rice, then back to work, then shuffled back to the barracks for another nearly inedible and inadequate meal.

Two weeks passed and it seemed to Sam that he'd never done anything else in his life. He realized quickly the Japanese didn't care if their workforce lived or died. The amount of work required far more calories than they were given. The results were weaker workers. The weaker a worker became, the less able to keep up and more likely they were to be beaten. The more they were beaten the quicker they died.

Sam understood the only way to survive was to maintain the workload. The only way to do so was to do as little as possible without drawing unwanted attention and finding more calories. He was resourceful. His grandmother had always told him there was plenty of food in the jungle if you knew what you were looking for. She'd taught him to forage for roots and bugs from an early age. He'd never eaten the bugs she pointed out, but he remembered which ones were safe and more importantly, which ones were poison.

When they stopped working for the midday meal, he always sat near a rotten log, or moist section of dirt. He'd peel bark, or dig and eat the beetles, bugs and worms he uncovered. At first Felipe watched him in disgust, but when he realized Sam wasn't dying as quickly as the rest of them, he joined in.

Sam's ankle was calloused and scarred just like Felipe's now. His body was in constant pain from the never-ending work and malnutrition, but he was young and becoming more adjusted to the day to day rigors. It allowed him to focus on his hatred.

He thought about the day the Japanese came and destroyed his family. He wondered if his sweet Yelina was alive, and if so, would she rather be dead. He also remembered Berto's role. His own brother had betrayed him to the Japanese. He doubted Berto thought his family would be treated in such a way, but he'd been the one that caused it. Sam dreamed of the day he took his revenge. It kept him moving forward. Kept him alive.

He started thinking of ways he could fight the Japanese. The bunker system he slaved over was expansive. There were interlocking tunnels. There were underground rooms filled with ammunition and food. The Japanese obviously thought they couldn't hold the city once the allies attacked and were preparing a fallback position.

One night after a particularly hard day of digging, Sam leaned over to Felipe and whispered. "You awake?" Felipe grunted and opened his eyes to slits. Sam was inches away. He carefully unfolded a piece of scrap paper he'd stolen off the top of an ammo crate. He'd scrawled a crude drawing of the bunker system using a whittled piece of charcoal from the cooking fire.

He showed it to Felipe. In the dim light of the moon shining through the holes in the thatch roof, it was barely visible. "I've been making this for a couple of days," he whispered. Felipe didn't react but stared at the drawing. "Keep your eyes open and add any information you think is missing."

Felipe shook his head and whispered back. "They will find that and you'll be tortured and killed. Get rid of it."

Sam shook his head. "I'll give it to the allies when they come. It'll help them destroy the Japs."

"You're dreaming. You think they'll let us live? When the allies come they'll dispose of us."

Sam hadn't thought of that. "What? Why?"

Felipe pointed at the map. "That's why, idiot. We know about the bunker. We built the cursed thing."

Sam folded it up and shoved it back into the fold of his shirt. He laid back and wracked his brain for a way to escape and get the plans to the allies. He took a deep breath and let it out slowly. He whispered to Felipe. "I've gotta get outta here."

"You're crazy and you'll get yourself and probably others killed."

Sam shrugged, "If they're going to kill us anyway, why not die trying to escape? I'd rather die fighting than kneeling."

"Go to sleep and put it out of your mind."

Sam shook his head. "I'll find a way out of here. I'll use my shovel, kill that scrawny guard, take his rifle and run. They won't follow an armed man without caution. I know the jungle, I can lose them easily."

Felipe leaned close and Sam could feel the anger in his voice. "You'll ruin everything, you idiot."

Sam pulled away. "What do you mean? What are you talking about?"

"I'll show you tomorrow."

THE NEXT DAY, Sam followed Felipe out of the barracks and into the bunker complex just like every other day. Sam watched his friend, waiting for some hint at what he'd talked about the night before. Felipe didn't let on until the midday meal. As they put down their shovels, picks and hoes, Felipe gestured for Sam to follow.

Felipe got into line for a ration of rice, Sam right behind him. Felipe whispered, "The water girl. Stay close to me."

Sam looked down the line of haggard workers and saw the small frame of a woman scooping out water from a large wooden barrel. He'd never paid any attention to her before, but now he scrutinized her and realized she was younger than he assumed. She kept her face down and moved slowly, but efficiently, careful not to spill. There was a bored looking Japanese soldier nearby watching the workers.

When it was Felipe's turn, he held out his cup and said, "Greetings. A fine day today."

The woman hesitated for a fraction of an instant and filled his cup. "All the days are pleasant."

Felipe nodded his thanks. "The boy behind me is thirsty."

He moved away and Sam took his place. He held his cup out and stared at the top of the woman's head. She looked up and their eyes met. He recognized her immediately and was about to speak but she did first. "We will quench your thirst." She poured a ladle full into his cup, but dropped the ladle. She crouched to pick it up at the same time he did. They lingered for an instant and her eyes bore into his. "Be ready, the hour is close. Do exactly as Felipe says and you'll have your revenge."

They stood together and she thanked him for helping her with the ladle. The Japanese soldier barely noticed. Sam nodded and sat down next to Felipe. As he scooped the rice into his mouth and drank the water, he leaned toward Felipe. "That's my old school teacher. Mrs. Cruz."

Felipe nodded but didn't look at him. "Yes, before the war she was a teacher. Now she's the leader of the resistance. We call her Major Cruz, now. She's second only to Colonel Cushing."

Sam nearly choked. "Major? She's a woman and so small."

Felipe grinned. "Once you see her fight, you will not think her so small. Ferocious is the only word."

"How can she lead when she's here?"

"She's not on the work detail. She comes from the city. Informs us of developments, and we pass off anything we've learned."

"We?" Sam looked around at the pathetic assortment of humanity. "There's more like you?"

Felipe nodded. "Many. Most of the young men and some of the old. You're late to the game. Don't talk to anyone, some will give us up. The allies are off the coast. Any day they will attack. That is when we will strike."

"How will I know?"

"Stay close to me. You'll know."

THREE DAYS PASSED before Major Cruz spoke to Felipe again. Sam didn't catch her words but he noticed Felipe tense. Sam held out his cup and she filled it without a word. He lingered, hoping for something. She tilted her head up and gave him a quick smile. He saw her eyes twinkle. She was excited.

He sat next to Felipe. Sam noticed Felipe's hand shaking as he brought the cup to his lips and drank. Sam started to speak, but Felipe shook his head. He was staring at a man sitting in the dirt across from him. The dirty Filipino caught his stare and Sam saw Felipe flash him a quick hand signal. The worker's eyes lit up momentarily, but he went back to his meal. Seconds passed before Sam saw the man nudge the prisoner next to him. He flashed the same hand signal. He watched as each prisoner passed the signal. His heart swelled as he realized most of the work crew was part of the resistance. He'd been trying to survive day to day, while all along he'd had friends all around him.

Felipe was also watching. When the signal had traversed the entire group, Sam spoke. "What happens now?"

Felipe looked annoyed. "It'll happen in the barracks. As we enter tonight."

Sam felt the heat of adrenalin rush through his body. He wanted to ask so many questions, but knew Felipe was done talking.

The bunkers they'd been slaving over were nearly complete. Sam spent the rest of the day thinking how it would happen. They wouldn't have their tools, they always left them at the site. He wondered how they would fight armed soldiers with only their hands. He hoped there was a plan. He didn't relish the thought of charging headlong into machine gun fire.

The work day finally ended. Sam could feel a barely contained energy in the group. The normally sullen and beaten-down prisoners were more alert. They seemed to step a little lighter. He hoped the Japanese didn't notice.

He glanced at the nearest guard. The soldier had his long Arisaka rifle slung over his shoulder and he looked bored. The officer in charge walked at the front of the column. He looked crisp and efficient even though his shirt was soaked with sweat. He looked like an aristocrat among the bedraggled prisoners. Sam had seen him use the samurai sword which hung from his belt, to deadly effect. If a prisoner was too weak to work or was injured, the officer took great pleasure in dispatching them with a quick stroke. Sam pictured himself killing him, choking the life out of him.

As the column approached the barracks, a soldier with stripes on his shoulder jogged up to the officer's side and saluted. There was a quick exchange and the sergeant pointed toward the sea. The officer nodded and gazed in the direction, but the city buildings blocked the view. He spoke to the nearest guard who bowed and started yelling at the prisoners. He motioned and pushed them to hurry.

Sam tensed as he entered the barracks. His eyes darted around the familiar space looking for some clue as to how they would fight, but the space looked the same. He could see nothing different. He took a deep breath, readying himself for his death.

He followed Felipe, who acted as though nothing was about to happen. He stopped at his normal spot and the Japanese soldiers hustled to ready the chains. Sam thought, *surely we'll strike before we're chained.*

He wanted to ask Felipe, but knew he needed to keep quiet and follow along. The guard was about to string the chain through the first prisoner when a single shot rang out nearby. It was immediately followed by more until it was rippling all around the building. The soldiers in the room unslung their rifles and looked around like cornered rats. They backed away from the prisoners with their rifles leveled. There was shouting and more firing outside.

The soldier nearest the door turned as a bullet ricocheted off the metal wall. The nearest prisoner took the opportunity and leaped like a tiger. He tackled the soldier from behind and the soldier screamed in surprise. In an instant the rest of the prisoners were up and attacking. There were four guards inside. One swung his rifle and fired into the charging group. The sound of a bullet thunking into flesh was drowned out by the rising yell of men fighting back.

Felipe ran for the door and Sam followed. The guards were down with a mass of angry prisoners on top, tearing them apart. The gunfire outside continued. The awful sound of a machine gun opening fire nearby made Sam crouch, but he kept running behind Felipe. When they got to the door, a rifle was thrust into Felipe's hand. He checked the weapon like he'd done it before and crouched beside the open doorway.

It was sunset, the day darkening quickly. Felipe moved to the opening and brought the rifle to his shoulder. He fired and the sharp crack made Sam flinch. Felipe chambered another round in a blink of an eye and fired again and again until the clip was expended. The machine gun stopped firing. Felipe stood and motioned the rest of the prisoners forward. Sam noticed the men nearest were brandishing the other three rifles. Their eyes sparkled with excitement. Felipe said, "Move out, I see the major."

Sam stayed crouched but followed Felipe out the door. The rest of the prisoners filed out and spread out. Sam noticed the machine gun that normally covered the road to the barracks was pointing straight up. The crew was sprawled in various death poses, fresh blood seeping from multiple wounds.

From the city he saw shabbily dressed Filipinos armed with multiple types of rifles and sub-machine guns streaming toward them. Leading the charge was a small figure wielding a stubby burp gun. Sam realized it was the woman from the water-line. She crouched, aimed and fired off a short burst. Sam saw her target, a fleeing soldier, throw up his hands and fall face first into a rock pile.

Felipe called out and the woman motioned her fighters to continue forward. She veered toward the group of prisoners. Felipe pulled up short and snapped off a quick salute. "Major Cruz, it worked perfectly. Just as you said it would."

She nodded and gave a quick smile. Sam was mesmerized by the woman who'd taught him English. He'd never thought of her as more than a diminutive school teacher, but now he saw her in a brand-new light. She was beautiful and deadly. She noticed Sam staring. "Good to see you, Sam." She pointed behind her. "The weapons are forty meters that way. Gather weapons and ammo and join the fight." There was firing all around them, mostly from Filipinos. "The enemy are running, but they'll regroup. We must push them out of the city." Felipe nodded and she gripped his shoulder and pushed. "Go."

Felipe nodded and waved the prisoners to follow. Sam watched Major Cruz trot to catch up to her troops. She moved like a graceful tiger. He cringed when a bullet whizzed over his head. He crouched and followed the group. The light of day was gone, but the area was dimly lit by fires from burning Japanese vehicles. He jogged past a fiercely burning jeep with a charred soldier still gripping the steering wheel. He could smell burnt flesh and it turned his stomach.

They approached a two-story building. There was a Filipino standing beside the doorway motioning them. Felipe ran to him and they embraced. Sam was behind him. The man said, "It's good to see you my old friend. There's no time to waste." He pointed inside the lit room. "You'll find what you need inside."

Felipe gripped his shoulder and nodded. He entered the room with

Sam close behind. His eyes lit up when he saw the room was filled
with an arsenal of weapons. They were propped along the far wall and
arranged in order. The left side was rifles. There was everything from
Springfields to shiny new M1 Carbines. The next bunch was small submachine guns, including Tommy guns, which Sam recognized from
watching American gangster movies. The heavier BARs were the final
weapon.

There were three Filipino fighters inside handing them out. Felipe
stepped forward and took a Thompson. He hefted it and smiled. He
checked the action, then scooped up a magazine, checked it and slid it
in. He pulled the priming handle and put the stock to his shoulder and
looked down the sights. Satisfied, he slung it over his shoulder and
scooped up a satchel filled with more magazines. He slung that over
his other shoulder.

Sam stared at the arsenal. The other prisoners were grabbing
weapons like they knew what they were doing. They were disappearing quickly. Felipe noticed his inaction and reached for an M1
Carbine. He stepped forward and handed the light weapon to Sam.
"Listen carefully. This is the safety. When it's on," he pushed it and it
went from black to red, "it's ready to fire. When it's black," he pushed
it the opposite way, "it's on safety and won't fire. Keep the safety on
until you're ready to fire. You don't want to shoot someone in the back
on accident while your running down the street. Got it?" Sam nodded.
He picked up a magazine and held it up. "This is your ammo. You've
got twenty rounds. Put it in like this." He pushed it into the bottom of
the weapon and it clicked into place. "Then you pull this back." He
turned the weapon so Sam could see the top. "That's the breech. See
how the bullet is propped there? It'll slide in and be ready to fire when
you release this." He released the handle and it snapped into place. He
handed the loaded M1 to Sam. "Safety off, aim and shoot. Got it?"

Sam swallowed and nodded. He held the weapon. It was light but
felt good in his hands. He looked at the stack of Thompsons. Felipe
shook his head. "You're not ready for one of those. They've got more
punching power, but you won't be able to hit anything until you've
practiced with it." He pointed to the M1. "You'll be better off with
this." Sam nodded and took the offered satchel of spare magazines.

The lesson over, Felipe looked around the room. The prisoners were all armed. Their emaciated bodies looked small holding the deadly weapons, but their eyes burned with ferocious light. Felipe yelled, "let's go!"

They streamed out of the building and into the night. Sam's eyes darted around, wondering what to do. What would he do if he saw a Japanese soldier? He thought of his grandmother and his sister and knew exactly what he'd do. The thought passed, *what if I see Berto?* The answer wasn't as clear. Perhaps he was already dead. He hoped so.

They jogged back the way they'd come. There was firing everywhere. Small firefights starting with intense, constant fire and occasional explosions, and ending with sporadic shots. Sam didn't know what it meant. He only knew he wanted to fight.

The group of prisoners came up behind a line of Filipinos stacked up along the side of a house with their backs against the wall. The roof was smoldering and was putting off a lot of smoke. Felipe crouched near the corner and addressed the Filipino at the corner. "What's going on?"

The fighter gestured with his head. "There's a machine gun in the middle of the road. We need to get behind them."

Felipe nodded and licked his lips. "We'll move through the houses. I know this neighborhood. You keep them occupied."

The fighter nodded. "They know we're here." As if to punctuate his words the machine gun fired and tracer bullets streaked down the street and tore up the walls and road. The sound terrified Sam. It sounded like a ripsaw.

Felipe moved to the center of the block and kicked in a door. Sam was beside him. He was pushed to the side as three fighters moved into the house with their weapons ready. There was no firing. Sam followed Felipe inside. The building seemed to be abandoned. They moved through it quickly and found the back door. Felipe said. "There's an alley. I'll lead." He opened the door and poked his head out. "It's clear." He hustled out the door and the others followed. Sam was the fourth man out.

The fighters moved to another alley which went off at a ninety-degree angle. It would take them the direction they wanted to go.

Shooting erupted from the street, quickly answered by the Japanese machine gun nest. The other fighters were keeping them occupied.

Felipe crouched at the corner of the alley and peered around the corner. It was dark. He couldn't see any Japanese, but there was so much debris littering the area, he wouldn't be able to distinguish soldiers using it for cover. He looked at the low rooftops. It looked clear. He motioned men forward. "Use the cover."

The fighters moved into the alley. Sam was near the front. As he rounded the corner his eyes darted in every direction, looking for danger. There were too many hiding spots. If the Japanese were there he wouldn't know it until it was too late.

He ran in a crouch keeping his eyes looking down the alley. He saw a pile of debris off to his right and he angled for it. There was a sudden flash from the end of the alley. He flinched as a bullet smacked into the man in front of him. He stood paralyzed as the man stumbled and fell. More flashes, and bullets were snapping past his ear like angry hornets. The sound of gunfire in the tight alley added to the chaos. He heard Felipe yell, "get down!"

His voice cut through Sam's fear and he leaped for the debris pile. The pile was closer than he'd thought and he slammed into the wall it was stacked against. His face ground into the wall and pain lanced through him. He curled into a ball as bullets smacked into the walls and ricocheted off the pile. He whimpered and held his weapon tight to his body, as if it could offer him deliverance.

There were flashes from the alley he'd just left. The fighters were returning fire. It was quickly answered by more fire from the Japanese. He heard Felipe yelling. "Return fire, return fire!" He didn't know if he was talking to him or not, but he had to do something. He took a deep breath and knew he was about to die. He forced his body into action. He had to help his friends. He did a mental countdown, *one, two, three.* He stood and aimed the carbine down the alley. He pulled the trigger but nothing happened. He pulled harder, still nothing. The realization hit him as bullets thunked into the debris, *the safety.*

He pushed the button and pulled the trigger. The M1 fired as quickly as he pulled the trigger. He kept firing until he felt something bite him in the cheek. The pain seared through him and he dropped to the ground clutching his cheek. His hand came away sticky and wet.

He thought he was dying. He could feel blood flowing down his neck. Something crashed into the space beside him and he grasped for the carbine. He felt a hand on his shoulder. "Are you hit?" It was the familiar voice of Felipe. Sam nodded, afraid to test if his mouth still worked. "Answer me."

Sam muttered, "Yes." When he knew his jaw still worked he raised his voice, "In the face, I think."

There was a flurry of firing as Filipinos raced past the debris pile and fired down the alley. The volume of fire forced the Japanese to take cover and the Filipinos advanced steadily. Sam tried to get up and join them, but Felipe pushed him down and in the dim light, inspected his face. It only took a couple seconds before he said, "You're fine. The bullet grazed your cheek. It's bleeding a lot, but you're fine." He yelled, "Juan, bandage."

Another fighter slid in beside them and reached into a satchel hanging around his neck. He pulled out a strip of cloth. Felipe squeezed Sam's shoulder. "He'll take care of you. Then get back in the fight. We're going to need everyone tonight." Sam nodded and Felipe stood and ran down the alley toward the fighting.

Juan handed Sam the bandage. "Hold this tight against your wound until the bleeding stops. I can't secure it for you." Sam took the bandage and pushed it against his cheek. It sent pain through his jaw but he forced himself not to show weakness. He felt his body start to shake. Juan looked him in the eye. "You okay?"

Sam felt shame at his weakness. He nodded. "Fine." Juan nodded back and unslung his carbine. He stood and darted away after Felipe. Sam noticed the firing had stopped. Keeping the cloth pressed to his cheek he stood and looked down the alley. He could see running shapes. He gritted his teeth, put the bloody cloth into his ammo pouch and on shaky legs, followed.

He ran past a body sprawled in the center of the alley. It was one of the men from his work detail. The man's back glistened with fresh blood. The sight made his wound seem trivial and he increased his speed.

At the end of the alley, Sam stopped. He was the last fighter. There were more bodies in the alley, but they were Japanese soldiers. The nearest body was only feet away. The fighters were stacked against each wall, peering around the corners. Sam couldn't tear his eyes away from the dead Japanese soldier's eyes. They were glazed over, unseeing, but it seemed to Sam they were looking into his soul.

The ripping sound of a nearby machine gun brought him out of his trance. The walls of the buildings in front lit up with the muzzle flash. Sam realized they were close to the gun. He went to the center of the alley and moved past the line of fighters. He got to the corner and saw Felipe. He crouched beside him. Felipe grinned and pointed to the right. When the machine gun stopped he said, "They're set up in the intersection. We'll come around the corner and kill them." He looked at the men. "Check your ammo." Sam looked at his weapon. His face flushed as he realized he had no idea how to change the magazine. Felipe said, "Ready?"

There were nods and grunts throughout the group. Sam was too embarrassed to admit he wasn't ready and gave a quick nod. *How many shots did I fire?* He thought he must be close to running out. Felipe stood. "We'll attack the next time they fire." There were nods up and down the line.

They didn't have long to wait. The machine gun crew opened up, the walls lit up with muzzle flashes. The fighters rushed around the corner. Sam was beside Felipe. When he entered the street, he could see the sandbags protecting the machine gun crew. The crew didn't notice the horde of fighters rushing from the side, but Sam saw movement to the left. It was a Japanese soldier bringing his rifle to his shoulder. Sam crouched, aimed, pushed the safety off and pulled the trigger. He pulled the trigger repeatedly and watched the soldier lurch and twitch as his bullets found their mark. As the soldier crumpled and fell, Sam continued pulling the trigger but the Carbine had stopped firing. The rush of killing the soldier quickly vanished as he realized he didn't know how to reload.

The rest of the fighters were upon the machine gun crew. Sam watched as the Japanese soldiers were shredded with concentrated fire. Sam trotted up to the soldier he'd killed. He looked young. The expanding pool of blood threatened to flow over his sandals and he stepped back. *I killed a man.* Sam took stock of his feelings. He felt satisfaction. He'd done something to avenge his Lola and his sister, Yelina.

The former prisoners were hooting and celebrating their victory. Sam watched as they dismantled the machine gun from the mount and hefted it away. The rest of the fighters from up the street joined their group. Sam trotted up to the group but didn't join in the celebration. Surely there was much more fighting ahead. The entire city was full of Japanese. He wanted to kill more, but first he had to figure out how to reload. He saw Juan standing nearby. He went to him.

Juan saw him and grinned, "Good shooting back there."

Sam couldn't help smiling back. He held out his carbine and whispered, "I don't know how to reload."

Juan's grin turned to a full smile. He took the weapon and gave him a quick lesson. When he was sure Sam knew how to eject and reload, he marveled, "It takes a brave man to enter a fight without knowing if he has any ammo in his rifle."

AFTER TAKING out the machine gun nest, the group of fighters held their ground. The Japanese soldiers had been plundered of anything useful. The machine gun was set up and pointed down the street in the other direction. Sam was antsy to keep attacking. He wanted to kill more Japanese. He saw Felipe talking with a small group of Filipinos. Felipe nodded and the men ran back up the street, the way they'd come.

Felipe addressed the remaining fighters. "The Japanese are in full retreat. Major Cruz wants us to form up with her and the rest of the resistance at the city center." The fighters manning the machine gun stood and started dismantling it. Sam and the others moved along the dark streets. As they passed, windows and doors were flung open as the residents of Cebu City realized their day of liberation was upon them.

Sam found himself near the front of the pack. He was trotting, watching the doorways and windows for Japanese. He came to an intersection and slowed. He went to the corner and peaked around. He saw scurrying movement on the right side. He squinted, but in the dim light couldn't tell if he was seeing friend or foe. The answer came with a muzzle flash and a zinging bullet.

He pulled back. There was another shot and the wooden wall beside his head shredded with a bullet impact. He crouched and pressed his back against the wall. He took a deep breath and was about to lunge around the corner when he heard a commotion. The closest fighter put his hand on his shoulder and held up a hand for him to wait. Sam nodded. There was yelling coming from down the alley. At first Sam thought it was Japanese, what he expected to hear, but then realized it was in his own language.

The fighter beside him smiled and slapped his shoulder. "It's been taken care of." Sam went around the corner with his M1 leading and saw a group of Filipinos huddled around a dark form. Sam trotted the twenty yards and was met with excited back slaps. At the feet of the group, a Japanese soldier was crumpled. An expanding pool of blood spread from his back. He was bleeding from multiple wounds. The Filipinos held up their bloody knives. Sam could see their teeth gleaming in the low light.

Felipe was beside him. He grinned and slapped Sam's back. "Our people are taking their revenge tonight."

3

Platoon Sergeant Carver sat on a bunk below decks of a troop transport ship playing cards with Sergeant O'Connor and other men of Able Company. Most of the 164th Regiment occupied the cramped ship. He'd been back a week. His leg felt good, although he still had a slight limp.

Sergeant O'Connor threw down his five cards. "Four of a kind." Moans all around as GIs flopped down their hands in disgust. Carver held his close to his chest. O'Connor said, "Well? What you got?"

Carver grinned and laid his cards down. "Straight flush."

O'Connor's jaw dropped. "Best hand I've had all night and you pull that shit? It's like you've got a damned horseshoe shoved up your ass." As Carver shrugged and scooped up the dollar bills, O'Connor asked. "Your gal teach you to play or something?"

Carver leveled his eyes at O'Connor. "What gal? What're you talking about?"

O'Connor stood and grinned. "It's pretty damned obvious, Platoon Sergeant. You haven't said anything, but since you've returned, you're always getting that far-away look, like your lusting after your school teacher or something."

Carver looked at the other sergeants and corporals who looked down at their boots like they were the most interesting things in the world.

He put his arm around O'Connor and pulled him away from the others. When they were alone he separated and said, "Don't bring that shit up in front of the men again, Sergeant. We're invading that Jap island any day now. They don't need shit like that distracting them."

O'Connor's eyes narrowed. Carver felt a chill as he looked into the eyes of a killer. O'Connor said. "That's exactly why I brought it up. We've been through a lot together. You outrank me, always have, but I'm addressing you as a friend." He paused and Carver gave him a slight nod. O'Connor continued. "Your head's in the clouds. The men need you here, leading them. Not thinking about some dame you've been..." he paused when he saw Carver's eyes turn icy. "You've met." He shook his head. "I don't want you getting whacked cause you can't focus."

Carver took a step back. He looked at O'Connor and tilted his head. "That obvious, huh?"

O'Connor nodded, "May as well be wearing a sign:" he framed his hands as if designing a marquee, "Pussy-whipped."

The corners of Carver's mouth turned down, but he saw O'Connor grinning. Carver rubbed his chin then looked his friend in the eyes again. "Her name's Lilly. She's an officer nurse and I love her more'n words can say."

O'Connor shook his head once. "Officer? That's dangerous ground." Carver nodded and O'Connor laughed. "Always wanted to fuck an officer, but not quite in that way." He put up his hands when he saw Carver ball his fists. "Whoa, just kidding."

Carver said, "She's special. I'm gonna try to lock her away though. You're right, I've gotta come back to ground level." He reached out his hand and said, "Tell you what. I'll keep that side of my life hidden and locked down as long as you *never* utter her name in the same breath with the word 'fuck' again."

O'Connor grinned and gripped Carver's hand. "Deal."

～

MARCH 26TH 1945

THE NAVY WOKE the men early with cruisers and destroyers shelling the coast of Cebu Island. Elements of the 164th Regiment alongside the 182nd, offloaded to LCPVs and motored towards Talisay Point. The air smelled of burnt gunpowder and thousands of unwashed men.

Platoon Sergeant Carver and Sergeant O'Connor were on separate LCPVs for the short ride to Talisay Beach. They were the leading elements of the regiment. Carver was near the front, staring at the back of the man in front of him. He looked up at the bright sky. He glanced at his watch, eight A.M. He shook his head.

The man next to him barked, "What's the matter Platoon Sergeant? Got you up too early?"

Carver looked at Lieutenant Swan and shook his head. "No sir. Just don't like assaulting a beach after the Japs have had breakfast."

Swan laughed and slapped Carver's back. "Don't worry sarge. The Filipino resistance assured us we're not facing an organized group of Japs. They said most of the veteran combat troops were moved weeks ago to defend Manila."

Carver nodded. "Yes sir. I got that word, but any Jap with a rifle can kill you just as dead, even if he's some malnourished private."

Lieutenant Swan turned serious and nodded. "We'll hit the beach running. I'm sure they'll have some surprises for us, they always do."

Carver nodded and thought about the changes he'd seen in Lt. Swan. When they'd invaded Bougainville Island months before, he'd been a brand new, green as grass, second lieutenant. He'd joined the regiment after Guadalcanal and trained with them for eight months on the island paradise of Fiji. He was solid in tactics, he just didn't have much of a backbone.

On the hell of Bougainville, he'd done his job, putting up a formidable defense of the hills around the landing zones and airfields. Carver didn't think he had the hard constitution to survive combat, but the lieutenant had proved him wrong at every turn.

Swan was tall and gawky, but he'd lost the awkward shyness. He'd survived where many others had fallen. That was enough to earn him a promotion and respect. He was leading 2nd platoon of Able Company with his two sergeants, Carver and O'Connor.

A sailor yelled, "Two minutes!" His shipmate pulled himself into the steel ring of the .50 caliber mounted machine gun and racked a round. Only his helmet and the slit of his eyes were visible above the metal. He moved the muzzle side to side.

Carver stood on his toes and extended his chin. He could just see over the edge. The beach was close. Except for the smoking craters and shredded palm tree leaves, it looked idyllic. He searched the tree-line for signs of the enemy but didn't see any bunkers or muzzle flashes. Maybe the landing would be unopposed.

"One minute!"

The heavy thumping of a .50 caliber machine gun opened up from the LCPV beside them. Carver flinched when the gunner beside him joined. The sailor was sending out short bursts. Carver could see the tracers lancing into the jungle, but there was no return fire. They were seconds from the beach. Lieutenant Swan yelled to the men. "Remember our objective is to push into the tree-line and set up a perimeter while the armor lands." The helmeted heads nodded.

Carver felt the LCPV lurch as it hit shallow water. The ramp dropped and slammed into the clear water. "Go!" He yelled. The men charged off the boat and sprinted up the beach. Carver had his Thompson ready as he ran in the white sand. He scanned for targets, thinking any second he'd hear the chattering of a Nambu machine gun. He made it to the tree-line without firing a shot.

He leaped for the cover of a downed palm tree. Men were stacking up along the length of the beach. A nearby explosion made him cover his head. Bits of debris and sand rained down on him. He looked down the beach and saw the fresh, smoking crater. Beside it two GIs were down. Carver heard someone yell, "Mines."

He watched a medic dart from cover and slide in beside the casualties. He quickly assessed the first then moved to the second. He shook his head and ran back to cover. He heard Lt. Swan. "Move up, push forward."

Carver peeked over the palm and got to his knees. The GIs around him got to their feet and took the first tentative steps into the jungle. Gunfire erupted off to the right and he dove behind another palm tree. There was return fire. He waved the men forward. The brief firefight ended and the entire company moved forward.

There was a road leading into the jungle off to Carver's left. It was well used and led directly to the Pailua airfield two miles ahead, then into Cebu City, three miles after that. It was the obvious route for the armor to take, which is why Carver avoided it. Command assumed it was heavily mined. The minesweepers would be coming in with the armor. He called to the nearest GIs, "Stay off the road." They nodded and moved forward.

Gunfire erupted to the front and the familiar snapping of bullets passing close made Carver and the GIs dive for cover. Carver looked to his right and saw Lt. Swan cowering behind a thick palm. Carver peaked his head around his own palm and saw the winking of a muzzle flash. He pointed his Thompson and squeezed off a short three round burst, then pulled back. The GIs followed suit, popping from cover and firing. The Japanese fire dissipated. He yelled to Lt. Swan. "Light resistance, sir."

Swan nodded and had a look for himself. He aimed and fired his M1 Carbine in quick succession, sending his bullets into likely hiding spots. He pulled back and yelled. "First Squad move up. Second squad, covering fire."

Carver yelled, "You heard the man. First squad on me." He stood and waited for the increased fire from second squad, then moved quickly around the palm and into the open. He jogged forward to the next bit of cover and went to one knee. He had his Thompson at his shoulder, looking for targets. When the GI behind him, passed on his right, he kept scanning. There was movement. He put the muzzle on the spot and fired off another short burst. The bushes shook and splintered and the shape disappeared. He followed the GI.

There was a sudden increase in fire and Carver saw the lead elements of first squad pouring rounds into a stack of cut logs. They moved around the structure and the firing stopped. Carver trotted to it, his Thompson at the ready, but the tangle of bleeding bodies told him the work had already been done. He yelled to the rest of the platoon. "Clear. Move up."

The rest of the GIs caught up and moved beyond, watching for more enemy. Lieutenant Swan trotted up and crouched beside Carver. "The heavy weapons company is coming off the boats now. They've got the four-inch mortars. We'll wait until they're set up then move forward."

Carver nodded. "So far it's light resistance. Hope they hurry, don't wanna lose the advantage. It's like they didn't expect us or something."

Lieutenant Swan nodded. "Looks like the feint at Leyte worked. That's where they were expecting us."

Carver grabbed the shoulder of a nearby private. He pointed to the right. "Run over there and tell Sergeant O'Connor to hold up for a while." The private took off, zigzagging through the sparse jungle. There was a single rifle shot and the private dove to the ground. Carver yelled, "Sniper. Fire up the tree tops."

There was an immediate hail of bullets shredding the nearby palms. Carver saw the medic, Private First-Class Haley dart from cover and slide next to the messenger. Carver watched as he worked and was relieved when they both got to their feet and sprinted towards the second squad's position.

The firing died down and he heard someone yell, "I got the bastard." Carver leaned from cover and saw the dangling form of a Japanese soldier. He hung upside down from the rope he had tethered around his ankle. He swayed and slammed into the tree trunk, leaving a smear of blood.

After a few tense minutes, the radioman, Private Hanks reached forward and handed Lt. Swan the handset. He spoke then listened and nodded. He pulled out his folded map and relayed their position. He signed off, stuffed the map back into his tunic and addressed Carver. "Mortars are in place. Move up."

Carver was relieved. He stood and motioned for the platoon to move. The GIs moved between points of cover for a couple hundred yards. There was sporadic firing from other units up and down the line, but nothing to their front, and nothing heavy.

Carver looked up as a flight of P-38 lightnings passed over-head. He watched as they angled down and saw the winking and flashing of their nose mounted machine guns. He looked to Swan fifteen yards behind him. Swan said, "Must be strafing the airfield. We're close."

The platoon moved forward steadily for another three hundred yards. Lieutenant Swan kept in contact with the rear, letting them know of their progress. Soon, the mortars moved up to keep pace with the quick advance. Swan called for a halt and the GIs found cover and crouched. Carver tapped the GI beside him. "Water break, pass it along." The message went down the line and the soldiers took long gulps of warm canteen water.

Carver wiped his brow. Although it was still morning, the day was heating up. The jungle steamed as it warmed making it seem like a sauna. The men were well acclimated to the heat but moving through enemy infested jungle made the effort that much more difficult. Staying hydrated was a major chore. Once you felt thirsty, you were already dehydrated.

Carver screwed the lid back on his canteen. He'd drained half of it. Even though it was warm and infused with the flavor of the canteen metal, it tasted like sweet nectar.

Lieutenant Swan handed the radio back to PFC Hanks and motioned Carver to join him. Carver stayed low and trotted to his side. Swan showed him the map. "We're here. The airfield's here and the road's off to our left," he moved his finger to the winding line, "here." Carver glanced that way but couldn't see the road. He nodded. "They've offloaded some Shermans and half-tracks. They're moving up the road with elements of the 182nd. We're holding their right flank. We'll wait here until they catch up, then move on the airfield en masse." He mashed his finger on the open area to their front. "The airfield, that's our objective. The mortars will start hammering it when we're approaching. We'll call in targets as we see 'em, but the flyboys have already destroyed the few Jap planes they saw on the ground."

Carver nodded. "So we wait. I'll spread the men out and have 'em eat something." Swan nodded and stuffed the map back in his shirt.

∾

THIRTY MINUTES later the sound of clanking tracks and the revving of powerful engines could be heard moving along the road. The distinctive snapping and crunching of palm trees told them the armor wasn't only sticking to the road. The sparse jungle allowed the Shermans easy movement. If the heavy tank couldn't go around something, it simply went over it.

Carver heard the radio crackle and Swan listened, then nodded and handed the receiver back to Hanks. He caught Carver's eye and motioned him forward. Carver stood and the whole platoon moved forward with their weapons ready.

The sound of the tanks drowned out the jungle sounds. Carver was glad he wasn't facing the advancing armor; the sound alone would be enough to freeze a man in fear. He thought the Japs at the airfield must be shitting themselves about now.

Another fifty yards and Carver could see the outskirts of the airfield. The jungle stopped and the dirt of the cleared airfield began. He licked his dry lips and crouched a little lower, anticipating the coming battle. He hesitated for an instant as the sight of Lilly lying naked in the hammock crossed his mind. He shook his head, trying to focus on the job at hand, but he slowed his pace, letting the line of soldiers move ahead.

There was a deafening explosion from the left, mixed with the rending of metal. The force of the explosion sent the GIs scampering for cover. Carver held his helmet tight, as debris rained down through the jungle canopy. He listened for small arms fire, but there was nothing but the memory of the explosion. He pushed to his knees and saw the glowing remains of a large vehicle burning on the road. He yelled. "Get ready. Probably a mine. Japs might follow up with an attack." The men scooted to their knees and aimed their weapons into the jungle.

There was yelling and hollering coming from the road. Lieutenant Swan called out from behind the line. "Stay put til we figure out what's going on." Carver could hear him using the radio. He pictured Captain Flannigan, the company CO, back at the beach all safe and sound, surrounded by support staff taking the radio call.

A minute later Lt. Swan was off the radio. He waved Carver over.

Staying in a crouch Carver went to his side. Private Hanks gave him a nod and a smile like they were old friends. Carver scowled and focused on Lt. Swan. "Armor ran into a mine. Flannigan wants the company to advance to the airfield while they clean up the road."

Carver spit and nodded. "Yes sir."

"We're the left flank of Able Company. Baker Company's on the other side of the road. We've got plenty of support. We can take the airfield without armor."

Carver kept his mouth shut, recognizing the signs of stress. He knew Swan tended to over-explain things when he was nervous. Carver nodded. "Yes sir. No problem." Swan licked his lips and nodded.

Carver moved forward. When he was to his old position, he stood up and leaned on a palm tree. He could see the edge of the airfield. The men watched him and he waved them forward. They stood and with their weapons ready, slithered through the thinning cover.

It didn't take long before the company was pressed to the edge of the airfield. There was no movement. There were deep bomb craters all along the airstrip and burning husks of Japanese Zeros, but no enemy soldiers. Able Company was spread from the middle of the airfield to the right edge. Across the dirt airstrip there was a cluster of single story buildings. Some had taken direct hits and were charred, but some were intact and could be hiding Japanese soldiers.

Lieutenant Swan came up beside him and assessed the situation. "What do you think? Looks abandoned."

Carver pointed at the buildings. "I'd like some mortar fire on those buildings before we try to cross. One machine gun nest could fuck up our day."

Lieutenant Swan cringed at Carver's language but had grown to expect it. He nodded and motioned Private Hanks to come forward with the radio. Carver listened as he made contact with Flannigan and requested a mortar strike. Carver gritted his teeth as he heard the tirade coming through the radio. He couldn't understand the words but he damn well got the gist. Swan's face reddened. He signed off and spoke to Carver with barely contained rage. "Flannigan wants us to attack now." He shook his head. "Thinks we're stalling."

Carver wanted to get on the horn and tell the pissant Captain to get up here and lead the charge if he was so hot on attacking, but instead he gritted his teeth and nodded.

Swan looked at his watch. "We attack along the entire line in two minutes. I want first platoon to put covering fire on those buildings while we advance. Pass the word."

Carver nodded and pointed to a nearby private. "Pass the word to Sergeant O'Connor. Second platoon's going across with first covering us." The private nodded and scampered off to pass the word.

Lieutenant Swan pulled his M1 Carbine off his back and looked across the open field. The buildings across the way looked dark and abandoned. "Probably empty."

Carver flicked off his safety and said, "We'll soon find out, sir."

Two minutes later Carver waved the men forward. He thought about letting the platoon move out in front of him. As a Platoon Sergeant, he had that right, but as he looked into the scared eyes of the soldiers around him, he couldn't do it. He had to lead, even if it got him killed. *Sorry Lilly.*

He took the first step into the open field. He kept his eyes glued to the buildings across the open space, ready to throw himself to the ground at the first movement. First platoon opened fire to the right and Carver saw the front of the buildings erupt as bullets slammed into them. Carver waved and yelled. "Move out, let's go."

He started running, weaving back and forth to throw off any enemy sighting on him. The mass of men all around him, sprinting towards the goal filled him with pride.

They were a quarter of the way across when the buildings changed. Wooden front sections fell away exposing firing ports. Carver saw the dark shapes of muzzles poking out. The warning yell was caught in his throat as multiple machine guns opened up.

Bullets whizzed and snapped, but he was already going to the dirt. He heard the sickening sound of bullets slapping into meat. The screaming followed. He fast crawled to a nearby bomb crater and threw himself into the bottom, trying to catch his breath. The concentration of enemy fire was deafening.

More GIs fell into the crater with him. Their eyes were wide with fear. The fire from the jungle intensified. Carver crawled to the lip and peered over. They were halfway to the buildings and he could see the winking of muzzle flashes in the recessed windows, but they'd switched targets, slugging it out with the fire coming from the jungle. He looked left and saw GIs streaming across the airfield. They were taking small arms fire, but it seemed the main defenses were the buildings to his front.

GIs came up on either side of him. Carver said, "Need to get some mortars on the buildings."

Private Ethan looked behind them. "I saw the lieutenant drop into a hole further back. Hopefully he's on it."

As if in answer the whistling of incoming rounds mixed with the machine gun fire. Mortar rounds from the four inchers fell and exploded in front of the buildings. Dirt plumes arced up and rained down. More explosives followed, walking back until they were landing on and amongst the buildings.

Men that were pinned in the open moved forward, many rolling into the bottom of his crater. Carver looked them over. "Anyone hit?" There was no response. "The mortars are kicking the crap outta them. We'll be moving forward as soon as it stops. Check your weapons and ammo."

Carver peered back over the edge. The buildings were constructed of wood, but the mortars were wreaking havoc. Whole sections of walls were coming apart. There was no more firing coming from the machine guns.

Like a light switch the mortars stopped their deadly work. The silence was quickly ended with the crack of rifle fire from the left. There were GIs up and charging across the airfield, firing as they went. Carver crouched on the side of the hole and yelled, "Let's go!" He waved his arm forward and the men sprang up and ran past him, charging the smoking ruins.

Carver got to his feet and joined his men. He was ready with the Thompson, but there were no targets. His men streamed into the buildings and they fired into unseen targets. By the time Carver got there, the buildings were no longer a threat. He stood in the doorway of the center building and looked at the remains of one of the enemy machine gun crews. The tripod mounted Nambu was tilted up and the barrel was bent. There was a smoking hole directly behind it. The crew was sprawled back. He figured there'd been a three-man crew, but the shredded body parts made it difficult to identify where one body started and the other ended.

There was still sporadic firing. The GIs had learned to make sure the Japanese weren't playing possum. Lieutenant Swan came up beside Carver. "Report, Sergeant."

Carver didn't salute but said, "Sir, your mortar strike broke their back. We lost three men when that Nambu opened up." He pointed back the way they'd come. The dead were being put onto stretchers. "Once the mortars stopped, we moved up against light resistance."

Lieutenant Swan nodded. "This was the heaviest concentration of Japs." He pointed to the left. "The rest of the company didn't have as hard a time." The rest of the second platoon was trotting across the airfield, led by Sergeant O'Connor. Swan continued. "We're continuing to push forward to the next town. Place called Pardo, or something. It's another mile or so that way." He pointed west.

Carver asked. "They figure out the armor?"

Swan nodded. "Yeah, the mine sweepers are clearing the road as we speak. Found a lot of 'em apparently, along with camouflaged tank traps. They'll probably be another hour. We're not waiting though. Division wants us to keep the pressure on."

Carver nodded, "Yes sir. We'll be ready to move when you give the order."

O'Connor sidled up beside them and gave them a crooked grin. "That went pretty well."

Carver nodded. "Thanks for the covering fire. We'd have been torn up without it." O'Connor nodded, but kept his eyes scanning the surrounding area for threats. Carver thought, *he's got no off switch. Probably why he's still alive.* "We're moving out soon." O'Connor spit and moved off to inform his squad.

4

Captain Flannigan entered the outskirts of the airfield minutes later. He sat in the passenger seat of a Willys Jeep. He wore glasses and smoked a stogie. Carver poked O'Connor in the ribs. "Get a load of MacArthur over here."

O'Connor sneered. "Jesus H. Christ, does he know how ridiculous he looks? And talk about a nice target for a Jap sniper. They'd think they brought down the big one."

Carver grinned. "We're not gonna be that lucky."

The Jeep veered their way and accelerated. When it was close the driver slammed on the brakes and skidded to a halt in a cloud of dust that wafted over second platoon. The men lowered their helmets and put their faces into their shirts. Carver could hear cussing and yelling. He didn't do anything to stop it.

When the dust cleared Flannigan was standing outside the jeep with his fists on his hips and his shiny boots a bit wider than shoulder width. He moved the cigar from one side of his mouth to the other.

Lieutenant Swan hustled up to him and braced but didn't salute. Captain Flannigan looked him up and down. "Don't you salute superior officers, Lieutenant?"

Swan looked at the surrounding jungle. "Don't wanna give the Jap snipers a bigger target than you're already presenting them, sir."

Flannigan tore his green tinted, mirrored sunglasses off and looked at the surrounding jungle and sneered. "I was told this area was secure. In fact, I heard that from you." He leaned forward, using his height and athletic build to full advantage.

Swan stared back at him. "When you're dealing with the Japs, nothing's ever totally secure, sir."

Platoon Sergeant Carver and Sergeant O'Connor were close enough to hear the exchange. O'Connor leaned close. "I'll be damned. When did Swan get a backbone?"

Carver answered. "Bougainville, I guess." He grinned. "Hell, I remember when his biggest concern was shitting his pants. Now he's facing down Captain America."

"Captain numb-nuts more like it."

Captain Flannigan went back to his normal arrogant stance. His mouth turned down as he looked upon his skinny Lieutenant. Swan stared back and when Flannigan realized he wasn't getting his salute, he moved past him. He spotted Carver and O'Connor. O'Connor moved to walk away but Flannigan pointed at them and said. "Sergeants. I'd like a word."

They turned toward the striding captain, O'Connor much slower than Carver. Neither saluted. Flannigan gritted his teeth but decided to let it pass. He stood in front of them. "Tell me about the attack?"

Lieutenant Swan had kept pace with Flannigan. His face flushed with anger. Carver looked past Flannigan and got the subtle nod from Swan. It didn't go unnoticed and Flannigan flinched slightly but insisted. "Well?"

Carver didn't want to get into the middle of an officer pissing match. "Under Lieutenant Swan's guidance we advanced across the airfield." He pointed at the smoldering buildings behind them. "The Japs had hidden three MGs in there and when we came across they opened up on us. We lost three men, but with the help of O'Connor's covering fire and Swan's mortar strike, we were able to take the buildings without any more casualties." Flannigan raised an eyebrow and Carver threw in, "Sir."

Captain Flannigan nodded, happy with his small victory. "Thank you, Sergeant." He looked to Swan. "I like to get the story from men at the pointy end of the stick."

Carver couldn't help himself. "In that case you coulda asked Lieutenant Swan. He was in the hole beside me." He stared at Flannigan. *Where were you, asshole?*

Flannigan puffed up his ample chest and slapped Swan's back. "Good boy. It'd be nice to be able to fight alongside you men, but captains don't lead attacks unfortunately."

They all looked at the ground, embarrassed for the man. Flannigan sensed the awkward moment and put his sunglasses back on. He spun around and strode back to the waiting Jeep. Once he was seated, O'Connor trotted forward and waved for his attention. They had a brief exchange and Flannigan's lips went flat and he nodded slightly. He waved forward and the driver peeled out sending rocks and debris into the men.

Lieutenant Swan asked, "What the hell'd you say to the man?"

O'Connor smiled and brushed dirt off his face. "Told him he looked an awful lot like MacArthur and for his own safety and that of any one around him he should try to blend in more." Swan's jaw dropped. "Don't worry I said it so he thought I was concerned for his safety cause he's such a valuable part of the war effort."

Swan swatted him on the back. "You crazy son-of-a-bitch." He pointed at the Jeep tearing across the airfield. "You know he makes his driver drive like that? I talked to the kid about it. He hates it, but Flannigan likes to make an entrance."

Carver shook his head. "What an asshole." Swan gave him a stern look and Carver held up his hands. "Sorry sir, it slipped."

Swan nodded. "Just don't say it in front of the men. They have to respect their officers or they won't follow orders."

Carver nodded knowing the drill better than most. He pointed to the road leading from the airfield. "We taking that to the next town?" Swan nodded.

∼

TWENTY MINUTES LATER, Able Company was leading the way along the dirt road. It was hard-pack with occasional deep rivulets and potholes from the monsoon rains that raged through during the rainy season. The jungle was too thick to push through, so the company was spread out along the road. The men had their rifles ready.

The going was slow. The lead element was a squad from the mine-sweeper platoon. They swept the area with their metal detectors. The operators wore heavy, thirty-pound battery packs and headphones and slowly swept side to side.

Platoon Sergeant Carver was right behind them, ready to cover them at the first sign of trouble. The GI next to him shook his head. "Those guys sure have a lot of balls, walking out in front without so much as a pistol, and not knowing if their next step will be their last."

Carver nodded. "Keep a sharp eye out. We're their only protection."

They'd just rounded the first corner when the lead minesweeper stopped and crouched. The rest of them dropped and Carver and his squad put their rifles to their shoulders and swept the area. The mine-sweeper yelled, "I found one."

Carver looked to Lt. Swan. He licked his lips and yelled, "Second squad move up and cover them while they mark the mine."

Sergeant O'Connor and his squad stood and trotted forward. They moved alongside the minesweepers and watched the jungle. The mine-sweeper swept his metal detector over the area and marked the borders of the mine with red flags. O'Connor felt like his ass was hanging in the wind. If the Japs were waiting to ambush them, he wouldn't know about it until the bullets smacked into him.

It only took a couple of minutes before they were back up and moving forward. The GIs gave the mine a wide berth.

They found four more mines before they got to the outskirts of the town. Each time, O'Connor thought he'd be in the middle of an ambush, but it never happened.

Able Company halted and Lieutenant Swan got on the radio to Captain Flannigan. He listened and nodded, then handed the receiver back to Private Hanks. He motioned for the men to spread out and advance.

Carver nodded and stood. The GIs were careful not to bunch up, but it was tough in the confines of the road and surrounding thick jungle. When they were close to the first shack, they trotted in and spread out. It wasn't much of a town. It consisted of a row of thatch buildings on stilts and a few wooden shantys that looked like they'd been thrown together with leftover lumber of various types.

There was no one in sight and Carver thought it might be abandoned, until a shot rang out. A GI spun with blood spurting from his shoulder. He went down screaming. He dropped his M1 and held his right shoulder as blood seeped between his fingers.

The rest of the Company dropped and brought their weapons up. The crack of weapons firing filled the air. Bullets slammed into the buildings. The wooden shantys came apart with countless high velocity impacts, but the thatch buildings seemed to absorb the bullets, most passing straight through.

Carver yelled, "McGillis, get that BAR working." Seconds later the heavy thumping of the .30 caliber Browning Automatic Rifle joined the fray. The BAR from Sergeant O'Connor's squad opened up too. Return fire was sporadic, but another GI went down, his head snapping back as a bullet center-punched his forehead. Carver saw the red mist descend on his body like a gruesome fog. "Pour it on, pour it on!"

Lieutenant Swan yelled, "Grenade launchers and flame throwers up." GIs raced forward and went into crouches. They aimed their grenade launch modified M1s. The bulbous grenades mounted on the muzzle attachment made them look like the barrels had split at the end. They aimed at the nearest buildings on stilts and fired. The grenades arced, trailing thin streams of gunpowder and disappeared into windows and thatch walls. The explosions weren't impressive, but the resulting smoke billowing from the roof told of their destructive power.

Soon the dry thatch was on fire. The grenadiers reloaded and arced more grenades into buildings. The first thatch hut was burning with fierce ferocity. Carver watched as a Japanese soldier burst through a burning wall. The soldier ran straight for them. He was covered in burning thatch and his uniform was glowing with embers. Carver put three .45 caliber slugs into him and he dropped to the ground, sending sparks flying in all directions. The fire consumed him, turning him to blackened char within seconds.

The air was filled with billowing smoke as more buildings caught fire. Carver waved the men forward and they moved amongst the burning buildings firing indiscriminately. The heat was intense and soon they couldn't advance without burning themselves.

Lieutenant Swan called a halt and pulled them back from the inferno. There was screaming mixed with the roar of fire, but there were no more targets.

They waited at the edge of the town, watching it burn. The dry thatch burned quick and soon the buildings were nothing more than skeletal beams of wood. A stilt on the nearest building snapped like a gunshot and the men flinched. The building wavered, then came crashing down sending hot sparks soaring into the sky. A wave of heat slammed into them like a physical slap and the GIs moved back further. They were red-faced and sweat poured from their faces like they'd just dipped their heads in a shower.

Lieutenant Swan moved them further back, completely exiting the village. The platoon moved back along the road they came in on. The village was no longer in sight and the relief from the heat made Carver wonder how they'd stayed as close as they had. Swan stopped them and Carver ordered them to drink.

They'd just taken their first gulps when the welcome sound of clanking armor pulled them up short. The first vehicle was a banged up Sherman tank. It was dark green and the star on the side was faded and chipped. The turret swiveled as it rounded the corner and saw the GIs. The gaping black maw of the 75mm gun centered on the nearest man.

The platoon melted to the sides of the road and four Shermans thundered by. The ground shook as they passed and the GIs smiled and waved.

A jeep came flying around the corner and braked hard in front of the platoon. More tanks mixed with armored cars filtered past. Captain Flannigan jumped out of the jeep and strode to the GIs who were trying to make themselves look invisible.

Flannigan found Lt. Swan and yelled. "What's all that smoke ahead?"

Swan swallowed and his oversized Adam's apple bobbed. "The village of Pardo's on fire. We engaged snipers with grenades and those grass huts went up in a hurry. We're waiting for it to die down, sir. Hotter'n blazes."

Flannigan's face turned a bright shade of red and Carver thought his head might explode. Flannigan seethed. "Who told you to torch the town, Lieutenant?"

Swan shook his head. "No one did. Like I said it happened when we engaged the Japs."

"Dammit, Swan. Your orders are to take the villages, not destroy them. The natives will need someplace to live after this battle's over for chrissakes."

Carver was ready to step in and help his officer, he'd done it plenty of times before, but Swan spoke up. "Begging your pardon, sir, but my orders are to kill Japs. If there's a rulebook I need to follow, I wasn't aware of it."

Captain Flannigan stared into Swan's eyes sending daggers, but Swan stared right back, his gaze passive. It infuriated Flannigan more. He pointed a finger and laid into him like a principal dealing with an insubordinate student. "Your orders are to kill Japanese, but not at the expense of destroying the entire area. My God, man. What if there were natives in those huts?"

Lieutenant Swan tilted his head trying to make sense of Flannigan. "It wasn't intentional, but if burning the village kills the Japs and saves my men from being killed..." he let the thought finish itself.

Flannigan shook with anger. He liked the old Lt. Swan, the man he could push around and scare. This new officer seemed fearless. He removed his finger from Swan's face and lowered his voice. "Just be more careful next time."

He turned to leave, but Swan wasn't finished. "At the expense of the men, sir?"

Flannigan stopped, shook his head then continued to the jeep. He pulled his big body into the metal seat and said something to his driver. He floored it and the Jeep fishtailed until it was faced back towards the airfield. The jeep and the captain disappeared around the corner.

Swan grinned and turned back to the GIs. "Let's move up behind the tanks. The fire's probably dying down by now."

THE TANKS and the rest of the armor kept their distance from the town until the fires were smoldering. The hour respite allowed the GIs to eat and drink. Their dead and wounded were carted back to the beach where an aid station was set up.

The signal to continue the advance came when the Shermans fired up their 400 horse power Continental engines. The roar and the billowing white smoke brought the men to their feet. The lead Sherman's top hatch was open and a tanker in a steel pot helmet manned the mounted .50 caliber machine gun. He looked back to the other tanks and said something into his mouthpiece radio. The tank lurched beneath him and he held onto the machine gun handles. The rest of the tanks and halftracks lurched and ground forward.

The GIs filtered in behind and around the protective armor. Platoon Sergeant Carver stood as far away as possible, up against the edge of the road. Private McGillis was nearby and asked, "Why you way over there?"

Carver replied. "Those tanks are Jap magnets." McGillis shrugged but moved a few feet further away.

A few structures still stood, but most of the town was charred and smoking. Tongues of flames still licked wooden beams; not wanting to relinquish their destructive hold.

There was no sign of live Japs, or anyone else for that matter. Carver noticed the burning soldier he'd shot. His skin was gone, exposing his charred skull and teeth. Every shred of clothing was burned away, but a shiny metal object shone against what used to be the soldier's neck. Carver wondered if it was dog-tags or some memento from a sweetheart. He turned away as the lead Sherman's tracks ran him over and ground him into dust.

Carver felt hollow. A vision of Lilly smiling at him from the hammock came to mind. He shook his head; *how can I ever tell Lilly of such things?* The vision morphed and now Lilly's beautiful face was replaced with the charred Japanese soldier's. The vision was so powerful he stopped and took a knee. He pinched the bridge of his nose until it hurt.

Sergeant O'Connor kneeled beside him, his M1 ready. He whispered. "What's wrong? See something?" Carver stood and teetered slightly. O'Connor looked him over. "You okay? Look like you've seen a ghost."

Carver nodded and moved forward. "Get back to your squad, Sergeant. I'm fine. Just feeling the damned heat." O'Connor frowned and mumbled something under his breath. Carver ignored him and shook the image from his mind. *Gotta concentrate or I'll never see that girl again.*

They were almost through the village. The final buildings were still standing, saved by some inexplicable nuance of the flames. The lead Sherman's 75mm gun kept the nearest house centered. The tanker on the .50 caliber swiveled the gun back and forth.

Sparks suddenly showered the lead tank as bullets zinged and ricocheted. The gunner crouched low in the cupola keeping his hands on the handles of the .50. He yelled something into his headset and the tank lurched to a stop. The gun pivoted towards the middle building and stopped. It elevated slightly and fired.

The GIs behind the first tank stumbled into the stopped tank and when it fired they dropped to their knees. Carver saw Lt. Swan on the radio but couldn't tell if he was listening or giving orders.

Carver plastered himself to the ground as the Sherman fired. The 75mm shell traveled the short distance in the blink of an eye and detonated on the wall beneath the window. When the debris settled, Carver could see the front of the building was gone. The thumping of the .50 caliber filled the air and Carver watched tracers lancing into the dark building. He had his Thompson aimed, but doubted anyone could've survived such an onslaught.

The shooting stopped and there was a quick flash of light as the form of a Japanese soldier sprinted from the building. He dropped his rifle and ran for his life. Carver brought his weapon to his shoulder. He had a clear shot, but he hesitated. His finger was on the trigger, but the thought of killing yet another soldier suddenly made him feel sick. Shots rang out from other GIs and Carver watched the Japanese soldier's back blossom red. He fell into the short grass and was lost from sight.

Carver lowered his weapon and put his head on the ground. *What's wrong with me?*

5

After the airfield and the village of Pardo were taken, the road to Cebu City was wide open. Able Company along with mixed armored units and elements of the heavy weapons company advanced quickly and unopposed.

Lieutenant Swan allowed the men to glom onto the Shermans and they rode in ease and style for the first time. Carver reluctantly mounted a Sherman but made sure he had a quick and easy way off if attacked. He could see Sergeant O'Connor on the tank behind. He was standing, holding onto the turret. He had his helmet pulled low and was scanning the countryside. He looked as uncomfortable about riding the tank as Carver felt.

Lieutenant Swan was talking on the radio. He nodded and signed off. He got Carver's attention. "We're a quarter mile from Cebu City. We'll dismount as we approach and spread out. Regimental HQ doesn't seem to know what we'll find, but they seem to think the city's already pacified." Carver looked confused and Swan continued. "Thinks the Filipino resistance might've routed the Japs already."

Carver nodded and felt a weight fall from his shoulders. He hadn't realized it, but he'd been dreading the prospect of house to house fighting. His men were jungle fighters. They weren't trained to fight in a city. They'd have to learn as they fought and that meant a lot of men would die.

Minutes later the column slowed and Lt. Swan signaled for them to dismount. GIs sprang from the tanks and dispersed. Once clear, the tanks spread out to the surrounding countryside. The jungle had given way to agricultural fields. The heavy tank treads tore up the dark soil, sending plumes off the back-end. The GIs stayed clear, letting the tanks churn past them.

As the tanks approached the outskirts of the sprawling city they were met, not by Japanese but by cheering Filipino resistance fighters. They were holding up their rifles, an assortment of Japanese Arisakas, American M1s, and Enfields. Some were shirtless, but the majority wore loose fitting white shirts. A few looked like they were in uniform. Leading the group was a tall white man. He walked with a stiff back and Carver could tell right away he must be an officer.

The tanks stopped when they were yards from the group. With their engines at idle, Carver could hear the Filipinos cheering. They thrust their weapons over their heads and screamed and hooted. The tall officer's face was split into a wide grin. The top hatches of the M4 Shermans popped open and the tankers poked their heads out like turtles from their shells.

Lieutenant Swan waved the men forward and they advanced until they stood in front of the cheering Filipinos. Swan stepped forward and gave a quick salute. The tall officer saluted back and extended his hand. Swan shook it. "I'm Colonel Cushing and these are my merry band of cutthroats." He gestured to the Filipinos and their cheers went up a few decibels. He had to yell to be heard. "We've been anxiously awaiting your arrival. Welcome to Cebu City." With that, the Filipinos moved amongst them shaking hands and slapping backs. The GIs smiled and laughed and celebrated. The excitement and joy at being out from beneath the boot of the Japanese was contagious. No one noticed the jeep that skidded to a halt beside the closest tank.

Platoon Sergeant Carver tried to maintain his composure, but the celebratory feeling combined with not having to battle house to house made him smile and return back slaps and hugs. He noticed even Sergeant O'Connor was smiling.

The celebration was finally broken up by Colonel Cushing. He simply raised his booming voice above the din and the Filipinos went silent and separated themselves from the GIs. That's when Captain Flannigan made himself known. He strode up to Cushing and looked him up and down. Colonel Cushing's jovial demeanor disappeared in an instant and he raised his chin and looked down his nose at Flannigan. "I'm Colonel Cushing. Who might you be, Captain?"

Flannigan went ramrod straight and fired off a quick salute. "Captain Flannigan at your service, sir. I'm the C.O. of Able Company." He gestured to the GIs surrounding him.

"Well, captain you'll find Cebu City is mostly free of Japs. We struck last night and pushed General Manjome's troops into the northwest corner of the city. They took a lot of casualties, but around two thousand of them remain. They're surrounded behind a walled section of the city. Follow me." He pointed over his shoulder. "My HQ's in the center of the city. I'll show you the situation on the map."

Flannigan looked beyond him into the city. He shook his head. "I'm sure General Arnold will want to speak with you back at the HQ, Colonel."

Colonel Cushing shook his head. "I've been in contact with General Arnold, he's on his way in too." He put his hand on Flannigan's shoulder. Even against Flannigan's large frame, the gnarled hand looked huge. "Don't worry captain, it's perfectly safe."

Captain Flannigan's face flushed red and he muttered, "Yes sir." The nearby GIs couldn't contain their smiles. Flannigan's demeanor went from embarrassed to angry in an instant. He barked, "Lieutenant Swan." He swiveled trying to locate him.

Swan was beside him. He raised his hand. "Here, sir."

Flannigan shook his head. "There you are. Get the men sorted, this isn't some damned parade."

Swan noticed a sympathetic glance from Colonel Cushing. Swan said, "Yes sir. Right away, sir."

The men moved away from their new Filipino friends and formed a loose column without being told. Colonel Cushing moved to the front of the group with Captain Flannigan by his side. The large column of men, followed by tanks and halftracks streamed into town along the main street.

The street was lined with countless cheering Filipinos. They waved American and British flags and anything else they could find. They hung from windows and sang and smiled and laughed. Lieutenant Swan was leading the GIs who were in column behind the Filipinos. He leaned close to Carver's ear. "Looks a hell of a lot like a parade to me."

AFTER A BRIEF STOP in the city center to eat and resupply, they moved toward the northwest corner. The celebratory feeling ended as they neared the area. There were barricades manned by smiling Filipinos. Able Company spread out and hunkered behind cover. The Armor spread to side streets and aimed their turrets toward likely buildings.

Captain Flannigan crouched down beside Colonel Cushing. Lieutenant Swan, Platoon Sergeant Carver and Sergeant O'Connor were nearby. Colonel Cushing tapped a diminutive Filipino next to him. The fighter turned and noticed the Colonel. A smile spread across the fighter's mocha colored face. Colonel Cushing squeezed her shoulder and introduced her. "This is Major Cruz. She's been my second in command since this whole thing started. Without her, none of this would've been possible."

She nodded at the new faces and shook each man's hand as she was introduced. When she held her small hand out to Sergeant O'Connor he could only stare. His eyes were glazed over. The moment lengthened until Carver finally jabbed O'Connor in the ribs and said, "Snap out of it Sergeant."

O'Connor tore his gaze from her soft brown eyes and blushed. He took off his helmet as if it was a dress hat and held it to his chest. He took her hand. It seemed small and delicate, but he felt the hard callouses on her palm. She smiled and her eyes softened into ovals. She pointed at his helmet and in nearly accent-less English, said, "You're going to need that, Sergeant." Confusion flooded his face. She released his hand and took the helmet from him. She held it over his red hair and placed it carefully.

O'Connor pulled back and tore his gaze from the deep pools of her eyes and stuttered. "Th-thank you..." he suddenly remembered himself, "Major." He cleared his throat and felt he should do something. He straightened his back and snapped off a quick salute. O'Connor noticed Carver's grin and blushed deeper.

She smiled and turned back to the colonel. She pointed toward a walled section of the city. "The Japanese are inside the walls. They occupy the top floors and can see us when we move. They have snipers. Now that the Americans are here with their tanks, we can kill them."

Colonel Cushing nodded and addressed Captain Flannigan. "Call in your artillery and air assets. That's all we need to get inside and get in amongst them. It won't take long after that."

Flannigan jumped at the opportunity to get away from the front line. "I'll have to run it by General Arnold." He looked back the way they'd come. "I'll take a few of your men to escort me back to my jeep, Lieutenant."

Lieutenant Swan pointed at Private Hanks who was holding out his radio. "You can use this, sir."

Flannigan scowled and shook his head. "Nah, mine's more powerful. I'll need a clear signal." Swan called out three GIs to escort Flannigan back to his jeep. He took his leave. "I'll be in contact. Don't assault until I've given you the word, Lieutenant." Swan nodded and Flannigan trotted off surrounded by three GIs.

Colonel Cushing watched him go. "Doesn't enjoy the front line much does he?"

Lieutenant Swan was embarrassed for his commander. "No sir. Not really."

A bullet whizzed over their heads and slapped into the road beside Captain Flannigan. He went into a full sprint, pumping his arms and high stepping. The GIs escorting him trotted to the sides of the street and kept cover between themselves and the sniper. A dirt geyser erupted well behind Flannigan, followed immediately by the crack of the rifle. It was enough to send him into an even higher gear.

Colonel Cushing grinned. "That man's got a future in the hundred meter dash, if he survives this thing."

There was return fire up and down the line as the Filipino fighters engaged the sniper. Major Cruz pointed. "Those windows on the second floor of the nearest building are full of snipers."

Carver nodded and slapped O'Connor who was staring at Major Cruz. "Get your bazooka team up here. We'll put a crimp in their style."

O'Connor called out, "Vincent, Pullman, up!" the word passed through the company and soon two gangly soldiers were weaving towards them. The lead man, Private Vincent held the bazooka followed by Private Pullman carrying the satchel of bazooka rounds. They skidded into the cover and their eyes went wide when they noticed the beautiful major beside Colonel Cushing. O'Connor grabbed Pvt. Vincent's shoulder and pointed through a gap in the cover. "See that top floor window in the center?" Vincent squinted through the gap and nodded. "Think you can hit it?"

Private Vincent nodded and smiled. "Course I can, Sarge. Piece of cake." He stayed behind cover but put the bazooka tube on his shoulder and angled up slightly. "Load me up Pullman."

Private Pullman was already placing the high explosive M7 round into the back of the tube. As he pulled the wire from the rocket and wrapped it on the contact, he said, "Hold your damned horses." A second later he slapped Vincent's shoulder. "Ready." He stepped to the side away from the rocket blast.

Private Vincent adjusted his footing and rose up, aiming through the sight. He steadied and pulled the trigger. The rocket whooshed from the barrel and the white trailing smoke was easy to follow. The rocket went through the dark window frame hit the back wall and exploded inside. There was a bright flash followed by smoke and billowing dust. Major Cruz looked on admiringly. "Nice shot, soldier." The nearby Filipino fighters cheered and pumped their weapons into the air.

Private Vincent's smile threatened to break his face. "That was nothing. Give me something harder next time."

A blast from an M4 Sherman shook their cover. They ducked lower and saw the white plume of smoke billowing out from the alley to the right. The 75mm cannon was sticking into the street, trailing a thin strand of smoke. Carver looked over the top of the cover and saw the same window the bazooka had engaged. The shot had hit the side of the window and blown out a large chunk of the front wall. Pieces of concrete continued to peel off the wall and plunge to the ground. Smoke and dust continued to pour from the gap. Carver ducked back down and said, "Looks like your sniper nest's done for."

The other M4s opened up on the same building until it seemed to be erupting with great holes and explosions. Carver and the rest ducked down as bits of fine mist and debris rained down on them. Carver pulled his helmet down and pulled his shirt over his mouth.

When the Shermans stopped firing and the debris settled, Carver poked his head up again. The front of the building was pockmarked with large holes. The right side had completely collapsed.

He saw movement in the carnage and realized he was seeing staggering Japanese soldiers. He brought his Thompson to his shoulder but he didn't pull the trigger. The harsh cracks of M1 Garands and Carbines rippled along the line and he watched the soldiers stagger and fall as bullets slammed around and into them. He pulled back his Thompson, turned and sunk into cover. He had his back to the wall and he closed his eyes. *What's wrong with me? Am I losing my nerve?*

He looked to his left and saw Sergeant O'Connor watching him. He shook his head slightly and turned away. Carver stared at the sky and took a deep breath. He blew it out and pictured Lilly smiling at him. It soothed him and he felt the war disappear for a moment.

It came roaring back when he heard Lt. Swan chattering on the radio. Swan found Carver and scooted closer. "Listen up. There won't be an artillery barrage. Command wants to limit the damage, so we're going in behind the tanks. General Arnold is sending up more units but we'll be the head of the spear." He stopped and licked his lips. He glanced at his wrist watch. "We jump off in an hour. Get the men ready. It's house to house. Not our forte' but we'll figure it out."

Carver nodded. "We'll have to."

∿

ABLE COMPANY STAYED in cover while the Shermans plowed over the low wall surrounding the city district at various points. The mud and thatch walls crumbled as the thirty-ton monsters flattened them.

Sergeant O'Connor motioned his squad to follow, and he tucked up against the nearest tank. The Shermans advanced toward the sniper building. There were no more shots coming from it.

The streets and alleys were tight, not leaving much maneuvering room for the bulky tanks. The Shermans stopped short and idled. O'Connor saw Lt. Swan taking a call from the back of the tank he followed. It was a brief conversation. He hung up and signaled. They were to advance without the tanks the rest of the way. O'Connor cursed to himself. The tightly packed buildings could hold hundreds of Japanese soldiers and they'd have to enter and clear each one or risk being attacked from behind.

O'Connor turned to his wide-eyed GIs. "Okay, we cover each other all the time. One group enters the building while the other covers their backsides. Then we move onto the next with the first group covering the next." He watched the men nodding. "If we hear or see Japs we throw grenades first, then enter and take 'em out while they're stunned. Got it?" They nodded and waited for the signal to advance.

Lieutenant Swan waved his arm and he stepped from behind the Sherman. The Company was spread out, each squad responsible for the buildings to their immediate front.

O'Connor went around the Sherman and heard the footsteps of his men following. He went to the first door and stood to the side. He listened for any sound that would indicate the enemy. The Filipino resistance fighters assured them that all civilians had been evacuated, so anyone left were Japanese. The only thing he heard was the purr of the tanks. He made eye contact with the GI beside him, who licked his dry lips and nodded. Six men were lined up behind him. The remaining six were across the street scanning the roofs and windows for surprises.

O'Connor moved to the front of the door. It looked well built with heavy wood. He stepped back and kicked the door handle as hard as he could. The wooden frame shattered and the door swung open. With his M1 Carbine leading, he ran in. His mind was on overdrive as he took in the surroundings as quickly as possible. His felt his heart would leap out of his chest, but the room was empty. The rest of the GIs streamed past him and cleared the adjoining rooms. It was a single-story building. It looked to be some sort of store, but the shelves and counters were bare.

He heard shooting off to the right, in another building. It was intense but quickly faded to single shots. The GIs crouched and readied themselves for the next building. O'Connor hoped it went as well as the first. He trotted back to the front door and signaled the men covering them to move forward. They ran past him and into the cleared building.

They moved through to the back wall. The next building across the alley was a two story. There was a rickety back door they could enter through. It was partially opened. He whispered. "Now we switch." The men nodded. "I'll lead this one too." Relief flooded Corporal Mathew's face. O'Connor trusted him, he was a good soldier and had shown coolness under fire, but city fighting was new to all of them.

O'Connor looked both ways down the alley. It was strewn with debris but clear of enemy soldiers. With one last look to the windows above, he ran across to the side of the next door.

He waited until the men were ready. He was about to move, when he heard the clatter of something inside. He pulled back and put his finger to his lips. He pulled a grenade from his utility belt and pulled the pin. He released the handle and threw it into the room with a quick motion. He pulled back and cringed at the crack of a rifle. The bullet slammed into the side of the half-open door and splintered the thin wood. A second later the grenade exploded and sent the door flying into the wall across the alley.

Without exposing his head, O'Connor extended his carbine and pulled the trigger, moving the barrel side to side. He pulled back and yelled, "Go, go, go!"

Corporal Mathews moved past him and the shattered door frame. He darted left and went into a crouch. He saw movement deeper in the hallway and fired his M1 Garand. The heavy thud of a body falling was unmistakable. The rest of the men filled the room and fired down the hallway. There was screaming and yelling coming from deeper inside.

Mathews pulled a grenade and yelled, "Fire in the hole!" The GIs went prone and Mathews lobbed the grenade down the hall. It bounced off the right wall and went around the corner and disappeared. The explosion sent a dust cloud down the hall along with more screaming.

O'Connor took the moment to reload his partially used, thirty-round magazine. He pushed himself to his feet and ran down the hall with his carbine ready. He saw a body sprawled in front of him and before leaping over, he put three more .30 caliber rounds into it.

He came around the corner and saw the grisly aftermath of the grenade. Men lay in bleeding heaps. He pulled the semi-automatic trigger as fast as he could pull. The soldiers still alive were dazed and O'Connor poured bullets into them. The rest of the squad joined him. After a few seconds, he yelled, "Cease fire!"

Beyond the bodies there was another hallway and a stairwell leading up to the right. O'Connor saw an object hit the bottom step and bounce off the opposite wall. He dove to the right while at the same time yelling, "Grenade!" The GIs reacted instantly diving to the ground, using the Japanese bodies for cover.

The grenade exploded and the shock wave washed over O'Connor and made his already tortured ears ring in protest. The Japanese bodies had absorbed most of the blast, but he heard a GI screaming.

O'Connor got to his knees and shook the cobwebs from his head. He pointed at the ceiling. "Japs upstairs." There was firing coming from outside. O'Connor's ears were clear enough to hear the heavy thumps of footfalls above. He rolled onto his back and yelled. "Fire through the ceiling." He fired his carbine until the chamber locked in the open position. He released the magazine and reloaded. The rest of the squad was firing straight up. The ceiling was coming apart with large chunks of plaster and dust.

O'Connor got to his feet and signaled a cease fire. He listened for more footfalls but didn't hear anything. The firing from outside stopped. O'Connor pointed at Private Gilson. "Tell the men outside to cease fire, we're moving to the second floor." He nodded and ran off, plaster and dust streaming off his helmet and shoulders.

O'Connor pointed at Mathews then at the stairway. "Get up there and clear out any survivors."

Mathews stood and nodded. He adjusted his helmet and moved to the stairwell. The grenade blast had opened a hole in the wooden floor and the scent of scorched dirt and wood wafted from it. He waited until the men were behind him. He took the first step up the stairwell and started firing. He took the stairs by twos and was soon up and around the corner. The rest of the men followed, with O'Connor taking up the rear.

The firing stopped and O'Connor entered. It was a large room nearly covering the entire top floor. There were three dead Japanese soldiers in the center, victims of bullets coming through the floor. Tiny shafts of light streamed through countless holes. Near the far wall, beneath the windows were three more Japanese bodies.

O'Connor went to the window and poked his head out. He waved at the rest of his squad. "We've got a wounded man inside. Get Doc Haley." One of the GIs ran off in the direction of Carver's squad. O'Connor yelled, "Crenshaw, go with him." A short bandy-legged GI nodded and took off in pursuit. "The rest of you come inside." They nodded and moved across the alley.

The rest of the squad stood in the room with vacant looks. Their rifle's still smoked and the blood from the fallen Japanese seeped into the floorboards and dripped through the holes. O'Connor rallied them up. "Let's get downstairs and take a breather while we wait for doc Haley."

The men nodded and moved to the stairwell. O'Connor recognized the dazed looks. He needed to keep the men busy, keep their minds off how close each had come to dying.

Private First-Class Haley was coming through the door behind Private Crenshaw and Griffin. He slid in beside the wounded soldier. The GI was propped up against the wall clutching his right leg and moaning. Blood soaked his shredded pant leg. He was sweating and was white as a sheet. There were two other GIs hovering over him, trying to soothe him. Haley pulled a pair of scissors off his belt and cut the pant leg away. The soldier nearest turned white and vomited off to the side. Haley yelled at the GI. "Get the hell outta here if you're such a damned pussy. Doesn't help anything." The GI wiped his mouth and sulked away.

Haley redirected his focus to the wounded man. "Don't worry about that asshole. It's not as bad as it looks." He read his stenciled name-tag. "Private Lewis." He pulled out a bandage and sulfa powder. "Hell, it's barely bleeding. I've seen a lot worse than this, believe me." He poured the white powder over the meaty wound. He reached into his medic kit and pulled out a small white cylinder. He held it up for Lewis to see. "Gonna give you morphine, it'll ease the pain." Lewis nodded. Haley jabbed the syrete into his leg. The effect was immediate. Lewis relaxed and leaned his head back. Haley pushed the bandage onto the wound and tied it tightly around his thigh. He pulled out a marker and wrote the number '1' followed by the letter 'm' on Lewis's forehead.

Haley looked around at the rest of the squad. He noticed the pile of torn up Japanese soldiers but ignored them. "Anyone else hit?"

O'Connor shook his head. "Nah, that's it. Thanks doc."

Haley nodded, "Don't mention it. I've gotta get back. A few other guys got hit a few buildings over. You can leave Lewis here. I'll have a detail swing by and get him."

O'Connor nodded and pointed at the soldier who'd puked. "Stay with him, Montgomery." The soldier was still pale, but he nodded and crouched beside Lewis again. "The rest of you check your weapons and ammo. We've got more buildings to clear." As if to remind them, there was firing coming from another nearby building.

6

Sam Santos was exhausted but exuberant. He'd fought alongside his Filipino brothers and sisters all night long. They'd pushed the Japanese back steadily, routing them from buildings block by bloody block.

They'd succeeded in pushing them from most of the city, but the Japanese had set up a stout defense in the northwest corner. Sam and the rest of the partisans were ordered to stop and wait for the allies to come ashore.

He welcomed the rest. He sat with his back to a wall and recounted the night. He thought back to the men he'd killed, picturing their faces. He wondered about their families back in Japan. Would they ever know the fate of their loved ones? *Will I ever know the fate of mine?* The image of his little sister flashed across his mind and he felt a tear well up and roll down his cheek. It had been weeks since they'd taken her. He wondered if she was alive, and if she were, if she prayed for death.

The image of his grandmother bleeding on the floor, her normally bright eyes devoid of life, assaulted him. He ground his teeth and felt the hatred fill his soul. He hoped the Japanese suffered, the parents, the wives, sons and daughters, all of them could go to hell. His brother's face filled his mind. *What will I do when I find you, brother?* He knew. *I'll kill you myself.*

The sun was high when the Americans finally got to his position. He stood and watched their big tanks rumble forward and take up positions. The soldiers looked big and commanding and it seemed they all had smiles on their faces. Some had flowers in their helmet webbing where the locals had decorated. Sam thought they looked formidable in their green matching uniforms. Their weapons were shiny and looked new, unlike the M1 he carried.

He moved to the side of a building and watched with Felipe as the American GIs took cover. An impossibly tall GI walked by them and tipped his helmet. Sam smiled and gave him a salute. The GI laughed and continued walking.

He saw a group of GIs who looked like officers talking with Major Cruz, his old teacher. He pointed and asked Felipe, "Are those general's?"

Felipe laughed and shook his head. "They're officers, but not generals. Not every officer is a general. It looks like a Captain and a Lieutenant. The ones with the stripes on their shoulders are sergeants. The one with more stripes is a platoon sergeant, I think."

Sam lifted his eyebrows and shook his head. "How can you remember? It seems like there's too much to know."

Felipe slapped his back. "Don't worry about it. You're a private, the lowest rank. It's not hard for you. They all outrank you so do what they say."

Sam nodded, feeling better. "I think I'd like to stay a private."

One of the officers broke away from the group and was trotting down the middle of the street. Sam thought it was a bad idea. A shot rang out and he instinctually crouched. The officer took off running. Another shot and the officer ran even faster. Sam thought he was the fastest person he'd ever seen.

The Americans and Filipinos opened fire and the sniping stopped. Sam watched in fascination as the bazooka team fired into the building and the tanks followed soon after. When the smoke cleared he let out a long whistle. He pointed, "They destroyed the entire building with just a few shots. No wonder we were ordered to wait for them. They're like gods."

Felipe shook his head. "They bleed the same way we do, Sam."

AFTER WATCHING the Americans with their big guns and overwhelming firepower, Sam wanted to get back in the fight. The American tanks busted through the outer walls and flooded into the last Japanese holdout.

The Filipino fighters sat behind cover, unsure of what to do. Sam paced back and forth listening to the far-off sounds of fighting. He looked up as a low flying American fighter plane zoomed past. The guns on the wings blazed and he could see the empty shell casings falling to the ground. He was frustrated, he wanted to be a part of the action. He wanted to avenge his sister and grandmother. He wanted to kill more Japanese.

Finally, Felipe trotted up and assembled the large group of fighters. They formed loose rows and tried to look as militarily crisp as possible, but their non-matching, filthy clothes made it difficult.

Major Cruz appeared and she had to yell to be heard. "The Americans are meeting resistance and it will only increase the deeper they penetrate. Colonel Cushing has asked me for volunteers to act as guides for the Americans." Every hand in the group went up instantly. Her smile seemed to fill most of her face, and Sam thought she looked beautiful. He wondered how he'd failed to notice her beauty when he was a student. "We only need thirty volunteers." Hands went up higher some waving, vying for her attention. "The first row will go." Those in the first row cheered and trotted forward, unslinging their weapons from their shoulders.

Sam was in the second row and felt tears well up. He shook his head. *Warriors don't cry. I'm a warrior.*

Major Cruz felt the let-down of the remaining fighters. "This is not the end of the fight. The Japanese are not defeated on this island and certainly not the Philippines. You will have many more opportunities to fight." She flashed the 'V' for victory sign and the fighters cheered.

Sam felt dejected despite Major Cruz's assurances. He yearned to fight and fighting alongside the Americans would be a dream come true. They'd been kicking the Japanese like dogs for years. He could learn a lot from them.

TWO HOURS later Felipe came running into the building Sam was dozing in. He found Sam and kicked his prostate body. "Get up. You're needed at the front."

Sam was up like a flash. He grabbed his rifle and trotted behind Felipe into the evening light. He rubbed the sleep from his eyes. "What's happened?"

Continuing to trot, Felipe panted, "Juan Chavez was killed by a sniper. You'll be his replacement."

The news sobered him and he felt a flash of fear. He wanted to fight more than anything, but what would keep him from the same fate as Juan; a far more experienced fighter?

Felipe noticed Sam's pace slowed a fraction. "Having second thoughts?"

His tone angered Sam and he lashed out. "Course not. Juan was a good man. He'll be missed."

"Indeed."

Sam followed Felipe through the holes the tanks had left. They kept to the sides of the street, weaving in and out of cover. Soon Sam heard the rumble of idling tanks. Felipe looked back at him. "The Americans are just ahead. The streets were too narrow for their tanks."

They ran a few more blocks then came up on a group of American soldiers. They were sitting with their backs against building walls, sipping water. Sam saw a few Filipinos amongst them. He recognized them from the work camp.

Felipe trotted up to a group of soldiers. A red-haired GI with stripes on his shoulders greeted them. "Felipe, you've returned."

Felipe nodded and indicated Sam. "Your new guide. He knows the city well. Sam, this is Sergeant O'Connor."

Sam snapped off what he hoped was a snappy salute. O'Connor

reached out and pulled his hand down. "Don't salute out here, boy. Jap snipers will think I'm an officer and put a bullet through my head." Sam was embarrassed and lowered his gaze. O'Connor addressed Felipe. "Christ almighty. He's just a kid. You sure he knows what he's doing?"

Sam looked up and balled his fists. Before Felipe could answer, Sam seethed, "I know what I'm doing, Sergeant. I know the city."

Felipe backed him up. "He fought well all night. A real tiger." He slapped Sam's back.

O'Connor nodded. "Okay. Take it easy, kid." He pointed to his men. "We're awaiting orders to advance. This first block was well defended, slowed us down a bit. We're waiting for the rest of the company to move up, maybe get the tanks involved." He pointed down the debris filled street. "We took care of the sniper that killed Juan, but we can expect more of that shit. We have men in the next two buildings. They haven't run into anything more than snipers. Seems like the Japs have pulled back. Can you think of someplace they might be holed up?"

Felipe rubbed his chin. Sam nodded. "The plaza. It's in the center of this district. If they occupied the buildings on the far side, there's an open space you'd have to cross."

Felipe nodded confirming Sam's idea. "Yes, it would be a likely spot for a last stand."

O'Connor asked, "How far?"

"Two kilometers or less."

"Okay. You'll lead us there. We'll be moving forward within the hour. Make sure you have enough ammo."

Sam nodded, "I'm ready when you are, Sergeant."

AN HOUR later Able Company moved forward through the deserted streets. The going was slow, having to clear each block. They didn't run into any more snipers and resistance was light.

Sam was ordered to stay near the back and give any advice on their movement through the city. He felt useless. He wasn't able to give the Americans any advice. There was nothing to do but move from building to building. He felt confident they'd find the Japanese at the plaza. He wracked his brain, trying to come up with something that would help the GIs, but there was nothing to do but advance until they found the Japanese.

When they were a block from the plaza, Sam moved forward and found Sergeant O'Connor. He liked the American even though he knew he thought of Sam as a child. "The plaza is just ahead."

O'Connor waved his men forward and they leapfrogged through the buildings and streets, covering one another as they went. The rest of the company was spread out to either side, advancing carefully. Occasionally there'd be a shot, but nothing sustained.

Sam stayed on O'Connor's tail as he moved forward. They stopped at the entrance to the plaza. In the center, there was a fountain which hadn't seen water since the Japanese arrived. The space was wide and long. It looked like it used to be a park. There were play structures and sculptures which were overgrown with grass and vines. The jungle was slowly reclaiming the area. They crouched in a doorway. Sam pointed across the park. "Those buildings."

O'Connor nodded. "Yeah, that's where I'd set up." He studied the far building's windows. He couldn't see any obvious signs of Japanese, but he figured they were there.

A runner from Platoon Sergeant Carver's squad sprinted across the street and slid in beside O'Connor and Sam. O'Connor scooted into the back of the doorway. "What you got, Perkins?"

"The rest of the company is spread along this line. The flanks are going to move through the buildings surrounding the plaza. You're to stay here and provide cover. The tanks are maneuvering through the streets along the edge of the district with the help of the Filipino guides, but they won't be here for another half hour. Captain Flannigan doesn't wanna wait."

O'Connor licked his lips and nodded. "Okay, got it." Private Perkins ran across the street zigzagging all the way. O'Connor signaled the men watching him. They moved to find better cover and spots to shoot from.

O'Connor looked at the door behind him. He moved Sam aside and tried the handle, but it was locked. "Move back." He kicked the door at the handle level and it splintered. He moved into the building. It looked like an apartment. There was a bed, and a kitchen with a rusted sink.

A flight of stairs led up to the second floor and he was about to move to it when Sam grabbed his arm and held him. O'Connor shook him off and glared. Sam pointed. "Trap."

Two more GIs entered the building and crouched. They swept the room with their carbines. O'Connor studied the stairwell and saw the odd-looking pile of wood on the second step. It looked out of place, like it had been put there intentionally. He signaled for the men to move behind cover. He lifted his carbine to his shoulder and sighted in. He fired and pulled his head behind the corner. The stack of wood toppled and there was a dull thud of something heavy falling to the first step. The grenade blast reverberated in the enclosed space and made Sam's ears ring. Dust and debris filled the room.

O'Connor clutched the nearest GI. "Warn the others to look for booby traps." The GI nodded and sprinted out the door.

Another blast from the building across the street made them flinch. The screaming that followed, told them the warning came too late. O'Connor cursed, "Shit!" O'Connor stared into Sam's wide eyes and nodded. He didn't speak but Sam knew he was thanking him for saving his life. Sam tried to keep stoic and hard, but he couldn't keep the smile from spreading. "How'd you know?"

Sam swallowed against a dry throat. "We saw many of them last night."

Firing erupted from the buildings to their left. O'Connor walked up the shredded, smoking stairwell, looking for more booby traps. The second floor was empty except for a wooden chair. There was a blown-out window facing the plaza. A flower box hung from the outside of the window and weeds draped from it like green hair.

O'Connor moved to the side of the window, careful to stay hidden. He peered across the plaza at the far buildings. He saw flashes of movement in the windows. There was more firing from the adjacent buildings. The intensity, told him the rest of the company was meeting stiff resistance. He yelled, "Open fire!"

The GIs didn't need coaxing. M1s and .30 caliber machine guns opened up and the buildings across the plaza sparked and large chunks of plaster and wood splintered and tore. O'Connor leaned out his window and poured fire into the window seventy-five yards away.

Sam flinched at the roar of all the weapons. He was impressed with the sheer volume of fire the Americans were able to bring. He wanted to fire, but there was only one window and not enough room for both of them. He dove to the ground when he heard the buzzing of bullets smacking into the walls. A large chunk of wall behind him cascaded down. More bullets lanced into the room. He covered his head and moved to the back. O'Connor was on the ground too, holding his helmet.

The M1s and machine guns continued firing, not giving up the advantage. The intensity of enemy fire slowly diminished. The room was filled with dust and O'Connor choked and coughed. Sam shuffled to his side. "Are you injured, sir?"

"Nah, I'm fine." Staying low, he ran to the stairs and went to the first floor. Private Gilson was at the side door, leaning out firing his M1. O'Connor tapped his shoulder and spoke into his ear. "Find Vincent and Pullman. We need the bazooka on the top floor. If you see Craig, have him put grenades into the buildings directly across." Gilson nodded and fired again, then ran into the street. O'Connor watched him zigzagging his way to the next block. Geysers of dirt spouted up behind him. He dove into the recessed doorway across the street. He flashed O'Connor a thumb up and went into the building.

O'Connor went back up the stairs. The volume of fire had dropped off considerably. The .30 calibers kept hammering away in short bursts and rifle fire continued. The firing from the adjacent buildings had also subsided. O'Connor wondered about their progress. He knew Platoon Sergeant Carver was leading the left flanking maneuver. *Hope that love struck son-of-a-bitch is keeping his head in the game.*

An image of Major Cruz filled his mind. He wondered if she was safe. The thought of her injured or dead made him reel and he shook his head. *What the hell's the matter with me? I haven't spoken two words with her.* No matter how he scolded himself, he couldn't shake her image. There was something about her, something about the fleeting look they shared that made him care.

The clatter of GIs scrambling up the stairs pulled him from his thoughts. Private Pullman and Vincent entered the room. Vincent was leading, holding his stovepipe and grinning. "You called?"

There was an explosion at the base of the building across the plaza and O'Connor realized Gilson had found Craig and he was arcing rifle grenades where he'd directed.

"Stay down." O'Connor pointed through the window. "Think you can put a couple shells through that far window? The second from the right in the building directly across."

Vincent put the bazooka on the floor and looked at the target. There was a muzzle flash. He ducked but the bullet wasn't aimed at him. He grinned. "Does Betty Grable need chest support?" he answered his own question, "Hell yes." Sam stared at the duo as Vincent aimed, and Pullman loaded.

O'Connor noticed Sam's confusion. "Betty Grable has big tits." He pretended to bounce imaginary breasts.

Sam's confusion turned to an embarrassed smile and he repeated the word several times. "Tits."

His accented English made the soldiers grin. Pullman slapped Vincent's helmet and stepped to the side. He checked behind and motioned for Sam to move. "Don't wanna get your tits blown off." Sam looked confused again but moved. O'Connor moved back and Pullman said, "You're all clear."

Vincent was in a crouch, several yards back from the window frame. He found the window across the plaza and steadied his reticle just above and to the right. He blew out his breath and applied gentle pressure to the trigger. The whoosh surprised them all, despite knowing it was coming.

The rocket shot out the window and trailed a thin trail of white smoke. O'Connor watched it slam into the side of the window frame and explode. The explosion was small, but the effect was dramatic. Part of the wall broke away and crashed to the ground in a flurry of dust. Vincent cussed. "Dammit, load me again. I'll get it this time."

O'Connor shook his head. "No, get down the stairs, now!" He pushed Vincent to move and they ran down the stairs as bullets poured through the window. They took cover in the stairwell. Bullets smacked and thudded into the walls. The intensity of the .30 calibers increased, trying to suppress the Japanese. They stayed in the stairwell until the firing died down.

Private Gilson poked his head around the corner. "You guys alright?"

O'Connor nodded. "There's still a bunch of 'em over there." Gilson spit a dark stream of tobacco juice onto the wall and nodded.

Private Vincent spoke up, "I can get my next shot through that window."

O'Connor shook his head. "I need to know what's happening with the assault. Don't wanna fire on our own troops. Besides, you hit the target. That little piece of real-estate's unusable."

O'Connor moved to the doorway and watched his men continuing to pour fire across the plaza. The fountain was pockmarked with countless bullet impacts. He wondered when they'd be ordered to cross the deadly expanse.

His two-man .30 caliber machine gun crew was laying down behind a pile of rubble, the tripod perched amongst the debris. They were hammering out short bursts. O'Connor figured they were probably due for a barrel change out.

7

General Manjome wasn't happy with his current situation. The Filipino resistance had completely surprised him with their ferocity the night before. His troops were scattered, and in an effort to consolidate his remaining soldiers, he'd been forced to retreat to the far corner of the cursed city. Now his two thousand remaining soldiers were packed into a city block. The Americans had finally shown up and were threatening to overwhelm him.

"Captain Ito!" he yelled.

A thin officer with prominent cheek-bones appeared and went ramrod straight. "Sir."

"We need to keep the Americans off us while we move to our bunker positions in the jungle. The Americans will bomb us at any moment. We'll be slaughtered. If we get to the bunkers we'll be able to hold them off indefinitely." Captain Ito knew their situation and nodded. The general continued. "We need a diversion." He stared hard at his Captain. He'd served him well for many years and he respected his fighting spirit. "Choose a junior Lieutenant to lead an attack across the courtyard. We'll escape out the back before the Americans seal it off."

Captain Ito nodded his understanding and said, "Hai. I'll send

Lieutenant Sato." The General nodded and Captain Ito went to find his lieutenant.

CAPTAIN ITO FOUND Lieutenant Sato in the bottom floor of the centermost building. He had his submachine gun aimed and fired off a short burst. Captain Ito crouched and entered the room. The troops stiffened when they saw the officer in their midst. They weren't the hardened fighters he'd fought alongside for so many years. Those soldiers had been sent to defend Leyte weeks before. These soldiers were leftovers, but they'd served him well. He wondered if last nights debacle would have happened if he still had his veterans.

There was no use wondering, it hadn't happened that way. These men, had fought well, doing the best they could. Lieutenant Sato was the reason many of the men were still alive. He'd kept his company together and fought the damned natives well, making them bleed for their betrayal. Now he'd sacrifice himself and his men for the greater good of what was left of the division.

"Lieutenant Sato." The stocky Lieutenant stopped firing and looked over his shoulder. Keeping low he trotted to the doorway Captain Ito peered from. Captain Ito moved into the hallway, out of the direct path of bullets. He waved his underling to follow and went through another room. When they were both inside he shut the flimsy door. Lieutenant Sato saluted and he saluted back. "General Manjome is moving the rest of the division back to the prepared bunkers before the Americans succeed in encircling us here."

Lieutenant Sato nodded. "Good. We wouldn't last long here. I'll ready the men."

Captain Ito shook his head. "You and your platoons will stay here and keep the Americans occupied." Lieutenant Sato's eyes hardened and he looked the captain in the eyes. "General Manjome has ordered you to lead your men across the plaza. You're to attack the Americans."

Lieutenant Sato nodded his head then bowed. "It will be an honor, sir."

Captain Ito lifted his chin and looked down at the diminutive soldier. "You do me, General Manjome, and the entire Empire of Japan great honor."

Lieutenant Sato lifted his gaze and stiffened his back. His salute snapped into place and Captain Ito returned it. He looked at his gold watch, a gift from his wife he hadn't seen in three years. "Attack in ten minutes, Lieutenant." Sato looked at his own watch and marked the time. "Carry on."

Lieutenant Sato clicked his heels and went back to his men. He peered into the room and got the attention of his First sergeant. "Organize the men, we're attacking in ten minutes."

The suicide order had no effect on the sergeant. He simply grunted, "Hai," and followed the order.

The fire coming from the American lines tapered as the Japanese huddled behind cover and prepared for the attack. They reloaded and affixed bayonets to their rifles. They took long drinks of their precious water, knowing they'd not get another chance.

At eight minutes Lieutenant Sato addressed the men. "Second platoon will stay back and provide cover until our forward units reach the fountain. Then you will follow. We will not stop for anything. Once across the plaza we will skewer the Yankees and kill the murdering Filipinos. We will take no prisoners."

The men yelled in a lusty battle cry. Sato looked at his watch, it was time. He stood and raised his submachine gun over his head. "Attack!" The men yelled and surged forward while the soldiers of the second platoon fired into the buildings and streets beyond.

Lieutenant Sato pushed his way through the narrow doorway and sprinted straight ahead. He saw winking flashes ahead. He thought he could feel the heartbeats of the men following him. Bullets whizzed past him like angry hornets. He heard meaty impacts and grunts as his soldiers were hit, but he continued forward.

The fountain was his goal. He heard the sickening sound of the American machine gun opening up. He wondered why it had taken so long. The .30 caliber bullets ripped into his men, tearing holes in his advancing line, but the soldiers behind kept pushing past their fallen comrades. The fountain was only twenty yards ahead. He could see distinct faces behind the helmets of the Americans. They looked hard and wholly evil.

He dove the last few feet and slammed into the side of the stone fountain. He could feel it shuddering with countless impacts. He went to his knees and aimed his submachine gun at the nearest building. He could see winking flashes coming from the window. He pulled the trigger, sending a ten-round burst into the darkness. He didn't wait to see if he'd hit anything. He ducked beneath cover and came up shooting from another angle. His bullets smacked into the pile of rocks and wood in front of the American machine gun.

He ducked. The trail of fallen soldiers leading to the fountain gave him pause. His men were all around him, firing their long Arisaka rifles. Many had fallen, but more had made it this far. The second platoon broke from cover and started the long run. He yelled, "Let's go! Attack!"

He pulled a type 99 grenade from his belt and pulled the pin. He smacked the top against the stone fountain and hurled it in the direction of the machine gun nest. He leaped into the dry pool and shuffled the few yards to the other side. He leveled his machine gun and fired a burst from the hip. The stone wall of the fountain exploded in dust and rock chips as American bullets impacted, but nothing hit him. His exploding grenade sent a cloud of dust sweeping over the American position. He yelled and leaped over the fountain wall. There was forty yards of open space to cover. He could see the Yankee's eyes. He swept his muzzle across their lines as he ran and emptied his thirty-two-round magazine.

The dust and smoke thickened and he struggled to see targets. Bullets whizzed past and smacked into men behind him, but every step brought him closer to the American lines. He went to a knee and quickly swapped out the magazine. He waved his arm, "Follow me!" He'd take his men through the American lines and kill as many as he could.

The smoke cleared slightly and he noticed a hulking mass filling the street directly to his front. His heart sank when he realized it was an American tank. He had to get close enough to make the main gun ineffective. He had to get behind it. The great cannon erupted and sent a 75mm shell lancing past his head. He could feel the heat. The shell disintegrated the fountain, sending stone and flesh in every direction.

Lieutenant Sato could feel the concussive heat sweep over his back, but he kept running. The .30 caliber muzzle poking out the front of the tank slewed toward him. The muzzle looked immense. He leveled his MP34 and fired as he ran. The green metal sparked like it was sizzling, but had no other effect.

Ten more yards and he'd be beyond the arc of the gun. His hopes were shattered when the machine gun erupted in flame and the heavy bullets slammed into his soft flesh. Sato felt nothing, but suddenly his legs wouldn't work and he was falling. He tried to yell in frustration, but there was only silence. His head smacked the hard ground and his helmet rolled off his head. He watched it settle onto its back. The slow back and forth motion lulling his senses. Then only blackness.

General Manjome heard the attack start. The increased volume of fire left no doubt. "Move the men, Captain."

Captain Ito barked an order and the lead elements of what was left of the division moved out the back, led by one of the only remaining loyal Filipinos. Ito had his pistol out and ready. He was right behind the guide. In English he said, "If you betray us, you'll be the first to die, Berto."

Berto Santos looked Captain Ito in the eye. "I will be killed if my countrymen find me. Even if I helped them find you, they'd still kill me. My people do not forget, ever."

Captain Ito nodded. He doubted the treasonous scum would betray them, but traitors could never be fully trusted. The jungle was right up against the back of the city here. The Filipino moved along the edge, looking for something. Finally, he pointed and went seemingly into a wall of green. After a few yards a little-used path seemed to spring from nowhere. Berto led them through dense jungle.

The main road leading out the back of the city was lightly defended by Filipinos and the Japanese could have easily overrun the position, but the Americans would arrive soon to seal off the area, and there could be no delay. General Manjome wanted his troops to slip away without being noticed and the trail was perfect.

Berto trotted along the trail. It was well hidden and until today, the Japanese didn't know of its existence. Berto assured them it led deep into the jungle and passed close to the bunker system.

Soon the remaining troops of General Manjome's division arrived undetected at the bunkers. They quickly spread throughout the well-hidden and well stockpiled structure. Machine guns were placed in the gun ports, mortars were readied in the covered gun pits and for the first time that day, the Japanese soldiers ate without worrying for their lives.

General Manjome looked out the gun-port of his central bunker and nodded. "The Americans will find us soon enough, and when they do, they'll wish they hadn't. We have an excellent chance to keep them here indefinitely."

Captain Ito nodded, "Yes sir. The men are ready to stand and fight to the last."

8

Platoon Sergeant Carver stood beside Sergeant O'Connor and looked over the courtyard. It was littered with what looked like a full company of Japanese soldiers. "Looks like they got close."

O'Connor nodded. "They might've overrun us if the tank jockeys didn't show up when they did." He pointed toward the remains of the .30 caliber machine gun position. "Jap grenade took out our thirty crew, left us lacking some firepower." He looked at his boots. "Killed the gunner, Corporal Skinner. The loader, Watkins was shaken up, but he'll be okay."

"Any other casualties?"

"Crenshaw got knocked out. Bullet creased his scalp, but he's fine." He motioned behind him. "He's getting patched up with Doc Haley. Robertson took a round to the head. He's gone." He brushed some ash off his M1. "How'd you fare? I heard an awful lot of shooting coming from your direction."

Carver pulled the brim of his helmet back and wiped the sweat from his brow. "Lost Culligan and Frost. The Japs didn't wanna give up their flank. It'd just gotten quiet when they attacked across the courtyard. There was no one firing at us. It was like shooting fish in a barrel. Boys were whooping and hollering like it was opening day of duck season." He took his helmet off and looked over the mass of bodies. "They never had a chance."

"Yeah well, good thing."

"Fact is, they were a diversion. The rest of 'em squirted out the back and disappeared somehow. We've got men back there, a light screen that was being built up, but they didn't see a thing."

"Tunnels?"

"Nah, we found their tracks. They used a well-hidden little game trail. It cuts through a thick creek-bed, right through our guys." He shook his head. "They're holed up in some kind of bunker system in the jungle. Looks like a tough nut to crack."

Sam Santos perked up. "Did you say bunkers?"

Platoon Sergeant Carver noticed the young Filipino for the first time. "You know something about that?"

Sam nodded. "I helped build it, along with many others. We were forced to work. I know it very well."

Carver looked at O'Connor who gave him a nod, Sam could be trusted. "You think you could draw us a picture? Sure would help to know what we're getting into."

Sam smiled and nodded. "Piece of cake." He said it slow, unsure it was the correct phrase.

O'Connor laughed and slapped his back. "You got it, Sam. Need to get you to Lieutenant Swan."

SAM AND FELIPE were back in the warehouse where they'd been chained every night. The chains were gone, and the space was filled with tables and the hustle of a headquarters. The miserable hours spent in squalor and captivity seemed a lifetime ago, though it had only been a few days.

They stood at a table with a large map of the island spread before them. General Arnold, Colonel Cushing, Captain Flannigan, and Lieutenant Swan stood on the other side along with other high-ranking officers.

Felipe did most of the talking. Sam hoped no one would ask him a question. He wasn't sure he'd be able to talk. He was afraid he'd sputter and embarrass himself in front of the great men. How had he come to be standing in front of these towering, king-like Americans? Days before he'd been chained to the floor of this very building, eating worm filled rice. The difference was astounding and hard to wrap his head around.

Felipe circled an area on the map with the nub of a pencil. "The bunkers are interconnected by trenches and tunnels. They zigzag. Nothing's straight. There are ten bunkers, each have two machine gun ports. Just behind them are wider trenches with heavy wooden covers that can be opened and closed to fire mortars. I don't know these weapons but they have a lot of them and they're big."

Sam opened his mouth, trying to speak, but nothing came out. General Arnold leaned across the table. "You have something to add, son?"

Sam stared and managed a nod. He swallowed as all eyes were on him. His voice sounded small and weak. "Yes. Yes sir. They have twenty-four of them. The mortars. I counted them." He shook his head. "I don't know why I did that."

General Arnold grinned. "Well, I'm glad you did. Every bit of information's valuable. Tell us everything you know about it."

They spent the next hour filling in everything they remembered. Major Cruz arrived. She added her own memories. When they finished drawing up a detailed schematic of the bunkers, Major Cruz shook her head. "We should have known General Manjome would retreat to the bunkers. We could have occupied them ourselves and cut them to shreds."

Colonel Cushing shook his head. "It's my failure Major. Mine alone."

General Arnold shook his head. "Nonsense. No one can predict the future. Your Filipinos gave us this city with minimal casualties. I hate to think where we'd be without you." He returned his attention to the map. "We've got the precise coordinates of this place. We'll gather our forces tonight and let the navy and artillery boys pound the crap out of 'em all night. We'll see what's left in the morning."

～

THAT NIGHT, despite the coming battle, felt like a celebration. Able Company was spread across a city block. The locals pulled out food and drink they'd been hiding from the Japanese for years. There were fire pits with various forms of meat cooking on spits. The sizzle and drip of huge lizards didn't look appetizing, but the taste surprised the Americans brave enough to try. There was music playing on every corner and the Filipino women strutted around in their finest clothes trying to attract the attention of the Americans. It wasn't hard to do.

Platoon Sergeant Carver was sitting on a box of .30 caliber ammunition reading a letter in the dim light of a fire. His hands were black with dirt, grime and gunpowder, but he was careful not to smudge the precious paper. He'd read the letter fifty times through and had it memorized. He concentrated on the curved lines of Lilly's fine penmanship, thinking about her strong hands clutching the pen. Those same hands had brought him so much pleasure.

He brought the letter to his nose again and closed his eyes as he caught the hint of her smell. It seemed out of place here. It reminded him that the constant smell of rot and decay he'd become so used to, wasn't the only smell in the world. There was still goodness in the world beyond the war. It smelled like the future.

The whoop of a soldier brought him back to reality. Up and down the street he could see the forms of his men in silhouette. They were laughing, lifting bottles of local hooch and clutching at eager young Filipino women. The background noise of thumping artillery and the flashes of light to the west reminded him that while his men celebrated, the Japanese occupiers, less than a mile away were catching hell.

He thought about the morning. Able Company would be leading the attack again. He folded the letter and carefully re-inserted it into the envelope. He tucked it into his breast pocket and patted it. He took a deep breath wondering if he'd ever see Lilly again.

～

SERGEANT O'CONNOR WALKED amongst his celebrating men. The orders were clear, they'd be attacking in the morning. The men needed to rest and prepare, but that wasn't happening, and he didn't give a shit. The men needed to blow off steam. They'd spent the entire day in combat and would do so again in a few hours. Let them have their fun.

Many Filipino women had thrown themselves at him as he walked, but he'd quietly pushed them all away. He was as young and red-blooded as the rest of the men, but he was only interested in one Filipino woman. He hadn't been able to get Major Celine Cruz out of his head since meeting her the day before. He knew it was folly, she was an officer and a foreigner, but the fact remained.

He walked aimlessly through the many parties surrounding bonfires. He told himself he was keeping the men in-line. Making sure they weren't getting too out of hand, but he kept his eyes peeled for the fiery freedom fighter.

He'd come to the edge of the city and stopped at a raging bonfire surrounded by dancing and gyrating GIs and Filipinos. He had his carbine slung over his shoulder and he held his hands out to the heat. A drunk Private Vincent stumbled into him. "Sarge? That you? It is you." He held out a piece of white meat skewered on the end of a stick. "You gotta try this. It's delicious," he slurred the last word making it sound anything but.

O'Connor eyed the meat. He recognized the dark skin of a lizard. He shook his head. "No thanks, Vincent."

He pushed the stick away, but Vincent wouldn't take no for an answer. "You gotta try it. You gotta. It's delicious."

O'Connor eyed the soldier. He was swaying on his feet, held up by the small Filipino at his side whose smile could melt the icecaps. He was about to refuse again, when another voice he recognized joined. "It tastes like chicken, Sergeant."

Relief flooded O'Connor. He realized he'd been worried for Major Cruz's safety. He turned away from Vincent and faced the diminutive Major. He stared at her soft features. She wore brown, baggy pants and a rumpled brown shirt, two sizes too large. She looked like a child, but her eyes were those of a hardened combat veteran. She smiled and he thought his heart would burst from his chest. "You led your men well today, Sergeant."

He shook his head, reminding himself. *She's an officer.* "Thank you, Major, but we couldn't have done it without you and your fighters."

She nodded. "Walk with me, won't you?" She turned from the revelry of the dancers and walked down the street. He tripped but caught himself and walked beside her. They moved away from the bonfire. O'Connor could hear Private Vincent regaling the poor Filipino girl with war stories. Major Cruz smiled. "They deserve a little relaxation. It was a long day."

O'Connor replied, "They're acting like the whole thing's over. We attack the bunkers in the morning and that won't be an easy nut to crack." She looked at him curiously and he explained. "It won't be easy, that's what I mean."

She giggled and he thought it was the most beautiful sound he'd ever heard. Her face hardened. "I was married once. A good man, but foolish. He fought the Japanese when they first invaded." She stared at the ground, remembering. "They made an example of him. Strung him up in the center of town naked and whipped him. He bled to death." She stopped and looked into O'Connor's blue eyes. "He used to look at me the same way you do." O'Connor started to apologize, but she stopped him. "I miss that look."

He stared down at her. The distant firelight danced in her brown eyes. He bent forward, wondering if this was really happening. She pulled him to her and their lips touched tenderly, then with more force as the passion coursed through their bodies.

She broke away and he felt drunk. She clutched his hand and pulled him after her. In a lusty voice she murmured, "I know a quiet, comfortable place." O'Connor thought she could lead him straight into a meat grinder and he wouldn't care. He didn't think he could be any happier, but she proved him wrong.

LONG BEFORE THE MORNING LIGHT, Major Celine Cruz was out of bed and dressed. The dim light of a lantern glowed and she gazed at

Sergeant O'Connor. He was sprawled naked on the bed, his short cropped, red hair in stark contrast to the white pillow. She smiled, remembering the night of lovemaking. He had pleased her and made her feel things she didn't believe she'd ever feel again. Their first coupling had been lust-filled, almost violent. She could feel his need, his power, and she relished every second. The second and third were slower and more passionate. She thought he must be inexperienced, but he was a natural.

He felt her studying him and he opened an eye. He sat up and rubbed the sleep away. She smiled, "Good morning, Sergeant."

He grinned, "I think you can call me Sean, Major."

She giggled. "And you should continue to call me major, particularly when we make love."

He laughed, "Yes, sir … ma'am." He checked his watch and jolted, becoming fully awake. "Damn, that night ended far too quickly."

She nodded and threw him his dirty, smelly shirt. "Get dressed. As you said, the bunkers will be a 'hard nut?'"

He grinned. "Yeah, something like that." He swung his legs to the side of the bed and stood. He reached for her hand and she gave it to him. He looked into her eyes. "I'm hoping that wasn't a one-time thing?" She smiled but didn't respond. "I mean, if it was then fine, but … well I'm just hoping it wasn't."

Her eyes hardened and she gave his hand a squeeze. "I hope the same thing, but you know as well as I do … about war."

He stood and pulled her into his arms. They held each other tight. No more words needed to be spoken. They understood the dangers of the many days still to come.

9

Platoon Sergeant Carver and Sergeant O'Connor were huddled behind a rock outcropping, three-hundred yards from the edge of the jungle. The cruisers and destroyers had been hammering the bunker complex off and on all night. Now it was the flyboys turn.

In the early morning light, streaking fighters lanced in and dropped five-hundred-pound bombs. The ground shook with each detonation. When their bombs were gone, they circled back and strafed until they were completely dry, then another squadron of different planes would repeat the process.

Private Hanks held the radio out to Lieutenant Swan. Swan took the handset and after identifying himself, listened. He nodded and handed it back to Hanks. He relayed their instructions. "We're attacking in fifteen minutes. We're moving up with the light armor, the halftracks. Command is thinking the bunkers are knocked out from the pounding they took last night and this morning." He checked to make sure his carbine magazine was tight. "We're gonna find out."

Sergeant O'Connor shook his head. Private Hanks asked, "You don't think they're knocked out, Sarge?"

O'Connor glared at Hanks. "The Japs are never finished. We have to kill 'em one by one. They don't surrender and don't give up. Even if the bunkers are pulverized, I guarantee the Japs have plenty of fight left in 'em." He chambered a round. "You'd think command would understand that by now."

Swan ignored the comment. "Our company's going in right behind the halftracks. The mortars will lay down smoke, that's our signal to move out."

Carver and O'Connor nodded and started to move off to their respective squads. Carver reached out and clutched O'Connor's arm. "You okay?"

O'Connor shook his arm loose. "Yeah, I'm okay. Why you ask?"

Carver shrugged. "I don't know, just seem different this morning." O'Connor ignored him and moved to his squad.

The clanking of halftracks pulling forward and sitting at idle was all O'Connor could hear. A faint whiff of Celine's scent pierced the heavy smell of gasoline. His head spun as he recalled her body and the wonderful sensations from the night before. He shook his head, *gotta concentrate on the task at hand or I'm a dead man.*

He wondered what role she'd be playing, if any, during the attack. Surely, they'd leave this kind of assault to the more heavily armed Americans. The Filipinos showed their worth as fighters but they didn't know how to work with armor in an assault. Knowing she was out of danger eased his mind. *I've got enough to worry about without worrying about her.*

The arcing whistle of mortar shells shook him from his thoughts. He yelled over the din of the halftracks. "That's the smoke. Give it some time to work, then we go."

The jungle ahead disappeared in a thick layer of white and gray smoke. The halftrack engines roared and they lurched forward in a staggered line. O'Connor waved his arm forward and the men stood and walked, keeping pace with the armor. Atop each halftrack a soldier manned a .50 caliber machine gun with armor shielding. There were two more GIs riding inside, along with the driver. They were bazooka teams. The idea was to get them close enough to the bunkers to jump out and put fire into them. The infantry's job was to cover the bazooka teams and overwhelm the bunkers.

They entered the smoke screen and the smoldering jungle. The bunker system was another fifty yards. The halftracks slowed to maneuver. The jungle was sparse, but still a factor. The buzzing sound of a Japanese Nambu machine gun cut through the engine and tread noise. O'Connor ducked as he saw sparks tinkling on the side of the nearest halftrack. The gunner responded by swiveling the .50 caliber and depressing the trigger. The heavy thumping drowned out the Japanese guns. The halftrack spewed exhaust as the driver gunned it forward.

O'Connor waved the men forward. They had to stay close to the halftracks even though every fiber in his body was telling him to avoid them like the plague.

More fire ripped up and down the line. O'Connor yelled, "They're still kicking alright. Don't bunch up but keep covering the halftracks." He had to trot to keep up now. The smoke hung in the jungle like a thick web. The halftracks were dim silhouettes sparking with ricochets and muzzle flashes. He searched for the enemy positions but couldn't see any through the smoke.

The whistling of mortars froze his blood. "Incoming," he yelled. The halftrack directly in front of him suddenly blossomed with fire. It lurched to a stop and burned. The gunner was gone, the big gun pointing straight up. O'Connor instinctively dove to the ground. He still couldn't see anything, but he felt bullets whizzing over his head. More bright flashes in the smoke told him more halftracks were being obliterated.

He made a quick decision. He got to his knees and yelled, "Let's go, move up!" The men didn't hesitate. O'Connor held his carbine in front and ran in a crouch to a thick palm beside the burning halftrack. He could make out other GIs ducking into cover all around him. The half-track was charred and he noticed the front had a large, jagged hole. *Direct hit.* "Cover me!" He didn't wait for a response but got to his feet and ran forward to the next palm. He heard his men firing into the smoke. The ground shook as geysers of dirt erupted with mortar strikes. He heard GIs screaming in agony.

He brought his M1 up and fired a spread of five shots, while his squad leapfrogged past him. Then he was up and running. A light breeze sifted through and the smoke dissipated. The landscape was suddenly clear and visible. The pounding from the naval artillery and the air attacks had turned the area into a wasteland of smoking craters, but the heavily fortified bunkers still poked up with their deadly firing ports and slits. They were pockmarked, but for the most part, intact.

O'Connor took in the scene and yelled. "Bunkers front! Take cover!" The tree he was behind splintered and shredded as bullets slammed into it. He made himself as small a target as possible as the air to either side came alive with bullets. He watched in horror as Private Crenshaw tried to crawl to safety, but bullets stitched him from head to toe and he rolled out of sight.

He could still hear the roar of halftrack engines and the hammering of .50 caliber machine guns, but the two nearest his squad were burning pyres. The Japanese fire suddenly stopped and he took the opportunity to run forward and hurl himself into the bottom of a bomb crater. More GIs joined him and they huddled as the gunners finished reloading then continued to fire. Mortar rounds impacted randomly, sending shards of hot metal in every direction.

Private Griffin clutched O'Connor's shoulder and with wide, panicked eyes stuttered, "What do we do Sarge? What the fuck do we do?"

O'Connor shrugged out of his grip and crawled to the top of the crater. He peered out then ducked back down. "Listen up! The nearest bunker's forty yards away. It's got us covered, but I don't think they know where we are. They're firing at something off to the left, probably a halftrack." The huddled GIs looked pathetic, but they listened to their sergeant who'd gotten them this far. "We can take 'em."

Private Griffin was almost crying. "What about the halftracks and the bazooka crews? They're supposed to take 'em out, not us."

"The fucking halftracks are gone along with the bazooka teams. It's up to us now." He slid to the bottom of the hole and gripped Griffin's arms. He squeezed until Griffin tried to pull away, but O'Connor squeezed harder and leaned in close. "Pull yourself together, soldier. Now!" Griffin looked down and wiped his nose. He gave O'Connor a short nod. A mortar round landed near the front of their hole and sent thick, black dirt onto them. "We can't stay here."

O'Connor pulled a smoke grenade from his belt. "I'm gonna throw this, when it goes off I want you three," he pointed at the nearest GIs, "to lay down fire on the gun-ports." He gripped Griffin's shoulder. "Griffin and I will run to the side of the ports and throw in grenades." He gripped a fragmentation grenade. Griffin turned another shade of white but didn't say a word. O'Connor looked him in the eye and Griffin gritted his teeth and nodded.

The battle was raging over their heads. Japanese machine guns were now dominating the battle. A few .50 calibers were still in the mix, but O'Connor decided most must be out of business. He wondered how the rest of the company was faring. More men had rolled into the crater bringing their number to eight. Plenty to suppress the bunker while he and Griffin advanced. He shuddered to think what would happen if a mortar shell landed in the center of their hole.

O'Connor and Griffin crawled to the right side of the crater while the others filled in the rest. He poked his head up again for another look, then dropped back. He spoke into Griffin's ear. "Take a look." Griffin poked his head up and came down quick. "We'll run to the side. They don't know we're here." Griffin nodded, committed to his fate. He checked his carbine. O'Connor slapped his shoulder and looked to the other men. "Ready?" They were poised just below the lip, ready to move up and fire on the bunker.

O'Connor pulled his feet beneath himself. He primed the smoke canister and hurled it in the direction of the bunker. He took a deep breath and blew it out slow. He yelled, "One, two, three." He leaped out of the hole and took off like a jackrabbit. The smoke canister popped and spewed white smoke, but he'd thrown it too far to the left and he could still see the firing ports and the winking muzzle flashes of the machine guns. They weren't aimed his way, but they'd see him any second.

The firing ports suddenly erupted in dust and the metal frame sparked like someone had lit off a string of firecrackers. The machine gun stopped firing, but the muzzle was shifting towards him. He'd covered half the distance when Griffin streaked past him as if he were standing still. *Damn, that boy's fast.*

The covering fire continued to hammer the ports, but the muzzle continued to swing. Griffin reached the side of the bunker first and pushed his back tight against the concrete, breathing hard. O'Connor dove for the side at the same instant the Japanese gunner opened up. A stream of bullets grazed past his back and he swore he could feel their heat.

He rolled to his feet beside Griffin and out of harm's way. Griffin's eyes were wide. "Shit, I thought you were a goner, Sarge."

"Cover our backside." O'Connor put down his rifle and pulled a grenade from his belt and reached for one on Griffin's. With a grenade in each hand he kept his back pressed to the wall and scooted toward the firing slits. The GIs had melted back into their cover, and the nambu was sending hot metal their way. O'Connor pulled the pins. He could hear Japanese voices chattering. He leaned out and with a flick, sent the first grenade through the firing port, followed quickly by the second. The voices turned to yelling and when the grenades exploded, to screams.

O'Connor stepped closer and thrust his carbine barrel into the port and emptied his magazine, spreading his bullets. He pulled back and reloaded. There was firing coming from Griffin. O'Connor joined him in time to see him pouring fire into two Japanese soldiers who'd come out the back of the bunker. Another soldier burst out and O'Connor poured five bullets into him. He dropped like a sack of rice and blood oozed from his ruptured chest. O'Connor yelled, "Get a grenade into that door!"

Griffin clutched his last grenade and pulled the pin. The door was partway open, the hinges on the far side. He had a three-foot opening to hit. He reared back like he was delivering a fastball and hurled it. The grenade hit the side of the door and bounced straight back. Griffin yelled, "Shit!" and tried to move away, but he slipped and fell onto his back. The grenade came to rest at his feet.

O'Connor dropped his rifle and gripped a chunk of Griffin's shirt. He pulled with everything he had. The thump of the grenade came an instant later and Griffin screamed.

O'Connor thought he'd be mortally wounded at least, but Griffin got to his feet and repeated, "Holy shit, holy shit," like it was his new mantra.

"You okay?" O'Connor spun Griffin around to face him. Griffin stared blankly. "Hey! You okay?" He shook him and Griffin finally managed a shaky nod.

There was more movement inside the bunker door. O'Connor released his grip on Griffin and pulled his last grenade. He threw a strike through the opening. There was yelling coming from inside. He dove away, pulling Griffin along with him. The dull thud was followed by smoke billowing from the door.

The rest of the squad moved from the safety of the bomb crater and joined them on the wall of the bunker. There was fighting up and down the line. The chatter of Japanese machine guns still dominated. As far as O'Connor could tell, the bunkers to either side were still in Japanese hands. "We've gotta clear this bunker." He pointed to the front firing slits. Thin streaks of smoke leaked through. O'Connor pointed at the three GIs nearest the front. "Fire into the holes. The rest of us will go through the back. Once we're inside, cover the door." The GIs nodded their understanding and moved toward the firing slits. They thrust their rifles inside and fired until their clips and magazines were empty.

O'Connor pushed Griffin's shoulder. "Go." Griffin jumped down into the trench followed by the other four GIs. O'Connor took up the rear. Griffin grabbed the door handle and pulled it open all the way. Private Hughes was first through. He was followed closely by Pvts. Dawson, Muse, and Taggert. O'Connor took one last look down the trench. It traveled straight for ten yards then disappeared around the corner.

He ducked into the darkness. The smell of burnt flesh and blood assaulted his senses. His eyes took a moment to adjust to the dimness. He could see his men moving cautiously with their weapons ready. He stepped over a shredded body, glancing quickly at the soldier's blank eyes. The shrill yell of a Japanese soldier pierced the silence. Private Dawson fired his M1 carbine into the charging attacker. The muzzle flash lit up the concrete walls. The rest of the GIs spread out and fired into the main room. The bullets ricocheted and blasted dust from the walls.

O'Connor rounded the corner as the firing stopped. There were bodies everywhere. The light streaming through the firing ports illuminated their grotesque wounds. The soldiers were shredded with shrapnel and bullet wounds. There was no sign of life. O'Connor wanted to get out as quickly as possible. "Let's get out of here. We need to link up with…" A sudden flash of movement behind him caught his eye. The glinting of a long bayonet thrusting toward his gut. He parried the bayonet at the last possible instant. He went low and felt the weight of the soldier plow into him. O'Connor planted his feet and took the weight, then thrust forward and threw the Japanese soldier off him.

With some breathing room, he brought up his short carbine and leveled it at the soldier's chest and fired. The Japanese staggered backward, then yelled and charged forward. O'Connor kept firing, but his attacker kept coming, leading with the long steel pig sticker. O'Connor stepped inside the thrusting bayonet and swung the stock of his rifle into the soldier's face. He heard the skull crunch as it caved into his brain, ending the attack.

O'Connor was taking in ragged breaths. Griffin shouted, "You okay, Sarge?"

O'Connor nodded. "Where'd that guy come from?"

The men streamed past him and soon Griffin yelled. "There's a stairway leading down."

O'Connor collected his wits and strode to where his men stood on the edge of a stairway. He held up his hand for silence. The battle was still raging outside, but he thought he heard voices, lots of voices. He whispered. "Sounds like a lot of 'em down there." He felt for grenades but knew he'd used all he had. "Get ready with grenades. Hurry." The GIs pulled grenades off their belts. O'Connor held out his hand. "Give me one." Private Hughes accommodated.

O'Connor pulled the pin but kept the lever tight and took the first cautious step down. The stairway curved making it impossible to see where it ended. With each step the sounds of enemy troops grew louder. O'Connor was ready to run back up the stairs at the first sign of an attack. He'd be able to see around the corner in another step. He signaled for his men to stop and took the step. He crouched low, trying to see. His breath caught in his throat when he saw a mass of Japanese at the base of the stairs.

He didn't hesitate. He hurled the grenade and took off, taking the stairs by twos. "Throw 'em and get out of here!" The GI's eyes were big as saucers seeing their sergeant fleeing so quickly. They hurled their own grenades and took off after him. They were out the door when the soft thuds of multiple explosions went off.

The GIs waiting outside were startled to see the mass exodus. "What the hell's happening?" Corporal Mathews asked.

O'Connor spoke between breaths. "Shitload of Japs downstairs coming up. We don't have enough guys or ammo to stop 'em." He pointed toward the jungle. "Take the men back into the jungle and link up with Carver."

Mathews looked angry. "We're giving up the bunker?"

O'Connor nodded. "No choice, we can't hold it. No way." He pushed him along. "Get outta here. I'll cover you."

Mathews nodded and waved the men to follow. He jumped out of the trench and started running down the slope. A Nambu from an adjacent bunker opened up on the streaking soldiers. They dove for cover, but not before Private Taggert buckled and fell from multiple hits.

O'Connor didn't see it happen. He was too focused on the space in front of him. He heard the clanging of many boots slamming up the metal stairs. He thrust his M1 around the corner of the bunker and without seeing what he was shooting at, fired. He pulled back and Griffin took his place and fired another fifteen rounds. The doorway sparked and zinged as the Japanese fired back.

O'Connor pulled Griffin from the doorway. "We gotta go!" He jumped out of the trench and ran as fast as his feet would carry him. He saw the crumpled body of Private Taggert and the rest of the squad crawling downhill. He felt bullets whizzing past him and he realized he was about to die. He dove behind a thin layer of cover as bullets sliced only inches over his head. Griffin slammed in beside him.

Mathews was five yards ahead firing in the direction of the bunker. He yelled to O'Connor. "Nambu's got us pinned!"

O'Connor looked to the bunker they'd just left. Any second the

Japanese would fill the firing slits only yards away. They'd be cut to pieces. "We gotta go. We can't stay here!" He raised his head but saw the winking flashes of the other machine gun and felt the heat of more near misses. "Shit!"

He yelled. "I'll cover you. When I fire you gotta get the men back to that bomb crater."

Mathews shook his head. "There's no way, we'll be cut to pieces."

O'Connor screamed. "It's our only fucking chance!" Corporal Mathews licked his lips and nodded. He knew he was going to die.

O'Connor put in a fresh magazine and took a deep breath, readying himself. He was about to roll to a firing position when he heard the soft explosions of mortars. At first, he thought they were about to die in a barrage of friendly fire, but the mortars were firing smoke. Relief flooded him. He yelled. "Wait for it to work!" the firing from the Nambu's decreased and finally stopped. O'Connor could hear Japanese shouting from the nearest bunker. He got to his knees. The smoke was billowing, covering the area. "Now! Get a move on!"

The GIs sprang to their feet and ran down the slope. They didn't stop running until they ran into friendly lines. They took cover and laid on their backs gasping for breath. Platoon Sergeant Carver found them and laid beside O'Connor. "We thought you were finished. We lost track of you."

O'Connor finally got his breath back and sat up. He looked up the hill at the smoke screen. He couldn't see the bunkers at all. "We took a bunker but didn't have enough men to hold it. The bottom floor was filled with Japs. They must have underground connectors. There was no way to hold it."

Carver nodded. "You were the only unit that made any headway. Fucking Japs sliced us to ribbons with interlocking fields of fire. We're moving back to the city. Gonna let the navy and artillery boys have another go at it."

O'Connor shook his head. "Didn't work the first time."

Carver nodded and spit a stream of tobacco juice. "Nope."

10

A ble company moved to the safety of Cebu City. They walked single file. Most had their heads down, exhaustion etched into their faces. Alongside them another line of medics and soldiers carried stretchers with wounded and dead GIs.

Eventually they found an unoccupied area and milled about looking for places to sit. The other companies moved to different parts of the city and spread out to find cots and food.

Captain Flannigan strode up and looked the bedraggled bunch over. As they milled about he called them to attention. Most were too tired to comply, but it kept them from sitting down. In his booming voice, Flannigan addressed them. "The attack failed despite having detailed maps from the very men that built the complex." He paused for dramatic affect. He put his balled fists onto his hips. "To say I'm disappointed would be an understatement." Platoon Sergeant Carver stood with his fists clenched and his jaw set. Flannigan continued. "Tomorrow we attack again and this time I won't accept anything but total victory. Every man will give everything they have ... everything!" He screamed the last word. His face turned a deep shade of red, almost purple. "Dismissed!"

The men stood in stunned silence, then slowly broke up and moved to find the shade. Carver remained stock still. Lieutenant Swan was beside him and noticed his posture and his hatred filled stare. "Easy Carver. Easy. It's not worth it."

Carver shook his head and seethed. "The coward sat back all safe behind friendly lines while we died and he's got the nerve to question the men's will to fight? That doesn't sit right with me."

He took a step toward Flannigan, but Swan grabbed his arm and held him tight. Carver looked at the hand holding him, then at Swan. Swan leaned close. "These men need you tomorrow. You go spouting off to Flannigan, he'll put you in the brig. He's already got it in for you. Don't give him an excuse. That sumbitch ain't worth it."

Carver relaxed and shrugged out of Swan's grip. He watched Flannigan walking away but stayed put. He leveled his gaze at Swan. "You're right. He's a piece of shit. I just can't see how tomorrow will be any different than today."

Swan nodded, thinking about the men he'd lost and the men he'd lose tomorrow. He shook his head. "There has to be another way."

Sam Santos sat amongst the GIs. The joyous dancing and partying from the night before was long gone. There was barely any talking. Most GIs sat with their heads down. Some slept, others tried to sleep and still others cleaned and re-cleaned their weapons. As the evening progressed, everyone was thinking about the morning.

The thumping of navy guns slamming the bunkers gave them little comfort. It had barely put a dent in them the day before, and there was no reason to think tonight would be any different. At least it would keep the Japanese awake.

Sam wasn't involved in the assault, but he'd heard the intense clash and seen the wounded and dead GIs it produced. It tore at his heart to see the Americans who'd help free his people, looking so dejected and down. He knew the plan was another frontal assault in the morning. *How many more will die?*

A memory of walking along a path with his brother and father came to him. He remembered they were hiking and his father would stop often and point out various plants and explain their virtues or dangers. It was information Sam's father learned from his mother, Sam's grandmother. The memory made his heart ache, but it also made him spring to his feet and search for Felipe.

He found him getting ready for a snooze. When Felipe saw him, he smiled. "Sam, how are you? You look worried."

"I think I know a way around the Japanese. A way to hit them from behind where they won't be expecting it."

He told Felipe about the trail his father had taken him on. How it wrapped around the low hills then cut into the jungle and turned back toward town. The bunker system had effectively cut off the trail, but he assumed most of it was still there.

"It's a long march, but we could make it in a night and be behind the bunkers by morning."

Felipe snapped his fingers and got to his feet. "Let's talk with Colonel Cushing."

Colonel Cushing liked the idea. He'd watched the assault from afar and was frustrated he wasn't able to join in the fighting. This would be a way to involve his Filipino partisans and maybe the answer to overwhelming the Japanese. The trail wasn't on the map he had laid out on the table, but Sam assured him it was there. He drew an 'X' on the map where the trail began. He was confident he could find it.

Colonel Cushing rolled the map and tucked it under his armpit. "We'll talk with General Arnold. He's been looking for a way to flank the Japs, but the jungle is too dense. Your trail may be the answer."

Sam felt overwhelmed. He was being thrust into the middle of great and powerful men. Felipe slapped him on the back as they left the house that acted as Colonel Cushing's headquarters. He whispered into Sam's ear. "This trail of yours better be there." Sam flushed, and nodded, picturing it in his head. He was sure of it.

General Arnold was huddled around his own map of the island. The group was shown inside the tent and Sam was introduced. The general was tall, and his balding scalp was dotted with perspiration. His chin was strong, accentuated with a deep cleft. Sam thought he looked tired, but he immediately felt at ease despite his rank. Sam snapped off what he hoped was a proper salute. The general smiled and his eyes shone. He returned the salute. "I've been told you know of a trail that can get us behind the Japs?"

Sam nodded vigorously. "Yes, sir." He stepped forward to the map. He took a moment to study it. There were lines and arrows in red and black with symbols and numbers that made Sam's head spin. He panicked for a moment trying to get his bearings.

The general stepped forward and put his finger on a point. "Ignore all that other stuff. The bunker's here." He slid his finger down a little, "and we're here."

Sam nodded and ran his finger up the map. "The trail is here." He ran his finger along the map, laying out the general pathway he remembered. "It wraps around these low hills then cuts back for a ways then cuts back to the city."

General Arnold rubbed his cleft chin. "That's a mighty long trail. You say you walked it with your father?"

Sam gulped, "And my brother. We did it over two days. We stayed the night in the jungle. It's a good trail, although it's probably overgrown a bit since the Japanese invaded."

General Arnold nodded. "Looks to be about twelve miles." Silence filled the tent. He looked around the room at the other officers. "Any of our boys up to that kind of a march tonight?"

There was mumbling and lowered gazes. Captain Flannigan stepped forward and spoke up. "Able Company can make the trek, sir."

"Weren't your men at the front of the attack today?"

Flannigan nodded. "Yes sir. But they've been resting ever since."

General Arnold nodded and looked at his other officers. He centered his gaze on Captain Stark. "I want Baker Company to go too."

Captain Stark stiffened and nodded. "Yes, sir. We can make it."

Arnold continued. "As far as we know there's no Japs out there. They're all in the bunkers, which means you can use lights and you can move fast. You'll have to in order to be in position by morning. Take plenty of ammo, and water, but otherwise keep it light. No mortar units. The Navy guns and Army artillery will provide all the fire support you need. Be sure you have fresh batteries for the radios. The key will be coordination." He looked the map over then at Colonel

Cushing. "Can you spare some fighters for this excursion? I'd sure like to have some locals along in case our boys get lost out there."

Colonel Cushing nodded. "I'll send Major Cruz and her platoon." He put his large weathered hand on Sam's shoulder. "And Sam too, of course." Cushing gave the order. "Inform Major Cruz. Hurry."

Felipe snapped off a salute and ran from the tent. Sam watched him go, sudden doubt filling his head. *They're all counting on me.*

THE NEWS that they'd be marching all night along an unknown jungle trail did not go over well with the GIs. Platoon Sergeant Carver was stunned when he first heard the news from Lt. Swan. He'd started laying out all the reasons it was a bad idea, but it was obvious it would do no good. Lieutenant Swan was following orders and those orders called for speed. There was no time to discuss it, they had to get moving.

They rode in heavy trucks through Cebu City then along a well-used dirt road. They turned onto a smaller road and finally stopped when it got too narrow to continue. It wasn't dark yet, but the shadows were lengthening. In a few hours it would be dark. There was an urgency to find the trailhead before that.

They piled out of the trucks and the Filipinos took the lead, following the child warrior. Carver recognized the kid from the fighting in the city. He hoped he knew what he was doing, or they'd be spending the night in the hot, muggy jungle going in circles. Two full companies of GIs trudged after the guides. It was a long snaking line of soldiers.

Carver stood to the side as the GIs passed. None looked happy about the mission, but they were used to being abused. When there was a hard job to do, they'd put their heads down and do it. Whether they agreed with it or not was irrelevant, they followed orders and got it done. *That's why they call us grunts.*

Eventually they turned off the road and took another trail. Sam was obviously relieved when they found it. He couldn't keep from smiling. He, along with the Filipino platoon led by Major Cruz took point and moved fast. There was little danger of ambush, all the Japanese were concentrated in the bunkers.

Once darkness descended, they snaked along the trail with blazing lanterns and flashlights. Carver suspected they must have looked like a long lit up centipede from above. He glanced to the sky, hoping the flyboys had gotten the word they were out there.

The trail was narrow up front with vines hanging down and roots crossing, but with so many soldiers tromping past, it widened and cleared out quickly. By the time the last soldier passed, the trail was more like a highway.

SERGEANT O'CONNOR WAS the leading GI, walking alongside Major Cruz at the tail of the Filipino platoon. He was torn about her presence. He was overjoyed to be walking beside her, but terrified at seeing her engage in the coming combat.

When he first saw her joining their group, it was all he could do to keep himself from running up and embracing her. Instead he'd smiled and nodded at her. She'd acknowledged his presence but got on with the mission at hand. Once they found the trailhead and settled into a comfortable pace, she hung back until they were walking side by side.

O'Connor thought it must be obvious to the others that they had a history, but he didn't care. He was happy to be beside her again. She'd been the first to speak after they found each other. "I was worried about your safety today."

"You were worried about me? I was worried about you."

She shook her head. "I was in no danger. You were fighting in the bunkers."

"I didn't know where you were." He looked at his mud-covered boots. "I wasn't in danger either," he lied.

She looked up at him. "We are soldiers, both of us. Do not lie to protect me. I'm not a flower in a vase, but a weed in the mud. We are both in danger and will be until the Japanese are all dead." He tried to speak but she continued. "Our lovemaking was a brief respite from this ugly war, but it didn't uproot me and place me in a vase. I'm still very much in the mud ... alongside you."

He took a few steps in silence. Her toughness was the very thing that made her so irresistibly attractive to him. He'd never met a woman with even a quarter of her grit. He nodded. "I understand what you're saying." He leaned close to her ear, "But I think you're the prettiest damned weed I've ever seen."

She smiled and he thought his heart would melt. "You Americans ... so sentimental. Tell me more about where you come from ... Ory-Gun?"

He smiled. "Oregon. You'd love it. The woods are full of deer and the streams and rivers full of huge Salmon, Steelhead, and trout too." He gestured to the surrounding jungle. "It's not nearly as hot, and the trees are bigger and stretch as far as you can see. There's tall mountains that make the ones you've got here look like mole hills. It rains a lot, but it's not like the downpours you get here. It's more of a slow constant, not an all at once dousing." He looked into the growing darkness, imagining his home. "Seems like another world, another age."

"You will return there?"

The question startled him. He hadn't thought about his future beyond the war since landing on Guadalcanal back in '42. With death surrounding him all the time, he assumed he'd die long before the war ended, or get wounded so bad, he'd want to die. This woman beside him made him want to survive, if only to have the chance to spend more time with her. He grit his teeth; *this kind of thinking will get me killed.* He shook his head. "Haven't thought about it."

She sensed the change that overcame him and understood. "It's hard to think beyond the next day in this war."

He nodded. "The next hour even." They walked the rest of the way in relative silence, but it was okay. Her smell, the way she moved was all intoxicating to him. He was happy just to be with her and he sensed she felt the same way.

11

They marched all night, never stopping. They drank water and ate rations as they moved. If they had to take a shit, they did so quickly or risked being left behind. They carried light loads, ammunition, weapons and rations, but little else. Their rucks were light compared to the sixty pounds they normally marched with.

Platoon Sergeant Carver spent most of the march thinking about Lilly. He felt her letter in his breast pocket. He'd read it countless times. So much that he feared the paper would fall apart, or the words smudge. Despite being tired from the stresses of the day's combat, the march bordered on enjoyable. There was no danger of ambush. It was as if he were on a stroll, albeit at night and in a hellish, steaming jungle setting.

When the column finally stopped, he bumped into the man in front of him. He'd been walking so long, he was confused by the stop. He focused and got his head back into combat mode. All thoughts of Lilly vanished as he found Lt. Swan. "We're at the jump-off point," Swan whispered. He pointed ahead. "The Filipino kid says the bunkers are a thousand yards that way." He flashed a quick grin. "We're behind 'em."

Carver peered into the dark jungle and shrugged. "I'll take your word for it, sir."

Another figure approached from behind. Captain Flannigan said, "What's happening Lieutenant?"

"We've arrived, sir."

Flannigan looked around with wide eyes as if the jungle would come alive at any second and consume him. He looked at the glowing hands of his watch. "We're early." He nodded in satisfaction. "The men did well, have 'em take a fifteen-minute break before we move up to the attack point. I'll radio HQ."

Lieutenant Swan said, "Yes, sir."

An hour later both Able and Baker were spread out facing north. The jungle was silent as they waited for dawn. Major Cruz had sent scouts forward to pinpoint exactly where the bunkers were. They returned saying they could easily advance another couple hundred yards without tipping the enemy off.

Captain Flannigan was in contact with HQ. General Arnold wanted them to attack at precisely 0600. There would be no morning artillery to tip the Japanese to an imminent attack. They'd hit the bunkers at precisely the same time and take them by surprise.

After moving up, they hunched down in the darkness. Carver couldn't see the bunkers, still too dark, but he could smell burnt flesh and cordite wafting through the air. He licked his lips and looked at his watch. All there was to do now was wait.

O'CONNOR HAD his back against a palm. According to his watch they had ten minutes until the attack. He'd lost track of the Filipino platoon and Major Cruz, *Celine*. Even her name was beautiful. He spit and thought, *now I'm sounding like Carver*. The Filipinos wouldn't be a part of the initial attack. He was thankful for that. He'd only just met her, but somehow, she'd changed his life. The thought of her dying in a hail of Japanese bullets made him almost physically ill.

He shook his head. *I've gotta get my head in the game*. He closed his eyes and tried to put thoughts of her into a locked corner of his mind to access later. He looked around. The jungle was lightening and he could see dim outlines of his men surrounding him. He couldn't see their faces, but he could sense their fear and nervous energy. They'd fought in the bunkers most of yesterday then did a forced night march and now they were chomping at the bit to attack again. He blew out a long breath. *Where do these men come from?* All thoughts of the major faded. These fine men deserved his undivided attention. He'd do everything he could to get them through the next few hours ... alive.

He looked at his watch and leaned over to slap the GI lying a few feet away. Corporal Mathews flinched and looked at O'Connor. O'Connor flashed him three fingers ... three minutes. The signal went down the line and the GIs went from prone to crouching positions. There was no sound coming from the bunkers they knew to be only fifty yards ahead. The Filipinos assured them there were no sentries guarding the enemy rear. They would take them completely by surprise.

Dawn broke somewhere out over the sea and O'Connor could feel the slight dip in temperature even through the insulation of the jungle. He'd been careful to remind the men to drink plenty of water after the march. The constant struggle to stay hydrated was sometimes more difficult than fighting the Japanese. The constant sound of insects increased as the morning progressed. He felt insects crawling on him, but he ignored them.

Off to the left, there was movement. He glanced at his watch, it was time. He got to his feet but remained in a crouch. The plan was to advance to contact. There'd be no running charge, but a controlled steady advance, using the natural cover.

He took the first step toward the bunkers. It felt good to finally be moving again. He could feel the tightness in his muscles, but it faded with each step. Even though he was surrounded by a hundred other men, he moved quietly. He watched his step, instinctively using the outside of his foot and rolling forward, not making a sound. His eyes beneath the low brim of his steel helmet scanned for threats, but it was bare jungle.

He stopped abruptly when the sound of a machine gun pierced the morning stillness. He fought the urge to dive for cover. The gun was

firing away from them, toward the rest of the regiment attacking from
the front. More machine guns joined, until it sounded like one massive
orchestra of death. There was yelling ahead and O'Connor could see
movement, enemy movement. In the low light, less than thirty yards
away, he saw a flash and a puff of white smoke. He hunched lower
and recognized the unmistakable sound of a firing mortar. He
couldn't help grinning, they were coming up directly behind the
deadly mortars that had killed and maimed so many GIs the day
before.

He broke into a trot and the men did the same. He felt a surge of
adrenaline course through his body. He could see the structure hiding
the mortar pits. They were well fortified and well dug in. It would take
a direct artillery hit to take them out.

O'Connor ran up to stacked bamboo that formed the back wall of
the mortar pit. He nodded at Corporal Mathews and surged around
the corner with his Carbine on his shoulder. There were Japanese
soldiers scurrying everywhere. Some transported mortar rounds to the
waiting tubes, others hung the mortars and dropped on command. It
was an efficient killing machine.

O'Connor stood transfixed for an instant, taking in the scene. No
one seemed to notice him. A soldier transporting a mortar shell
suddenly stopped and stared at the tall, lanky American. It took him
an instant to realize he was looking at his own death. The soldier's
mouth opened to yell. O'Connor fired, sending the soldier stumbling
back into a steaming mortar tube. The soldier manning the tube yelled
out, cursing the dying soldier's clumsiness. O'Connor pumped rounds
into him too.

More GIs poured into the space. Corporal Mathews opened up
with his snub-nosed Thompson and swept the entire area with .45
caliber slugs. The Japanese never knew what hit them. Their bodies
crumpled and erupted with gaping wounds.

O'Connor pulled the trigger on an empty chamber. He'd burned
through his thirty-round magazine. He quickly swapped it out for a
fresh one. He let the rest of the GIs mop up any Japanese left alive. He
followed the trench out of the mortar pit area. He remembered from
the schematic, that the trench led directly to the back entrance of the

bunkers. He yelled. "Flame, up!" As he moved cautiously forward he heard the call for the flamethrower sifting through the ranks.

A Japanese soldier came around the corner pushing a cart stacked with boxes. He wore round glasses on his angular face. When he noticed the tall American he stopped and stared, trying to come to terms with what he was seeing. O'Connor shot from the hip. The soldier reeled back and clutched his belly. Thick blood seeped through his fingers and he looked into O'Connor's eyes with fear and confusion. O'Connor aimed and put a .30 caliber round neatly between his eyes. The soldier's head snapped back and he fell to the ground, his glasses still firmly attached.

O'Connor moved past the dead soldier with his carbine ready. Mathews touched his arm. "Flame's here."

O'Connor looked back at the GI holding the ominous flamethrower. The GI grinned at him like some deranged devil and pulled a pair of dirty goggles over his eyes. O'Connor nodded. "Get ready. I'll lead but be ready to blast the 'em." Private Hampton licked his cracked lips and nodded.

O'Connor got to the end of the trench. The machine gun fire hadn't let up, but the mortar pits were silenced. He peaked his head around the corner. He could see the back of a bunker. The door was shut. There was no sign of a sentry. *Japs aren't expecting us.* He trotted to the door. The trench continued straight for another twenty yards then made a left turn, no doubt leading to another bunker. He kept his eyes on the trench. The men knew what to do.

Corporal Mathews clutched the steel door handle and pulled. The door opened easily on greased hinges. He heard a Japanese soldier say something, perhaps greeting the returning ammo delivery soldier. Mathews fired his Thompson into the dimness. He heard a scream. He stepped away from the door and nodded to Private Hampton.

Hampton stepped beside him and pulled the front trigger of the flamethrower. Orange sparks spewed out the front of the muzzle. He stepped into the doorway, aimed low and pulled the rear trigger with a hard steady grip. Gasoline spewed out the nozzle and lit as it passed the sparks. The sudden light, lit up the inside of the bunker and Private Hampton could clearly see his victim's stunned faces. There were dozens of them. He clenched his teeth as he swept the flames side to side. The faces disappeared in fire. Flaming bodies scurried everywhere, trying to outrun their fiery fate. The flame lasted eight seconds before the spark ran its course. The roar of the flames mixed with the screaming of dying men filled the space.

Mathews followed him in. The scene nauseated him. The screaming agony, the smell of burnt flesh mixed with gasoline, it was too much. He lurched back but ran into another soldier directly behind him. O'Connor rasped, "Cover the stairway to the right." Mathews was glad for an assignment, something to get him away from the devastation being spewed from the nozzle of Hampton's cooker.

Mathews remembered the layout of the bunkers from the day before. The flames lit up the area and he could see the stairway leading down to the lower level. He crouched on the lip of the stairs with his Thompson ready. More men joined him. The sounds of screaming, dying men stopped, but the roar of the flames continued. Thick smoke moved on the ceiling and Mathews imagined he must be breathing their souls.

Private Dawson gasped. "Mother Mary, I think that crazy sumbitch is enjoying himself."

Mathews shook his head. "Just doing his job," but he didn't believe it. It took a certain kind of man to carry a flamethrower. The constant risk of burning alive from your own tank of gasoline on your back, matched with the firsthand view of your victims, was bound to change a man, and not for the better.

The roar of the flamethrower finally stopped, replaced with the banging of M1s killing any survivors. With the relative silence, Mathews heard voices filtering up from below. He tightened his grip on his Thompson and steadied his aim. He heard the clang of boots on the metal stairway. "Here they come!"

He could feel the presence of more GIs spreading out along the top of the stairs aiming into the darkness. When he saw the outline of a soldier, he squeezed the trigger. The Thompson bucked in his hand and he forced his grip downward, countering the upward kick. The others joined in and the hallway lit up with muzzle flashes. The faces of Japanese soldiers flashed as they grimaced in pain and fell. Soon the stairway was choked with bodies.

Mathews heard O'Connor yell, "Grenades!" Mathews kept his barrel sighted and heard GIs plucking grenades off their battle harnesses and pulling the pins. He saw the grenades disappear into the darkness. He lowered his muzzle and hunkered down. The grenades bounced over bodies and rolled down stairs. Within seconds there were explosions and the sound in the confined space was deafening. There were screams, barely discernible through the ringing in his ears.

O'Connor was saying something and soon he felt soldiers moving past him. He opened his eyes and saw GIs with flashlights moving over a mangled mass of bodies. A sudden burst of automatic weapons fire sent the men into crouches and they hunkered and returned fire down the stairs. Someone yelled. "Still a bunch of 'em holed up down here."

Mathews stood and was about to take the first step down, when Private Hampton stepped past him. His face was darkened with soot and his eyes behind the goggles were hard as steel. He caught Mathews staring and grinned. "Barbecue time."

The crouched GIs made room and Hampton and his mass of gasoline tanks moved past them. He'd fired half his thirty seconds of fuel. The sudden light from the new spark and then the flames made Mathews squint. He could see Hampton's stark outline. He looked like something out of a sci-fi comic book he remembered. He couldn't decide if he'd be considered a good or a bad guy.

There were screams of agony. Mathews put his hands over his ears, trying to drown them out, but it was no use. He'd hear those screams in his dreams for the rest of his life.

Eight seconds later the flames stopped and O'Connor went down the stairs with his carbine ready. He glanced back at Corporal Mathews. "Keep the rest of the men up here til I call you. Watch our backs." Mathews was relieved not to have to see the cooked carnage below.

O'Connor moved down the stairs and put his hand on Hampton's shoulder. He startled and started to swing the glowing nozzle toward him, but O'Connor spoke. "You okay?"

Hampton looked at his sergeant with wide eyes and gave a quick nod. He lifted the goggles off his eyes and they snapped into place on his helmet. His voice was raspy. "Think - think I'm outta juice."

The scene on the floor of the bunker was enough to make a hard man gag. There were multiple small fires and O'Connor realized each pyre used to be a man. The smell of charred meat was unmistakable. O'Connor swept his carbine around the room, but there was no one left alive. Flames licked up the walls, burning a tattered and soot covered Japanese flag. He looked back at Hampton who was rubbing the bridge of his nose. "Go on up and find more juice. We may need it again before the day's through." Hampton didn't respond, just kept rubbing his eyes. O'Connor raised his voice. "You hear me Hampton?" The private stared back at O'Connor and nodded. He turned to walk up the stairs, the other GIs stepping out of his way. O'Connor barked. "Hampton."

He turned, "Yes Sergeant?"

"You did good today. Saved a lot of GIs." Private Hampton didn't say anything, simply turned and slowly walked up the stairs, like his empty tanks weighed a ton.

O'Connor moved down the rest of the stairs and could hear GIs following. He stepped over a charred and still sputtering body. He averted his eyes, looking for the connecting hallway. He saw the door off to the right. He signaled for his men to advance and they stacked up to either side. There was dim light filtering through the cracks in the wooden door. It was blackened with fire and was warm to the touch. O'Connor pulled the handle and the door swung open on squeaking hinges. He crouched and aimed down the corridor, but it was empty. He could hear the dim sounds of fighting.

There was a clanging of boots on metal steps and he turned to see Private Perkins trotting toward him. He was breathing hard. When he caught the stench of burnt bodies he reeled back and put his hand over his mouth. O'Connor barked, "What's the message, Perkins?"

He caught his breath and relayed the message. "Platoon Sergeant Carver sent me. The Japs are routed. They're in full retreat."

12

———

General Manjome was furious. His men were dying, his intricate bunker system was falling. He gritted his teeth and seethed, *how did the Yankees get behind us so quickly? It's solid jungle.* The answer didn't matter. All that mattered now was saving the last remaining soldiers in his command. He bore holes into the Lieutenant standing before him, sweating. "Where is Captain Ito?"

The Lieutenant shook his head slightly. "He was burned by a Yankee flamethrower, sir. I saw him go down myself." The image of the fearsome officer as a flaming torch came rushing back and he fought off the fear.

General Manjome paused for an instant. "Leave the highest remaining noncom here with twenty men. They must hold off the Americans long enough to allow our escape. We'll head into the jungle and continue the fight."

Lieutenant Sato nodded and turned to carry out his general's orders. He'd wondered briefly if the general would choose surrender. They had little chance of survival and even if they managed to escape into the jungle, they didn't have enough food, water or ammo to last more than a few days. Surrender would be dishonorable and he knew the general to be an honorable officer. He also knew he'd never surrender himself, even if given the order. He'd take his own life long before that happened.

He noticed the cringing Makipili in the corner. There were six of the traitorous Filipinos huddled together. They were unarmed, completely at the mercy of their betters. "What of them, sir?"

General Manjome looked with disgust at the Filipinos. "We'll need a guide." He pointed at the nearest man. "That one got us here from the city. He knows the jungle. The rest put in front of our rear guard. Give them machetes. They'll slow the Yankee devils. If they don't fight, or try to run, kill them." The sounds of fighting from nearby bunkers hastened them. "Hurry. We leave now. They haven't sealed off this section yet, but they'll do so any minute."

General Manjome led his ragtag group of one hundred and fifty soldiers down the dimly lit underground corridor. It was well built. The dirt walls were held up with cut palms and bits of lumber. It was built as a way to enter the bunker system from the jungle without being noticed. The special Filipino work crew that built it was treated to better food, and housing. When they were finished, they were rewarded with a quick bullet to the back of the head.

Now he was using it as an escape route, a way to get beyond the Yankee forces. They'd surely find the tunnel and pursue them, but by then they'd be far away and able to mount another defense.

Each step took him deeper into the darkness. He looked at the low ceiling and wondered how many Americans were above him only feet away. If he'd had more time he could've used the tunnel to get a sizable force behind the Americans, but they'd attacked with lightning speed and surprise. He debated attacking them now with his remaining soldiers. They'd certainly inflict heavy casualties, but he shunned the idea. *I can deal more damage luring them into the jungle. We'll whittle them away.*

When they got to the end of the tunnel the line of soldiers stopped and Lt. Sato forced the Makipili, Berto forward. He pointed at the hatch which was at the end of a short set of stairs, hacked into the dirt. Sato kept his pistol aimed at the back of the swarthy Filipino, who's machete was out and ready. Berto went to the top step and had to crouch. He looked back at Lt. Sato who nodded and aimed his pistol at him. He nodded back.

Berto grasped the hatch handle and pushed. It gave way. Bright daylight streamed through, making him squint. He eased his head out and looked around. The jungle was gleaming green and shiny. He took a deep breath; the dank air of the bunkers and tunnel were making him sick. The urge to spring out and run through the jungle was overwhelming. The Japanese would never find him, but he knew Lt. Sato was waiting for that very thing. He could almost feel the muzzle of the pistol aiming at his back. Besides, where would he go? He was a traitor to his people. If and when he was caught he'd be tortured and hanged. He'd thrown his lot onto the losing side, and it was a decision he'd have to live with. He had little doubt he'd die soon, but he still had the chance to have a say in *how* he died.

He scanned the area. There were no GIs visible, but he could hear fighting in the bunkers. He wondered how his fellow makipili were faring. *Probably already dead.* He brought his head back below the hatch and looked in the direction of Lt. Sato. He couldn't see him, his eyes weren't adjusted to the low light, but he caught movement. He smiled and waved him forward.

Lieutenant Sato kept his pistol aimed at Berto's chest and moved up the stairs. He pushed the Filipino to the side and poked his head into the light. He blinked quickly and his eyes watered, but he didn't see any danger. He stood and stepped out of the tunnel. He motioned for Berto to come up and he did so quickly. More soldiers popped out and spread out in a defensive ring.

General Manjome came out near the end of the line of men. He nodded at Lt. Sato. "Have the Makipili lead us."

Lieutenant Sato gave a curt nod and prodded Berto. Berto sheathed his machete and moved into the jungle. He wracked his brain, trying to think of where he should lead them. He'd done lots of hunting and trekking growing up, but this was deep jungle and he wasn't exactly sure where he was. He decided he'd lead them upwards. He'd use the natural contours of the land to get them as lost as he possibly could. Maybe he could slip away some dark night and make his way to a different island where no one knew him. He thought about living out the rest of his days as a hermit on one of the many abandoned islands that make up the Philippines. He was bound to find one he could disappear on.

~

THE FINAL BUNKER fell by mid-morning. The GIs had suffered minimal casualties, unlike the day before. Now, jubilant GIs and Filipinos sifted through the smoldering remains of the bunker system.

Platoon Sergeant Carver sat on top of a bunker with his legs dangling over the side and took a long pull off his canteen. Sergeant O'Connor asked, "They find that Jap general's body yet?"

Carver screwed the lid on the canteen and shook his head. "Not that I've heard. He's probably part of all those burned bodies. No way to identify him."

O'Connor shook his head. "Even when those Japs had no chance of escape, I mean none, they still wouldn't surrender."

Carver nodded and pulled out a stogie. He bit off the end and jammed it into his mouth. He didn't light it but savored the dark taste on his tongue. "You've been fighting 'em long enough to know better'n that. Honor, country … all that bullshit."

"Yeah, I know. It just seems like we're rolling through 'em now. Thought maybe they'd realize they've got no chance and start acting like normal human beings." He spit off the side, "Save us all a lot of trouble."

"If they fight this hard here, imagine what it'll be like when we're in downtown Tokyo? It won't just be the soldiers, we'll have to kill every man woman and child able to hold a pitchfork."

O'Connor took off his helmet and rubbed his close cropped, red hair. "Ain't that the truth? Make everything we've done up till now seem like a fairy tale."

Private Perkins burst from the bunker door off to the right and looked frantically in both directions.

Carver called down to him. "Looking for me, son?"

Perkins looked up and shielded his eyes. Relief flooded his face.

"Lieutenant Swan and Captain Flannigan want you inside right away. They've found something."

Carver got to his feet. "Tell 'em we're on our way." O'Connor looked up at him. "You may as well come too."

Minutes later they were on the bottom floor of the bunker they'd taken last. There were still Japanese bodies in various death poses. They'd been pushed to the corners awaiting removal. The smell of death and decomposition was as familiar to the GIs as the daily rain showers, but it still made their nostrils flare in protest.

Lieutenant Swan and Captain Flannigan were standing around a group of Filipino fighters. O'Connor recognized Major Cruz and couldn't tear his eyes away from her. He'd tried to find her after the fighting ended but was told she was off in the jungle. Seeing her safe brought an involuntary smile. The boy, Sam was at her side.

Carver and O'Connor stepped into the circle. "Ah, there you are," stated Captain Flannigan, as if they were school kids up to no good.

Carver took the stogie out of his mouth. "Reporting as ordered, sir."

Flannigan pointed. "The natives found a tunnel. It's got signs of recent heavy use. It leads out into the jungle and is most likely General Manjome's escape route."

O'Connor stood beside Major Cruz. It was all he could do not to reach out and take her in his arms. The urge was overwhelming, but he settled for taking in her subtle scent. She smiled up at him and moved slightly closer.

Carver asked, "How many men you figure?"

Lieutenant Swan answered. "The Japs lost most of their men in the attack. Estimates are almost two thousand dead. We took a few prisoners, but only because they were wounded or knocked out. We figure there's at least a hundred that slipped out, probably led by General Manjome."

Carver nodded. "Let 'em rot in the jungle. They won't last long out there without food."

Captain Flannigan braced and put his fists. "We didn't bring you down here for your opinion, Sergeant. I want you and Swan to lead a platoon in pursuit."

Carver couldn't believe his ears. His men had fought the previous day taking massive casualties, then marched all night, attacked and destroyed the bunkers and now Flannigan wanted to send them out again. His men needed rest. He looked at Lieutenant Swan for help, but he was tight lipped.

Carver was about to put his military career at risk by questioning this jackass when Major Cruz stepped forward. "Captain, I will lead the pursuit mission." The silence hung in the dank air like a dark fog. Captain Flannigan's face went beet red as he thought about the chain of command. She was a Major and outranked him, but she was a Filipino under Colonel Cushing. Was she a part of the chain of command? Did she have a right to give him an order? Did a woman have a right to tell him what to do? She saw the conflict in his eyes and didn't wait for him to work it out. "Sam, get the platoon organized. We set out immediately."

Sam snapped off a quick salute and flashed a dazzling smile at Carver and O'Connor, then took off up the stairs, taking them two at a time. O'Connor cringed at what was happening but was also proud of the way the major handled the situation. Flannigan still looked confused and about to explode, but kept his mouth shut. Carver couldn't keep the grin off his face. Flannigan noticed. "Carver, you and your men are on clean-up. I want these Jap bodies out of here asap." He spun away and marched up the stairs

Carver put the stogie back in his mouth and muttered, "Yes, sir."

Lieutenant Swan looked apologetic. His face was soot and dirt covered and Carver thought he saw spatters of blood too. He'd fought beside him all morning. He'd led the men from the front and fought like a tiger. "I tried to talk sense into him before you got here, but he was adamant about sending the platoon."

Carver nodded. "Figured as much." He turned to Major Cruz. "Think you probably saved me from a court-martial, ma'am, thank you."

She smiled. She was short, but her presence made her seem much taller. "Doesn't make sense to send tired troops. My soldiers are well rested and know the jungle. We'll take our revenge on the general. He ruled with an iron fist, and we deserve to end his life."

The sound of many feet clanging down the stairs signaled the arrival of the Filipino platoon. They filled the space, making it cramped. The sweat of many bodies mixed with the putrid smell of death gave the air a tangy tinge that could almost be tasted.

Major Cruz looked up at Sergeant O'Connor who stared into her eyes. He wanted to hold her, to kiss her, to scoop her up and take her to the fresh air outside and make love to her but that was impossible. "I'll be back," she said. Her eyes left his and turned hard. She looked around at her soldiers, they were ready to follow her anywhere.

Without a look back she ducked into the dim tunnel and disappeared, followed by the rest of her platoon. When they'd all gone, O'Connor, Carver and Swan were left alone. The silence was heavy between them. Confusion flooded O'Connor as he realized he was in some strange new world where the woman went off to war while he remained behind.

Carver watched O'Connor's reaction and thought he saw something there. He shook his head and muttered to himself, "Well I'll be damned."

THE TRAIL WAS easy to follow. The Japanese made no efforts to cover their tracks. The Filipino platoon trotted along the path moving deeper and deeper into the jungle. The further they went the more chance they'd run into an ambush, at least that was what Felipe told Sam. The trail was relatively straight, leading toward the mountains.

Sam wondered who was leading the Japanese. Was it his brother, Berto? He'd looked for him amongst the bodies in the final bunker. He'd recognized a few of the shredded makapili, but Berto wasn't one of them. He didn't know quite how he'd feel if he found him amongst the dead. He wanted revenge, wanted him to pay for killing Lola and enslaving their sister, but he was also his brother and the final member of his family. *Can I kill him if the opportunity arises?* He had no idea, but he thought he might soon find out. He had a strong feeling that his older brother was still alive and guiding the Japanese.

Felipe stayed close to Sam as they followed the trail. He had his rifle slung over his shoulder. They were near the middle of the platoon. "Soon we will find the Japanese and destroy them. Then we'll have our island and our freedom back."

Sam furrowed his brow. "It seems like the Japanese have always been here."

Felipe nodded. "Yes, I forget how young you are. You were maybe ten? Eleven?" Sam shrugged, not liking the question. "Well, it doesn't matter. We will have to rebuild our country. Men like you and me will be responsible for doing so."

Sam gestured forward. "And will women like Major Cruz have a say?"

Felipe shrugged. "She and many more like her are heroes. I think there is always a place for heroes."

"And what of my sister?" He looked at his feet, then sideways at Felipe when he didn't answer right away.

Felipe looked down too. "If she's still alive, she will have a harder path. She'll be looked at as a collaborator."

Sam faced Felipe in a whirl and puffed his chest out. He had to remember to keep his voice down. "She's no collaborator. She was kidnapped and anything she's done she was forced to do."

Felipe nodded but kept his eyes forward. "It might be better if she died. Then she'd be considered no less than the major."

"She'll be considered a traitor if she survives? Is that what you're telling me?"

Felipe put up his hands, "I'm only saying she'll have a hard path."

"I pray every day she's alive. When I find her, I will not allow her to be mistreated. I failed her once, I won't a second time."

The trail angled into a canyon and Sam increased his pace, leaving Felipe behind. The thought of his sister being considered a Japanese collaborator, put into the same class as his brother, made him seethe. He closed his eyes hard trying to picture Yelina's face, but he saw her painted like a whore, a geisha, he thought they were called. He said a silent prayer and moved up behind Major Cruz. He wanted to ask her what she thought her sister's fate would be if he found her.

He was trying to get the nerve to speak to her when the soldiers in front suddenly crouched and the entire column stopped. Sam brought his carbine off his shoulder and scanned the surrounding jungle. They were in a creek-bed. There was a trickling flow of clear water moving through moss covered rocks and mud. Sam looked at the sloped ridges to either side. If the Japanese had doubled back and were above them, it wouldn't go well.

The scouts thought the same thing and Sam could hear them whispering to Major Cruz and pointing to the surrounding terrain. She nodded and looked back at Sam. She hadn't noticed him and gave him a quick smile. She signaled that he should move to the ridge to the right. He nodded and started climbing the gentle slope. Most of the platoon moved with him, but some moved up the left ridge too. The scouts and Major Cruz stayed in the creek-bed.

Sam realized he was the point-man on the right ridge. He looked behind and saw the next Filipino fighter ten meters away. Sam waited until he saw Major Cruz wave her hand forward. With his carbine at the ready he moved forward.

He'd grown up mostly in the city, but his father loved to hike and he'd spent many happy days at his side listening to him talk about various plants and animals they came across. This was entirely different though. Back then, the jungle had seemed a magical place, something he could leave behind and know was there for his pleasure. Now, the magic was gone, or had been replaced with a dark magic, full of danger and death.

He concentrated on trying to walk quietly. He remembered his father taking slow, careful footsteps when trying to get close to a deer. He tried to mimic that now, but he felt clumsy. Soon he was sweating more heavily than normal. The extra effort trying to stay quiet and maintaining concentration was taking its toll. He shook his head and felt drops of sweat fly off his nose and chin. He glanced behind and saw the fighter walking as if on a Sunday stroll. *How did I get myself into this?*

He gritted his teeth and saw the diminutive form of Major Cruz moving along the creek-bed. She moved effortlessly from boulder to boulder. She made it look easy and he wondered if she grew up hunting. He didn't remember her mentioning it when she taught him English. Of course, if someone told him his English teacher would one day be a great military hero, he would have laughed them out of the room.

He was brought out of his musings abruptly. He froze in place and concentrated on the jungle. He'd heard something, something out of place, but what was it? He played the noise back. *Was it metal scraping metal?* He squinted and focused every sense. Then he saw it, the outline of a barrel protruding from a thick copse of bushes. It wasn't aimed at him, but into the canyon, tracking Major Cruz's path. There wasn't time for a warning, he put his carbine to his shoulder, released the safety and pulled the trigger at the same instant the barrel in the bushes fired. The sharp crack sounded out of place in the serene jungle landscape. There was a pause as the Filipinos first froze, then found cover.

Sam ran forward. The muzzle had vanished. He had his carbine leveled at the spot. He sensed movement further along the ridge. He crouched behind a rock and aimed. He fired at the movement. There were suddenly shapes and movement everywhere he looked. He pulled the trigger until his magazine was empty. He dropped behind cover just as the crashing of many rifles opened fire. Bullets whizzed and ricocheted off the rock. Sam cowered, making himself as small a target as possible. The jungle around him shredded with bullets. The air seemed alive with steel.

He fumbled to insert another magazine, finally slamming it home and cycling a round into the chamber. He heard the sound of more rifles opening up, his comrades joining the fight. The volume of bullets hitting the rock he crouched behind, lessened. He peaked over the top and fired at movement and muzzle flashes then dropped back to cover.

There was a heavy volume of fire coming from behind him. His Filipino comrades were flooding the area with lethal fire. The Japanese firing subsided and soon the only sound was the crashing and popping of friendly fire.

Sam waited until he saw his comrades advancing past him, then moved forward to a thick palm and lay at the base. He struggled to calm his breathing and he wiped the stinging sweat from his eyes. He searched for more targets but didn't see any. The firing from the other

Filipinos died down and soon the silence of the sweltering jungle returned like an old familiar blanket.

Sam could feel his heartbeat throbbing in his ears. He heard yelling and realized they were giving the all clear. Keeping his weapon ready, he stood on shaky legs. Sam went to the area where he'd seen the muzzle. He nearly stepped on the body tucked into the thick bush. The Japanese soldier was on his back, his right leg tucked unnaturally beneath him. His helmet was still firmly attached and his blank eyes stared. He had dark red stains along his left side. The long Arisaka rifle that had given him away, was on the ground pointing down the canyon.

Felipe was beside him. He slapped his back and smiled. "Good job, soldier. You saved many men." He looked down the canyon and saw Major Cruz. "Oh no, the major's hit."

Sam followed his gaze. There was a cluster of men surrounding her. They were working frantically, applying bandages and pressure to a seeping wound. "I failed. I saw them too late. The major. How bad is it?"

Felipe shook his head. "You did everything you could." He pointed at him. "Stay here and watch the ridge. I'll see how she's doing."

13

With the bunkers secure, the GIs were sent back to Cebu City for a well-earned period of rest and relaxation. Platoon Sergeant Carver was looking for a place to rack out for a few hours. He couldn't remember a time he'd been more tired. He couldn't seem to stop tripping and bumping into things. He needed to sleep. He found a cot in a secluded corner of an open-air tent. He sat and unbuckled his boots. He barely had the strength to pull them off. He rubbed his aching feet and was about to lay down and check out for the rest of the day and possibly the night, when Private Perkins trotted in. He had a satchel over his shoulder. His eyes lit up when he saw Carver. "Glad I found you, Sarge."

Carver growled, "What is it, Perkins?"

He dug into the satchel and pulled out three letters. "Mail call."

Lilly. Carver reached out and snatched the letters before Private Perkins could get a look at them. The fatigue fell from his shoulders like shrugging off a heavy pack. Perkins said something, but Carver didn't hear him. He finally left and Carver turned the letters over in his hand, inspecting every millimeter like they held clues to all the mysteries of the world. Each letter had a faint, but distinct smell. Lilly.

He read each letter twice and fell asleep with them draped over his chest. He dreamed of her and the hammock in the jungle.

Sergeant O'Connor was exhausted, but restless. He laid on his cot staring up at the ceiling of the army green tent. The heat swept over him in waves, but his body was tired enough to sleep through a trip through hell itself. His mind, on the other hand, whirled and wouldn't shut down. The image of Celine disappearing into the tunnel wouldn't leave him. He wondered if she'd caught up to the fleeing Japanese. He wondered if she was in combat at that very instant. He told himself that she'd survived without his help for this long. She'd lived through much more dangerous situations over the past three years of occupation. But it still drove him crazy knowing she was in danger while he relaxed in safety. Sleep finally caught up to him and he slipped into a dreamless abyss of blackness.

He was awakened what seemed like only seconds but was actually six hours later. It took persistent poking and prodding by a nervous Private Perkins, but he finally cracked his eyes open and sneered. "This better be good, Private."

"Sorry Sarge. Wouldn't a done it if I had any other choice. Lieutenant Swan wants all the NCOs to report to the gymnasium as soon as possible."

O'Connor swung his legs to the side of the cot and put his head in his hands. He rubbed his eyes and nodded. "I'll be there in a few minutes." Perkins turned to leave. "You hear any news about those Filipinos chasing the Japs?"

Perkins shook his head. "No, sir. Not a word."

Ten minutes later O'Connor sat next to Carver and the other NCOs and officers of the 164th Regiment. Half the men looked haggard and tired, the other half rested and clean. Only half the regiment had been used, along with elements of the 180th, to assault the bunker system.

O'Connor looked Carver over. He looked tired, but he had a slight smile on his face, as if he knew some secret that no one else did. O'Connor felt like hell. "What're you grinning about?"

Carver snapped out of his reverie. "Huh? What?"

"You look like the cat that ate the canary. What's up?"

Carver shook his head. He still had dark stains of mud and gunpowder on his face, making his teeth look extra white. "Got some letters from Lilly. That's all."

O'Connor looked at his boots and shook his head. "Jesus, Sarge. You're like some love-struck rube."

The grin disappeared from Carver's face. "Watch your mouth, Sergeant. I'm still your superior."

O'Connor looked to the podium and shook his head. "You actually think we're gonna survive this don't you?"

Carver looked at his old friend. Neither of them thought they'd make it off the Canal in '42. When they did, they thought they'd never make it out of Bougainville in '44. Now they'd made it through the first phase of the Philippine campaign.

Carver realized his attitude had changed since meeting Lilly. He saw a possible future he wanted like nothing he'd ever wanted before. Was he losing his edge? Was the reason he kept surviving because he'd already accepted his fate? Would Lilly be his death? He wasn't able to ponder it long.

General Arnold strode in and the entire cadre sprang to their feet and saluted. He saluted back. "At ease men. Have a seat." He waited until they'd re-settled.

"We routed the Japanese today. The remnants of their shattered command are being pursued into the jungle where they will either be destroyed or contained. Either way, the southern part of the island is secure from a long and brutal occupation, thanks to your courage and valor. Fighting continues in the north, but we expect victory there soon. Convey my gratitude to your men."

He stepped to the map hanging from a board behind him. With a wooden pointer, he smacked it. "This is our next target. Bohol." There was sniggering from the fresh troops and a murmur went through the group. "Odd name, I know, but it has an estimated thousand Japanese soldiers that need to be dealt with." He smacked the bigger island to the north of Bohol. "We need to clear Bohol before we move on southern Negros. We don't want to leave any Japs behind us." He let that sink in. "Bohol is tiny, but well defended. The Japs are well dug in on the high ground. We don't think they have much in the way of artillery, at most some mortars, but they've honeycombed the island and we'll have to root them out one by one." He looked at the soldiers. It was nothing they hadn't heard before. "Portions of the 164th and 40th will be teaming up for this one. There's a contingent of Filipino fighters on Bohol. You'll link up and they'll guide you inland." He looked at his notes. "Major Ingencio is in command."

He looked the men over. "I know we're barely done with things here, but MacArthur wants Negros taken yesterday, which means we have to move fast. We'll be debarking two days from now. It's a short boat ride. We don't expect any hostilities on the beach, but our destroyers and cruisers will be standing by, just in case." He collected his notes and smiled at the faces staring back at him. "The Bohol operation will involve three companys. Able from the 164th, Easy and Charlie from the 40th."

It was all Carver could do not stand up and protest. He could see the back of Captain Flannigan's head a couple rows in front. He tried to bore holes in his skull with his eyes. He muttered under his breath, "Son-of-a-bitch."

O'Connor leaned back in the metal folding chair and crossed his arms. The thought of leaving the island before knowing the outcome of the Celine's mission, made him nauseous.

General Arnold stepped away from the podium. "I know we've been through a lot, but we have to keep our foot on the gas pedal. The Japs are reeling and the harder we push the quicker we can end this thing and get home." He turned and strode out the way he'd come.

The room broke into varied conversations and started to clear out. O'Connor was on his feet. Carver started to walk away, he had a lot to prep for the coming mission. O'Connor shook his head. "I can't leave without knowing how Celine ... I mean Major Cruz is faring in the jungle. I can't leave it hanging like that."

Carver remembered the look O'Connor and Cruz had shared in the tunnel. He'd forgotten all about it in his extreme fatigue and joy at reading Lilly's letters. He looked hard at O'Connor. "Hell, I'd forgotten about that. Obviously, something happened between you two. Look, I'm sure she …"

O'Connor interrupted him. "Doesn't matter. She's off chasing Japs and I'm leaving the island to fight on another." He looked at his feet. "Probably better this way." He spit a stream of clear spit.

Carver knew he was hurting. "She'll be alright. She's been doing this shit for years now. She's an impressive soldier."

"I know all that." He cut his eyes at Carver. "Doesn't make it any easier."

Carver nodded. "I know. I think about Lilly every damned day. I…"

O'Connor cut in. "Lilly's safe back at the hospital. All she's gotta worry about is getting groped by horny doctors. Celine's out chasing Japs in the jungle."

Carver's jaw rippled as he gritted his teeth. He was going to say something more but realized nothing he could say would make it better. *He's confused about his feelings.* He put his finger in O'Connor's face. "When we get to butthole, or Bohol or whatever the hell island, you stay focused on doing your job. The men need your leadership. Understand?" O'Connor pushed his finger away and stalked off like a scolded child.

THE NEXT DAY was spent resupplying and getting ready for the assault on Bohol Island. Most of the regiment lounged, but Able Company soldiers were busy.

Carver was making the rounds, making sure the disgruntled GIs were staying focused. He came across a group of GIs hand loading magazines with bullets. Private McGillis looked up at Carver. "Why we always get the shitty end of the stick, Sarge? There's other companies seen half the combat we have, but we're always picked."

Carver felt the same way but couldn't let on. "Because we're the best, McGillis, that's why."

Private Gilson chimed in. "That's bullshit and you know it, Sarge.

It's Flannigan. Always volunteering us, trying to get promoted by putting us in harm's way."

Carver knelt beside the men and spit a stream onto the muddy ground. "Look, I know it's a shitty deal. You're probably right about Flannigan, I don't know, but we've got a job to do and the quicker we do it the quicker this war ends and we all go home." The GIs kept loading their magazines. "We've got a good officer in Lieutenant Swan. He'll do what's best for us, despite the captain."

Private First-Class Haley squinted at Carver. "Why is it we never see Cap'n Flannigan when the shit hits the fan?"

Carver stood and looked over the harbor. A steady stream of supplies were being loaded onto troop ships. He grinned at the GIs but didn't answer.

SERGEANT O'CONNOR MADE sure his men were ready and getting what they needed. He did his duties on auto-pilot. His thoughts were elsewhere. He kept glancing toward the heavy jungle to the north where the Filipino guerrillas were chasing the remnants of the Japanese forces.

A full day had passed since he'd last seen Major Cruz and not knowing if she was alive or dead was tearing him up. He'd caught Platoon Sergeant Carver watching him and felt embarrassed. He knew he was acting like some love-struck child. He immersed himself in over preparing for the coming landing, but Celine was never far from his thoughts.

That evening, after the men had eaten, he wandered around the beach. The gentle lapping of the waves against the white sand was soothing. He watched the sun disappear into the sea. The day suddenly transferred to night. He shook his head. *There's no dusk here, only day and night.*

He found himself walking past HQ. It was set up in a large, open air tent. General Arnold had moved out of Cebu City in order to be closer to the developing operation.

The coming landing on Bohol was a minor show. The real push

would come from the main forces of the 40th and Americal Divisions landing on the southern and northern ends of Negros Island. Negros was due North from Cebu, but the ships had to move west until they cleared the tip of Cebu before they could turn north. The assault on Bohol would happen first, a couple days before the first landings on Negros.

O'Connor stopped to watch the hustle and bustle around the tent. Runners were darting into and out of the area like ants on urgent errands. *The machine never rests.* He listened as a flight of distant bombers streaked overhead. There was still sun up there and he could see light reflecting off the aircraft. He wondered where they were headed. There were any number of Japanese bases and occupied islands within range of the multiple American airfields. *Can they strike Japan from here?* He shook his head.

He was about to move on when he saw a different soldier running toward the HQ. He wore a khaki top and shorts and his skin was dark. A guerrilla. O'Connor became alert and without knowing he was doing it, ran toward the lit up interior of the tent.

He got to the guard posted outside and stopped when he was challenged with an outstretched rifle. "Halt."

O'Connor eyed the man. "Let me through, Private. I have business inside."

"Sorry, Sarge. My orders are to limit entry to everyone except runners and officers."

O'Connor looked into the tent and could see the guerrilla speaking urgently to an officer. He recognized Colonel Cushing. O'Connor was desperate for news about Major Cruz. He eyed the soldier and squinted. The GI looked competent and ready to enforce his orders at any cost. O'Connor imagined himself taking him out but decided it would do no good to be put in the brig, and perhaps the hospital. He moved away from the guard, but stood a few yards away waiting for the runner to come out.

He could see the animated conversation continuing beyond the guard. Soon Cushing conferred with other officers then came back and relayed a message to the Filipino, who snapped off a crisp salute and moved to the door.

O'Connor stopped him as he was about to run past. The slight guerrilla stopped and focused on Sergeant O'Connor. His face lit up when he recognized him. "Sergeant O'Connor. Hello."

"Sam, I didn't recognize you at first." He grasped Sam's shoulders and squared him up to himself. "What's happening out there?" He forced himself not to ask about Major Cruz.

Sam's smile faded. "We've been fighting a running battle with the Japs. They continue to retreat, but they leave small units behind to slow us down." He looked into O'Connor's eyes. "The Major is wounded."

All color drained from O'Connor's face. He almost staggered as his legs threatened to give out. "What? How bad?"

"A sniper." He looked at the ground. "It was my fault. I shot an instant too late."

O'Connor shook Sam's shoulders. "Is, is she dead?"

Sam looked up abruptly and shook his head. "No, but she's hurt bad. The others are bringing her out." He pointed toward the tent he'd just left. "Colonel Cushing ordered me to bring a doctor and a medic to keep her alive while they move her."

O'Connor nodded and released him. "Go! What are you waiting for? Go!" Sam looked confused but darted away.

O'Connor went back to the tent and the guard tilted his head. O'Connor said, "Is Lieutenant Swan or Captain Flannigan in there?"

The guard shrugged. "What's it to you?"

O'Connor had had enough. He lunged and got right up to the guard's face before he could block him with his rifle. He put his finger close to his nose and seethed. "Don't fuck with me, soldier." The guard blanched, sensing O'Connor's malice and deadly intent.

There was movement just inside the tent flap and a familiar voice said. "Sergeant O'Connor is that you?"

O'Connor stepped away from the guard and replied, "Yes sir, Lieutenant Swan, it's me. Can I have a word, sir?"

"Of course." He addressed the guard. "At ease soldier." The guard looked relieved and stepped aside. O'Connor moved past him. "What's up, Sergeant?"

"Sir, that Filipino runner that just came in, Sam," Swan nodded.

"He had news about Major Cruz."

Lieutenant Swan nodded but looked grim. "Yes. She took a sniper's bullet. She's in critical condition. They're bringing her here as quickly as they can."

O'Connor's eye twitched, and his voice broke. "I know. I need to go out with the medic to meet her on the trail. I could help."

Swan frowned and his forehead wrinkled. "What? Why? What's this all about?"

O'Connor shook his head, wondering what to say. "Sir, I … well, I just need to help her. It would mean a lot to me."

Swan shook his head. "They won't be here until tomorrow morning at the earliest. You'll be on a ship steaming toward Bohol." He saw the anguish overcome O'Connor. O'Connor looked around like a caged animal.

The sudden realization came to Swan. *My God. He's in love with her.* He put a hand on his shoulder and could feel the tension of his sinewy muscles. He wracked his brain for a solution. "I don't know what went on between you and it's probably best I never do. You're obviously frantic. Maybe I could put you on sick call?"

The thought of bailing out on his men with a fake sickness nearly made him sick for real. Swan saw the disgust creep across his face. He was fascinated as he watched O'Connor sift through the decision. It was like watching a well-matched tennis game. Finally O'Connor shook his head. He looked into Swan's eyes and he would've sworn he saw the beginnings of tears. *Nah, can't be. This son-of-a-bitch is tough as nails.*

O'Connor shook his head in defeat. "I can't do that, sir."

THE BOAT RIDE from Talisay Bay to the beach at Tagbilarin on Bohol only took a few hours. To the relief of everyone, the landing was unopposed. In fact, they were met with joyous cheering from hundreds of Filipino guerrillas and townsfolk. They met up with units of the 40th Infantry Division soon after landing.

Bohol looked identical to the island they'd left that morning. The air was muggy, the beaches sparkling white, and the rolling hills covered with low, dense scrub and palms. Platoon Sergeant Carver thought it would be beautiful if not for the war.

Carver watched from a distance as the cheering guerrillas quieted at a command from a stocky guerrilla wearing a cocked jungle hat. They quickly formed into ranks and snapped to attention. They wore khaki tops and shorts that covered their dark skin and hard, sinewy muscle. Despite their broad smiles, they looked like a lethal force.

The stocky guerrilla stepped up to Captain Flannigan. "I'm Major Ingencio." He gestured to the men forming up behind him. "And these are some of my men. We are at your disposal."

Captain Flannigan braced and saluted the guerilla. Even from a distance, Carver could see the indecision in Flannigan's salute. He was still unsure if the Filipino guerrilla officers used the same military courtesies.

While the officers conversed, the offloading of men and material continued. Carver studied the town situated on the bay. It was small by comparison to US towns and built from different materials, but it looked like it wouldn't be a bad place to live before the Japanese came. He guessed the Filipinos lived a happy existence of fishing and farming. There was no sign of the Japanese occupation and he wondered if the guerrillas had already eradicated them.

That thought was dashed when Private Perkins approached. The short kid always reminded him of the pet ferret he'd owned when he was a kid. His squeaky voice cemented the thought. "Lieutenant Swan says the guerrillas have the Japs pinned down in the hills about three miles inland. Wants us to push forward immediately."

An hour later Able Company along with the 40th Division's Charlie Company moved through the small fishing village. Every doorway was filled with smiling brown faces. Children ran up to them and marched beside them. Carver kept his eyes forward, looking for trouble. He had his Thompson slung over his right shoulder. He glanced back at Sergeant O'Connor, leading second squad. O'Connor's face was an unreadable mask to most, but Carver could see the pain just beneath the hard surface.

A child ran up to Carver and tugged on his pant leg. Carver

ignored it and kept scanning for threats. The tug persisted and he finally looked down. The tiny face beaming back at him looked to be that of a five-year-old boy. "Git outta here, kid." The child kept on smiling and tugging. "Where are your parents, dammit?" The boy kept tugging, not speaking, but the intent was clear. Finally, Carver shook his head and reached into his pocket. He pulled out a chocolate bar and handed it to him. The boy took it. The bar looked huge in his tiny hand. His smile grew impossibly big. Carver thought the kid's cheeks would burst. He shooed him away. "Now leave me alone. Get outta here." The boy stepped away and snapped off a salute. He kept walking beside him with his hand saluting, staring at Carver. Carver ignored him, but the kid persisted and finally Carver stopped and faced him. The boy squinted up at him. Carver looked at the men streaming past. He cursed under his breath but braced and gave the kid a perfect salute. The boy's face went serious and he dropped the salute, saying something Carver couldn't understand. "Don't mention it." Carver continued walking and the boy stayed in place and watched him go, the chocolate bar melting in this hand.

Corporal Mathews trotted up next to him. "You getting soft on us, Sarge?"

Carver growled, "Fuck you, Corporal. Damned kid wouldn't leave me alone."

Mathews smiled. "Cute kid. Glad he doesn't have to live under the boot of the Japs anymore."

Carver grunted and kept walking. Mathews continued beside him. "Something on your mind?"

Mathews stole a glance behind him. "I'm worried about Sergeant O'Connor. He's been quiet all day. Didn't say more'n two words the entire boat ride. Seems preoccupied with something."

Carver glanced back. O'Connor was staring straight ahead. "Got some bad news just before we left. He'll be alright, just give him space."

Mathews nodded. "Figured it was something like that."

14

Major Ingencio's guerrillas led the two companies of GIs three miles inland along a well-used dirt road. The guerrillas walked like they were on a Sunday stroll. They weren't worried about being attacked.

They stopped at the base of a small hill. There was a large, well established base full of more Filipino fighters. They greeted the newcomers with smiles and backslaps. Platoon Sergeant Carver thought it felt more like a party atmosphere than a war zone.

There were small cooking fires sending white wisps of smoke through the sparse tree canopy. The green hills beyond the camp were easily visible and the obvious signs of human activity were everywhere. Carver smacked Cpl. Mathew's arm and pointed. "Those are Jap bunkers." He squinted and noticed the same wispy smoke coming from the hills. "They're occupied too." He looked around the camp, no one seemed concerned about the Japanese forces less than a quarter mile away. Mathews nodded and shrugged his shoulders, unable to explain the odd situation. Carver continued. "Japs must be out of mortars, otherwise they'd have a field day."

An hour later the officers and NCOs were brought into a large central area of the camp. It was well fortified, which made Carver feel better. They sat on stumps and rickety wooden chairs.

Soon Major Ingencio stood and addressed them. "As you can see, the Japanese sit on the high ground, not far from our position. They are completely surrounded by my forces. I have five-thousand men keeping them penned inside their small perimeter. The hill you see is the only land they hold. We figure there are five-hundred troops defending the area." He let that sink in. "We have them completely cut off from resupply, however they have an unlimited supply of food stores, and the rains keep them supplied with water. They sit inside an intricate bunker system. The bunkers are strong and will be able to withstand a frontal assault with ease."

Carver looked at O'Connor and gave him a confused look. The major's light, almost happy tone didn't match the dire report. O'Connor shrugged back at him.

Major Ingencio finished his briefing. "Now that you're here, we're ready to end the Japanese presence on the island."

Captain Flannigan looked confused as well. He stood and addressed the major. "Have you already tried an attack? It seems five-thousand men could overwhelm a force of five hundred beleaguered Japs, no matter their defenses."

Major Ingencio smiled. "We have not attacked them as it would be a waste of lives." Captain Flannigan's face turned beet red and he was about to explode, but Ingencio continued. "We finished wiring the hill only yesterday. We thought we'd wait for you Americans before setting it off."

Captain Flannigan voiced all their questions. "Wired it? What do you mean?"

Major Ingencio gestured toward the hill. "The bunkers the Japanese sit in were built by us. For the past year, they've forced us to work under their horrible conditions. Many men and women died in the process." He paused and looked down, then raised his eyes and continued. "There's a large ammunition depot deep beneath the bunker system. As soon as we learned of it we started tunneling toward it. The entrance to that tunnel is over there." He pointed toward the hills again. "The invaders have long since used up what was stored there. It is empty now and lays forgotten and sealed off from the bunkers above." He looked over the group of dumbfounded GIs and smiled. "With the explosives you have brought, we can wire the depot and send the hill, along with every murdering Japanese soldier, to hell."

~

PLATOON SERGEANT CARVER didn't know if he believed Major Ingencio. He had no reason to doubt him, but the claim they could destroy the bunker system without exposing themselves to danger seemed like a fairy tale, and he knew fairy tales could easily turn to nightmares. So, he kept his men on task, not allowing them to become complacent, as the Filipinos seemed to be.

The American officers weren't taking the Major's word at face value. They insisted on a first-hand view of the tunnel and depot. Carver assigned the task to Sergeant O'Connor.

O'Connor was glad for the distraction. He'd been having trouble taking his mind off Major Cruz. Not knowing if she were alive or dead was agonizing. He didn't know what to do or how to act. He was living in a nightmare. He desperately wanted to know her condition, but at the same time feared the information.

He swapped out his M1 Carbine for a Thompson submachine gun. If the Japanese were waiting to spring a trap, he wanted the firepower. He teamed up with two swarthy and lethal looking Filipino guerrillas. They told him their names were Stuart and Donald. They waited until dusk, then left the camp and approached the sloping hill.

O'Connor let them lead. They moved carefully once they were outside the camp. It was the first time since landing, he'd seen the natives acting like they were in a combat zone. The change from happy-go-lucky to combat ready brought O'Connor out of his stupor and he felt his senses become razor sharp. He didn't simply stop worrying about Celine but tucked it away until he was out of danger. The change felt better, less complicated.

The Filipinos moved like ghosts through the jungle, not making a sound. O'Connor had instant respect for their skills.

A few minutes later they stopped and crouched in front of a mass of bushes. O'Connor searched their faces. The one named Stuart inched forward and slowly pulled the bushes aside. He exposed a hole leading into the ground. He flashed a smile and disappeared into the hole head first. He wiggled his hips and was soon gone. Donald stepped aside and nodded at O'Connor. He slung his Thompson and adjusted it so it was tight on his back. He got on his belly and inched toward the hole. He had broader shoulders than the Filipino and had to shimmy his way side to side. He finally squeezed through and could feel the hole opening up in front of him. He arrested his slide downward, not liking the sensation of falling into dark space. A light came on and lit up the area. He could see Stuart smiling back at him. He held a small lantern.

O'Connor got to the end of the short entrance and squeezed his way out and onto the dirt floor. It reminded him of taking a shit, and he was the turd.

He made room as Donald slithered through and rolled onto the floor. Stuart didn't wait for Donald to stand but lifted the light above his head and moved down the straight tunnel.

O'Connor pulled his Thompson off his shoulder and held it in front. They moved fast. The ground was well trod and hard as concrete. The dirt above was supported by thick chunks of palms. O'Connor tried not to think of how many tons of earth were above his head. The tunnel was relatively flat, taking them deeper into the rising hill.

It took ten minutes before Stuart stopped and crouched. He waited for O'Connor and Donald to stop. He hung the lantern on a nearby hook. It seemed the tunnel came to an abrupt end but upon closer inspection, O'Connor could see a kind of thatch door. It covered a much smaller tunnel than the one they sat in and he wondered if he'd be able to fit through. He couldn't see how far the little tunnel went. Stuart gave him another grin and entered the tunnel like he was diving through rings in a pool. He slithered and gyrated until his feet were the only thing still in the larger tunnel. He paused, then disappeared quickly. O'Connor slung his weapon and looked back at Donald. He gave him a smile and indicated he should enter next.

O'Connor took a deep breath and took the lantern off the hook. He ducked down and peered into the hole. He was relieved to see it was only six feet long. He could see another opening and this one opened up onto a larger room. He hung the lantern and slithered his way through the tunnel. It took all his strength to move the six feet. When he entered the weapons depot, he was sweating profusely and breathing hard.

He somersaulted out of the hole and lay on the ground trying to catch his breath. Stuart put his hand on his shoulder. A second later another lantern was lit and Stuart held it up to shine on the room. It was square and there were broken crates and discarded pieces of equipment strewn around. There was a large crate blocking the tunnel they'd just come through. Stuart put the lantern on top of the crate and picked something off the ground. He placed it next to the lantern. O'Connor thought it looked like an oversized cork and realized it was used to stopper up the hole they'd just come through. It looked like a part of the wall, a clever disguise.

O'Connor watched Donald slither through. When he was back on his feet, O'Connor stepped into the center of the room. He marveled at the engineering feat. He wondered how many Filipinos had died building this room. Had there been cave-ins? He shuddered thinking of a suffocating death.

He strode to a door on the other side of the room. It was heavy iron and when he tested it, it didn't budge. It was locked and barricaded from the inside. He wondered about that. *Do the Japs suspect our intentions? Why lock it?*

Stuart and Donald stood in the center of the room and tilted their heads. Stuart pointed to the ceiling. Tiny particles of dust danced in the flickering light as vibrations from feet in rooms above, knocked them loose. The sound was hauntingly close, and O'Connor had to fight the urge not to pull his weapon off his shoulder. He pictured the hill they were beneath. He figured it rose over four-hundred feet from the base camp, which meant the Japanese had tunneled deep. They were right above their heads clomping around in their split-toed boots.

The thought of all that earth coming down around them made him feel uneasy. He nodded and stepped away from the door. He whispered and his voice sounded loud. "I've seen enough, let's get the hell outta here."

~

PLATOON SERGEANT CARVER watched the Japanese held hill through binoculars. It was early evening and he could see smoke from small cooking fires. Occasionally he noticed darting shapes he assumed to be Japanese soldiers. He shook his head and spoke to Lt. Swan. "Poor bastards have no idea what's about to happen."

Lt. Swan took the binoculars from him and nodded. "Definitely gonna be a big blast. We'll need to evacuate this position. We'll move back once it's dark." He looked at the scratched face of his watch. "At 1900 hours." He took in a deep breath and let it out slow. "You confident with the explosives?"

Carver nodded. "The demo guys walked me through it. They know what they're doing and assured me it'll work. The hill will be a smoking crater in the morning."

"Almost doesn't seem fair. I thought about bringing up surrender to the captain. You know, give them a chance before we blow it, but they'd never go for it and would probably do a suicide attack, or fake a surrender." He shook his head. "They're gonna have to die like rats."

Platoon Sergeant Carver's mouth downturned. "You're right. No way they'd surrender that way. Against their bullshit code."

Another sergeant from the demolition platoon showed up and snapped off a quick salute. "Charges are ready, sir. We've extended the wires well back. The plunger's back there." He pointed behind them. "We can blow it whenever you're ready."

"Thank you, sergeant. Captain Flannigan wants a 2200-hour detonation. Wants to be sure the Japs are all tucked in for the night."

A few hours later, the Filipino guerrillas and the GIs were well back from the base of the hill. The camp was abandoned, but there were still smoldering cooking fires dotted here and there. If the Japanese were observing them, it didn't look any different from any other night.

Captain Flannigan sat on a rickety chair beside the box-plunger, staring at his watch face. There was one minute until 2200 hours. He looked at Lt. Swan beside him. "This is gonna be something to see."

Swan could hear the excitement in his voice. He was like a kid about to open presents on Christmas morning. "Yes sir. Something to see." Under his breath he murmured, "God have mercy on our souls."

Flannigan held up his hand like he was starting a hot-rod race. The demo sergeant crouched in front and put both hands on the plunger handle. He watched Flannigan with dull eyes. He knew what he was about to unleash on the men on the hill.

Flannigan dropped his hand and said, "Now!" The demo sergeant tensed and pushed the plunger. It generated a satisfying charge which raced instantly through the wires, igniting the blasting caps beneath the bunker, and igniting the stack of high explosives.

Everyone ducked and held their helmets, expecting a huge geyser of flame. Instead, there was a dull thump and a slight shaking of the ground. Carver lifted his head and looked toward the hill. In the pitch dark of night there wasn't much to see. He could sense something happening, however. Suddenly dots of flames erupted all around the hill, like power lines falling during a wind storm. The thumping of distant explosions rolled past in concussive waves, rocking the trees and foliage.

Captain Flannigan stood and with his balled fists on his hips asked, "Is that it? Did it work?"

The demo sergeant nodded. "Oh yeah. It worked perfectly. I'll bet the whole hill is collapsed in on itself."

"I was expecting a bigger bang."

The demo sergeant unhooked the wires from the box. "With that much earth above there was no way the blast was gonna penetrate all the way through, but believe me, the force went straight up and carved out the inside of that hill. There'd be nothing to keep the top from falling into the center." He shook his head. "Those Japs that survived the initial blast were buried under tons of dirt soon after." He pointed into the darkness where small spots of flame flickered. "Ground's gonna be real unstable up there. Your men will need to be careful sifting through, may be some dangerous pockets."

15

W hen it was light enough to see, the devastation was obvious. The hill was a mass of jumbled, smoldering earth. Platoon Sergeant Carver thought he'd feel good about the easy victory, but instead, dreaded the prospect of having to move through the wasteland. How many twisted and destroyed soldiers would he have to uncover?

The Filipinos, on the other hand, were in high spirits. They danced around, slapped each other's backs and laughed. Major Ingencio slapped Carver's back. In broken English, he said, "What's the matter? Would you rather attack the bunkers head-on?" Carver just shook his head. "You feel pity for them? Is that it? You pity the Japanese?"

Carver looked the major in the eye. Major Ingencio put his hand on Carver's shoulder. He pointed to the smoldering hill. "When the Japanese first came here, many feared them. They hid out in the hills, waiting to see what would happen. Those who stayed knew where they were, but never told. At first the Japanese did good things. They patched up leaking roofs and even rebuilt a schoolhouse. They improved the roads. After a month they gathered us in the center of town and told us they'd freed us from our Imperial masters. Told us we were free. They wouldn't interfere with us as long as we followed their easy rules. They promised that once the war was won, we could govern ourselves. They asked us to relay their goodwill to those that fled." He looked at his feet, remembering. "We were fooled. We brought them out of the hills." His voice caught in his throat. "The next day we were again gathered in the center. First, they tore the women and girls away from their husbands, sons and parents. They forced us to watch as they raped them. Then they hung them. All of them. Every man, woman, and child." Bitter tears formed in the corners of his eyes. "Do not pity them. I only hope their deaths were slow and painful."

Carver nodded and unslung his Thompson. He pulled the bolt and checked he was locked and loaded. "When do we move up?"

Major Ingencio smiled and wiped his eye. "Now. We move up now." He walked away and yelled for his men to form up. They snapped into a loose combat formation and moved toward the carnage. The GIs followed.

As they moved past the site of the base camp, the ground became uneven. Sergeant O'Connor pointed at a gaping, burnt hole in the ground. "That's the tunnel entrance." Carver could see half charred wires snaking into the hole. "Looks like the blast shot out the hole. Everything's burnt."

Carver nodded. "Wouldn't wanna be too close to that last night."

They moved up the slope. The ground felt different, like walking on sponge cake. Carver's leather boots sank into the soft, churned soil. As they moved further up the hill, the walking became more difficult. There were holes, where it seemed the ground had simply sunk. It reminded Carver of the sink holes he'd seen back in South Dakota. He'd seen one swallow an entire house.

The main line of bunkers loomed ahead. Some were obviously destroyed, torn apart. They were scorched with fire. He pointed, "The blast must've shot through their tunnels like water through a hose. Cooked 'em all inside."

Sergeant O'Connor nodded. "Never knew what hit 'em." There was movement twenty yards ahead and O'Connor brought his M1 to his shoulder. Out of a smoking hole, a silhouette rose like an apparition. O'Connor kept his rifle trained on him. The form staggered and nearly fell on the torn ground.

Carver had his Thompson leveled and moved forward. As he got closer he could see it was a Japanese soldier. His clothes were burned away and he was charred black. Red and pink spots of flesh showed where his skin had sluffed off. Half the skin of his face remained. The other half showed white where the skull poked through. The soldier staggered forward, but his eyes were clouded white and Carver figured he was probably blind.

Carver cursed under his breath. He dropped to his knees when he heard the shot. It came from O'Connor.

The Japanese soldier fell and bits of charred flesh cracked and oozed red. O'Connor's voice sounded cold. "I wouldn't let a dog suffer like that. Needed to be put down."

Carver moved forward and stood over the smoldering mess. The stink made him wince, but it was a familiar smell. He looked beyond the soldier and saw a gaping hole. He dropped into a crouch and pointed his muzzle into the hole. Black smoke curled out and disappeared in the daylight. The smell of burnt flesh was strong.

He moved to the edge and peered inside, but it was too dark. He felt the hairs on his arms stand up, it was like looking into the very pits of hell. Some of the other GIs spread out around him and crinkled their noses in disgust. Private McGillis suddenly arched forward and lost his breakfast. Corporal Mathews shook his head. "Must be a lot of 'em down there."

Carver stared into the abyss. "It'll be their final resting place."

They searched for two more hours. They found more holes beneath destroyed bunkers, but no more survivors. The stink was suffocating. Carver got the word to return to the jungle. The men wasted no time. They trotted off the hill, glad to get away from the hellish landscape and relieved they didn't have to investigate the gaping tunnels and holes.

SERGEANT O'CONNOR WAS glad to get away from the mountain of death. He blew his nose and looked at the black sludge on his kerchief. *Jap goo.* The smell permeated his body and seemed to ooze from every pore. Even though they'd been off the hill for hours, the smell lingered. He guessed it was tattooed forever in his skin.

He took off his helmet and wiped his brow. He glanced back at the hill. It smoldered and looked like a dying animal breathing its final breath. The thought made him think of Celine. Had she breathed her final breath? The thought made his own breath come up short. A wave of nausea swept through him and he thought he might vomit, but it passed. He closed his eyes, but the image of the staggering Japanese soldier filled his vision. *What a nightmare.*

He was relieved when he heard Private Perkins. "The lieutenant wants to see you."

O'Connor nodded and stood. He swayed for a moment but moved forward. *Why does every part of my body ache?* He found the other NCOs gathered around Lt. Swan. His faded olive drab uniform hung off his rail-thin frame and O'Connor wondered how he managed. He wondered if he ached as much as he did.

"I've heard from Division. They're falling over themselves congratulating one another. They didn't expect this operation to go so smoothly. We only had two casualties, some idiots from the 40th put their jeep head on into an unyielding palm tree. No combat related casualties at all and the complete destruction of the Japanese forces on Bohol." He looked the men over. They looked tired despite the easy victory. "That was a nasty scene up there. I doubt we'll ever wash the smell off. Division wants us to stay here a few days and watch for any more enemy activity." The men glanced back at the smoldering, stinking hill. "They didn't specify where, so I'm moving us out of here and back to the port town. We can rest up and try to wash the stink off." The men nodded, glad to get away from the area. "Don't get too comfortable though. We'll be shipping out soon to join the rest of the 164th assaulting Negros Island. It's only a couple miles that way." He pointed North. "Around the tip of Cebu. Negros will be a tough nut to crack. The reports from the Filipinos aren't good. The Japs are well dug in and once again, own the high ground. There won't be an easy victory. The Filipinos have sustained heavy casualties trying to roust them. We'll be in for another hard fight." He let that sink in. "We won't be alone though. In fact, we'll probably be held in reserve since we weren't slated to finish up here for at least another week."

Carver shook his head. "Reserve? Maybe in a perfect world, sir." He looked to the others. "I wouldn't count on that."

THE GIs ENTERED the port town of Tagliab and were greeted like conquering heroes. The Filipino natives lined the streets much the way they had when the GIs first arrived only days before. This celebration was even more joyous. Their Japanese tormentors were finally gone.

The GIs walked in two parallel lines. Carver was beside O'Connor. He talked over the din of cheering and singing. "We hardly did a thing. Just brought the damned explosives." A young Filipino girl ran up and shoved a bright colored flower in Carver's belt. It was the fifth one. "I'm starting to look like some kind of parade float." He patted the girl on the head and she beamed up at him with a broad smile.

O'Connor responded. "I need to find the radio room."

Carver could see the worry on O'Connor's face. It was making him look older than his twenty years. "Once we get the men settled, we'll go to the port. See about a radio."

O'Connor squinted at Carver. He shook his head. "You look like a damned marionette. Or a piñata." His face turned serious. "Thanks, Sarge. The not knowing is killing me." Carver nodded, knowing O'Connor wasn't big on conversation. Particularly about his personal life.

An hour later the throngs of GIs were happily sprawled in the southernmost part of the town. The residents had taken them in by twos and threes, happy to share their homes with the men who'd helped destroy the hated Japanese.

Carver, O'Connor and Sergeant Levy were given an empty house whose occupants had been hung in the town square three years before. There were still family photos hanging on the walls. Carver felt like he was trespassing.

Carver studied a photo that was bigger than the rest. It showed a family. A proud man with his chest puffed out and his right hand on the shoulder of a beautiful woman, whose smile threatened to break the glass from the picture frame. His left hand rested on a young girl with long hair. The epitome of innocence and goodness. They all wore their best clothes. Carver thought they looked happy. So happy. They couldn't foresee the storm brewing that would ultimately sweep them away like so much dust.

O'Connor stepped beside him. He glanced at the photo but didn't dwell on it. "Let's get to the radio center."

Carver jolted and nodded. "Yeah, sure." He tore his eyes from the picture. He grabbed his Thompson as he left the house.

It was midday and hot, but the clouds forming on the horizon were a sure sign of rain. The closer they got to the port the more GIs and sailors they saw. There was a celebratory attitude. He thought it might be a wild night in Tagliab. He wondered if there were any MPs or Navy Shore Patrol personnel around. If so, they'd have their hands full tonight.

It was easy to find the communications area. He searched the skyline until he saw antennas swaying in the gentle breeze. He pointed and O'Connor nodded and picked up the pace. Carver held him back. "Let me do the talking." O'Connor brushed him off and kept his pace.

The antennas came out the sides of an expansive tent. The heavy burlap sides were rolled up, giving the men inside some relief from the sweltering heat. There was a guard looking bored at the entrance to the tent. He had bright letters painted in white that said, 'MP,' on his helmet. *Guess that answers that.* Carver had heard about the MPs and SPs but hadn't come across any since he'd left the states. *Guess they finally caught up to the war.*

O'Connor stepped up to the MP and tried to walk past. The broad chested cop stuck his meaty hand out and placed it on O'Connor's chest, stopping him. O'Connor's eyes went dark and Carver had to act fast or his sergeant would spend the next few days in the brig. "We have urgent business inside, Corporal."

The MP had a Texas drawl. "You can't just walk on by me, Sergeant." He locked eyes with O'Connor. "I've got my orders."

Carver could see the cauldron about to explode in O'Connor. The big texan was overconfident that his size would protect him, but

Carver knew the man's life hung by a thread. "Look, *Corporal,* we need to use the radio to check on some wounded we left back in Cebu City. Men we fought with since the Canal."

The reference to Guadalcanal had the desired effect. Everyone knew about the battle and everyone knew the men that fought there were hardened veterans. "You were on the Canal?" His hard cop demeanor melted away and suddenly he looked like a child hoping for a bedtime story.

Carver nodded. "Course we were."

The MP whose nametag said 'Blake,' looked back inside the tent. O'Connor took advantage of the hesitation and slipped past the big man. The MP reached for him, but Carver put his hand on the MP's shoulder. "Yeah, it was really something. Japs everywhere, marauding Zeros, Jap cruisers pasting the beach every damned day and night."

The MP turned back to Carver, forgetting about O'Connor. "Is it true about the suicide charges?"

O'Connor ignored the storytelling session and bee-lined it to the bank of radios with the lone operator sitting in front. He put his hand on the dozing man's shoulder. He nearly jumped out of his skin. "Need to get through to Division back in Cebu City."

The corporal looked O'Connor up and down. He saw the Platoon Sergeant chatting up the MP. "Guessing this isn't official business?"

"Look, Corporal…" he looked at his nametag, "Wicker. I need to be patched through. Now."

Corporal Wicker evaluated the hard stare from the sergeant. His eyes widened when he saw the venom that seemed to shoot from them. He noticed the sergeant's uniform was sun-faded and his boots were scuffed and nearly worn through at the toe. He looked like a man who'd killed many times and wouldn't hesitate to do so again.

It wasn't the first time he had GIs come in and want to use the radio, but he was usually able to get some loot from them. He thought demanding loot from the sergeant wouldn't be a sound life choice. "Sure, sure thing Sergeant. I know the guy on the other end, Corporal Charlie Kent. He's a good guy. Shoot the shit all the time."

"Ask Charlie to find a Filipino guerrilla, someone that has information on a Major Cruz. She was wounded in the hills outside the city and I wanna know how she's." He hesitated. "I wanna know how that soldier's doing."

Corporal Wicker gave him a sly grin. "Sure thing, Sarge." He put the headphones on and fired up the radio. It gave off a high-pitched whirring sound as it warmed up. He noticed O'Connor breathing down his neck and pulled one head phone off an ear. "You may as well wait over there. It's gonna be awhile. He'll have to round someone up that knows the major."

Corporal O'Connor nodded and stepped away. He found a wooden chair and slumped down in it. He listened as Corporal Wicker called in. He adjusted a dial and nodded his head. He looked back at O'Connor and spoke into the hand-set. O'Connor couldn't understand what he was saying but he could tell by Wicker's laughing that he was buddies with the GI on the other end. He wanted to tell him to get on with it, but decided he'd let it play out. Wicker seemed like he'd get around to it when he could.

After a minute or two he pulled the headphones off his ears and turned back to O'Connor. "He's checking. Said he knows a guy that's been hanging out around the base a lot. A kid. He'll give him the scoop. Shouldn't be long."

O'Connor stood up. "He say what the kid's name is?" Wicker shook his head. O'Connor wondered if it was Sam, the boy-soldier who'd helped lead them to the Japanese flank. He could still hear Carver regaling the MP with bullshit stories from Guadalcanal. The MP hung on every word, like he was listening to MacArthur himself.

Five minutes passed when Wicker put down his girly magazine he'd been drooling over and picked up the headphones. He motioned for O'Connor who was already moving to his side. He kneeled beside the corporal.

Wicker listened for a moment then said, "Yeah, yeah, I'm here. What you find out?" He listened and nodded his head, but before he got any information, O'Connor ripped the headphones off his head and pulled them over his ears. "Goddammit, sergeant. You nearly pulled my ears off," complained Wicker.

O'Connor ignored him and spoke into the hand-set. "Corporal Kent, this is Sergeant O'Connor. What you find out?"

There was a second of confused silence then Cpl. Kent's tinny voice came through. "What happened to Percy?"

O'Connor looked at Corporal Wicker and winced, *Percy?* "He's fine, just want to hear it first-hand."

The tinny voice came through like it was a thousand miles away. "Suit yourself. My boy Sam knows the major real well. He helped bring her out of the jungle, he says. He's pretty upset about it, could hardly speak when I asked. He's a tough kid, it must really be tearing him up to affect him like that. I wonder how he knew her…"

O'Connor interrupted and yelled into the head-set. "Tell me how she is, goddammit!"

There was a two second pause that seemed to take an eternity. "Boy says he thinks she's dead."

O'Connor could feel his guts heave and he had to swallow the bile threatening to spew from his throat. The bitter taste stung his nasal cavity and his eyes watered. The world went blurry. He gripped the set and his voice cracked. "Put, put the boy on. Put Sam on. Is he there?"

Charlie could hear the anguish in O'Connor's voice. He spoke quieter. "No, he's not here. Had to run off. I was lucky to find him as quick as I did."

O'Connor shook his head. "You, you said he *thinks* she's dead. Is that exactly what he said? He used the word 'think?'"

There was a pause as Charlie thought about the conversation. "Yeah, he said 'think.' I'm sure of it."

O'Connor shook his head. "Why? Why's he unsure?"

He was trying to process. Charlie answered. "I'm sure he meant she's dead. You know these Filipinos fuck up English all the time. He meant she's dead. I, I'm awfully sorry, Sergeant. I … "

O'Connor ripped the headphones off and didn't hear the rest of Corporal Kent's condolences. Corporal Wicker picked the headphones off the ground and checked they weren't damaged. He muttered under his breath about ungrateful sons-of-bitches.

O'Connor stumbled to the door. Carver saw him coming and knew he'd gotten bad news, the worst news possible. He broke off his conversation with the MP and stepped aside. O'Connor shuffled past him like he wasn't there. He left the MP watching his back as he trotted to catch up. He didn't try to speak, he knew there was nothing he could say that would make any difference.

He guided him to the little house they were staying in and made sure he found his bed. He left him staring at the ceiling. O'Connor hadn't spoken a word. Carver broke the silence. "I'll be in the next room. Need anything, just holler." O'Connor didn't reply and Carver didn't wait around. He'd seen a stack of letters on the dining table and he noticed they were all addressed to him. *Lilly.*

16

C arver didn't hear anything from O'Connor's room. He sat at the tiny dining table and went through each letter. They carried her faint essence and he felt drunk each time he re-read them. They were mostly mundane, telling of the daily life of an Army nurse.

He got his blood up when she told him how the doctor who'd signed off on his leg had come on to her soon after he'd left. She teased him that she was considering it, since he was a rich doctor, but decided she liked her rugged sergeant's larger member. He had to re-read that line a few times. He shook his head and almost laughed out loud at her crassness but shoved his fist in his mouth and ran outside. He didn't want O'Connor to hear. His joy wouldn't help him.

He read the letters over and over until he thought he could recite them from memory. It wasn't the content, but the fact that she'd touched the paper he held. He could smell her. He could imagine her wry smile as she wrote about the doctor and his imagined inadequacies. It was like she was sitting right beside him, and it was intoxicating.

Sergeant Levy came into the house and saw him sitting there. Carver put his finger to his mouth and gestured to the shut curtain leading to the bedroom. He whispered, "I moved our stuff to the other room. Sergeant O'Connor's sick, been puking all day. We don't wanna sleep near him tonight. He's asleep. Expect he'll be better in the morning."

Sergeant Levy shook his head. "That's a damned shame to be sick on your day off." He pointed at the well-worn letters. "Looks like you found your letters. They came this morning."

Carver smiled and nodded. "Like a little piece of heaven."

CARVER DIDN'T SEE O'Connor until the next morning. He hadn't been out of the room once, not even to pee or shit. He'd reported him sick and made sure he wasn't slated for any duty. He'd had nearly twenty hours to grieve, but now it was time to get up and get ready for the next shitty battle. Carver had no idea what he'd find inside the room. He was sure it wouldn't be pretty, but he had to get him moving, or he really would get sick.

Sergeant Levy was sitting on a chair cleaning his rifle, with parts spread out on the table. Carver knocked on the wall and pulled the curtain. He pushed past it quickly and entered the darkened room. The smell of sweat, stale breath and musty clothes hit him and he crinkled his nose.

O'Connor was sprawled on the bed, his long body filling the space entirely. Carver didn't think he'd moved from the day before. *Is he in a coma?* He took a few steps and stood on the side of the bed. O'Connor's eyes were shut, but he could tell he wasn't sleeping. "Time to get up and get some food, soldier."

O'Connor opened his eyes. They were red rimmed and bloodshot. He looked at Carver and shook his head. "Not hungry."

Carver grit his teeth. He'd never seen O'Connor so out of it. It made him uncomfortable. He decided the only way to get O'Connor out of his slump was a swift kick in the pants. His voice was gravelly, as he barked. "Out of the rack, Sergeant. There's a war on."

The tone and direction acted like a starter button. The long hours being yelled at during basic were instilled deeply in all soldiers' psyches. O'Connor sat up without realizing it and swung his feet onto the floor. The moment passed, though and he slumped his shoulders and glared at Carver. "Fuck you, Carver. I ain't going nowhere till I'm good and ready."

It was too late for Carver to retreat now. "Get off your ass, or I'll kick it for you. Men are depending on you for their very survival and I'm not gonna let you let 'em down. Now get on your feet!" He yelled the final sentence.

Sergeant Levy stuck his head in the room. "You still sick, O'Connor?"

O'Connor looked confused, but before he could react Carver barked. "He's not sick. Sickness has passed. It's traveled its course and now it's time to get up."

O'Connor glared, and Carver could see raw hatred seething from his eyes. It startled him momentarily, but he ignored it and continued barking. "Get your shit together, and be in the dock area at … " he looked at his watch, "1300 hours. That's an hour from now. Plenty of time to pull that tampon out from between your thighs." He turned and strode out of the room without looking back. He pushed past the stunned Sergeant Levy.

AN HOUR later Platoon Sergeant Carver was standing at the docks discussing the upcoming debarkation from the docks. They'd be leaving in the morning, rejoining the rest of the 164th Regiment as they assaulted the beaches on Negros Island. Negros was a much bigger island than Bohol and had many more Japanese. By all accounts it looked like it would be a bloody battle. Nothing like the Bohol operation. The brass expected casualties, but the island had to be liberated. It was the final major island in the Talisay region.

Men and machines hustled around the docks loading crates that had been offloaded only days before. Howitzers that hadn't fired a shot on Bohol were being hoisted and secured in the holds of rusty ships. The ship they'd offloaded from was anchored off the docks ready to sweep in and take the GIs to the next shit-hole island.

Carver was watching the hive of activity. Nearby, Lt. Swan talked with Captain Flannigan about who knows what. *Flannigan's probably trying to figure out how to take credit for Bohol.* He caught a fast movement out of the corner of his eye. He instinctively crouched and felt someone bowl into him. He sprang up and launched the body backward with his shoulder. He turned with balled fists and saw O'Connor's seething red face. O'Connor spewed hatred "You no good piece of shit."

Carver stepped back and held up his hands. He nervously looked toward the officers but they hadn't seen the attack. "Calm down O'Connor. I had to say those things to light a spark under your ass. You have to pull yourself together, there's no time to mourn. We sail in the morning."

O'Connor was breathing hard. "Easy for you to say. Your woman's alive and well. Sending you scented letters from somewhere nice and safe, while mine's rotting in some jungle grave." Before Carver could do speak, O'Connor lunged again, but this time he faked going right and Carver crouched to tackle him, but O'Connor sprang left and hit Carver with a left cross that left him seeing stars. O'Connor didn't hesitate, he reared back again and repeated the left cross, connecting again.

Carver shook off the second bell ringer and stepped away as O'Connor swung with his right and narrowly missed. He saw O'Connor over-extend, and took the opportunity for a right jab that slammed into the side of O'Connor's chin. O'Connor shook his head and faced Carver who had both hands up like a boxer.

A crowd of soldiers saw the action and quickly surrounded the pair. It didn't take long until money was out and betting started. Carver was a heavy favorite, but the quicker O'Connor was known as a scrapper and tightened the odds a bit.

Both men were bleeding from their lips. O'Connor kept his fists low and danced around the ring. "I'm gonna kill you, Carver."

"Give it your best shot, son." O'Connor feinted left and when Carver went to defend, shot in low to the right. He got under Carver's right hook and put two upper cuts into Carver's hard belly. O'Connor sprang out of the way and jabbed a quick left that landed on Carver's nose, sending a spray of blood.

It wasn't the first time Carver had his nose broken, but the pain searing through his head crazed him. Keeping low and well covered, he moved in like an unstoppable tank. O'Connor darted around left and right landing punches that lost their power against Carver's arms. Carver kept moving forward waiting for his chance, absorbing blows. O'Connor feinted left again, trying to get beneath and into Carver's belly again, but Carver was ready and didn't bite. O'Connor committed to the move and came in low. He was met with Carver's hard left hook. The blow snapped his head back and he stumbled away. He didn't have time to block the right cross that slammed into his jaw and sent him to the ground.

He was on his knees, his breath blowing in gasps, blood bubbles popping like thin bubble gum. The tank that was Carver moved forward for the coup de grace. His eyes were bloodshot and he looked like a crazed demon from hell.

He stepped over O'Connor and bared his bloody teeth. He had his fist cocked and ready to deliver oblivion, but he staid his hand when he saw the pain in O'Connor's eyes. It wasn't the physical pain of being beaten but the pain of loss. It was like a switch had been thrown. The rage melted, and he only saw his friend in agony before him. He kneeled and put his arm around O'Connor like a father giving his son condolences after a heartbreaking football game loss.

O'Connor spit blood and shook off Carver. "Get off me," He sputtered. He stood and swayed, scowling at Carver. "She's gone. She's fucking gone. I might've saved her if you'd let me go with her. You fucking killed her."

The crowd went silent, not having a clue what he was talking about. Money stopped exchanging hands. Carver was about to speak when the crowd split and Captain Flannigan and Lieutenant Swan burst into the center. Flannigan looked at both bleeding men. "What in the Sam hell is going on here?" No one spoke. Flannigan pointed at O'Connor. "You some kind of crazy man? You attacked the Platoon Sergeant. I'm gonna court-martial your ass. You hear me Sergeant?"

Lieutenant Swan touched Flannigan's arm and whispered in his ear. "We need every veteran NCO we can get our hands on. Taking O'Connor out of the line won't do us any good sir. We're already pretty thin."

Flannigan put his fists on his hips and considered. He nodded. "You're out of Able Company, soldier." He let that sink in. He stepped in front of O'Connor and poked his chest with his finger. It took all of O'Connor's thin self-restraint not to remove the finger from his hand. "You're no longer a sergeant … corporal." He turned to Swan. "See he's demoted. You fill it out and I'll sign the paperwork."

Swan nodded. It wasn't what he wanted to happen, but at least O'Connor wasn't headed to Leavenworth.

17

Sam Santos wanted to return to the fighting in the jungle. He'd helped bring the critically wounded Major Cruz out and delivered her to the hospital. She'd lost consciousness halfway back. When they rushed her into the hospital, she still wasn't awake. The last Sam saw, the Army doctor was ordering her onto the operating table. As a Filipino nurse pulled the curtain, he heard the doctor say, "There's no pulse and she's not breathing. We need to operate."

The curtain was pulled and the door shut. Sam knew he'd never see his school teacher turned guerrilla, again. He felt an ache grow in his heart. He made up his mind. He needed to return to the jungle and kill his brother, Berto. He was responsible for so much pain and suffering. He had to pay.

Despite his despair he felt his belly twisting in hunger. He veered toward the chow hall. As he was passing a tent, he saw a GI running from soldier to soldier asking them something then running to the next man. He recognized the soldier, it was Charlie from the radio room. He'd met him before he led the GIs into the Japanese rear. Charlie's eyes lit up when he saw Sam.

"Sam! There you are. You're just the guy I was looking for." He trotted over to him and placed his big hand on Sam's small shoulder.

He could feel the strength of his grip. "I've got someone on the radio, asking about a guer - I mean a Filipino officer. A major. A woman, I think. Major Cruz?"

Sam dropped his head and felt a tear forming in the corner of his eye. He looked up at Charlie and shook his head. "I think she's dead. The doctor said she doesn't have a pulse and wasn't breathing."

Charlie stepped back, surprised by the boy's sudden grief. "Sorry kid. This war stinks."

Charlie trotted off to the communications tent and Sam dragged himself to the chow hall, looking for a free meal before he retraced his steps into the jungle. The Americans were always willing to feed him with their great tasting food that never seemed to run out. He hoped there'd be mashed potatoes and butter again. He'd had a large helping last time and he still remembered it as one of the greatest experiences of his young life.

The chow hall was nearly empty. It was between lunch and dinner it seemed, but an American saw him peeking into the kitchen and recognized him. "Hey, how you doing?" He didn't wait for a response. "You want something to eat?" Sam nodded. "Sure, sit down. There's leftovers from lunch."

Sam marveled at the American's generosity. He thought their country must be very rich indeed to have so much food all the time. The cook brought a heaping plate and placed it in front of him. He stared at the mass with his mouth open. It was more food than he'd seen on one plate in his whole life. "Thank - Thank you, sir."

"Don't mention it." He gestured to another GI coming through the door. "Looks like you've got company."

Sam looked up and saw an officer taking off his hat. He hailed the cook. "You got anything leftover, Corporal? I missed lunch."

"Of course, sir. No problem." He pointed at Sam's diminishing pile. "You want as much as I gave him?"

The officer shook his head and patted his belly. "Nah, I'm not a growing boy anymore. Half that'll do."

"Sure thing Major." The cook spun and reentered the kitchen. Sam could hear dishes clanging.

The major stood beside the table Sam sat at. "Mind if I join you?"

Sam sprang to his feet and tried to swallow a mouthful of food. He couldn't speak but nodded his head and saluted. The major returned the salute with a smile and pulled a chair out and sat. He blew out a sigh and wiped his brow. "Your country's hot compared to mine. Not used to it."

Sam finally swallowed what he was chewing. He sat down and asked. "Are you new here, sir?"

He stabbed a piece of meatloaf and brought it to his mouth, inspecting it. "Yeah, kinda. I was here a while ago but got wounded on Guadalcanal." Sam looked at him, not understanding the word. "It's an island we took from the Japs." He decided the meatloaf was edible and shoved it into his mouth. After he swallowed he continued. "How old are you?"

"Fourteen, sir. I fight with the Filipino Army."

"You're a soldier?" Sam nodded and picked up his M1 carbine that was leaning on the table.

The major nodded. "You fought the Japs?"

Sam returned the weapon carefully. "Yes, sir. I helped take back Cebu City. I killed many Japs." To prove it he held up his arm and showed him two wristwatches strapped to his thin upper arms.

"Well, I'll be damned. Trophy hunter, huh?" Sam nodded proudly. "By the way, you can call me Toby, or Major Toby if you like." Sam repeated the name, testing how it felt in his mouth. Major Toby pointed at Sam's pile of food. "You better finish that or the corporal will be angry."

Sam looked at him like he was crazy. "Of course I'll finish it - it's food." The major laughed and Sam scooped great heaps into his mouth until it was gone.

"Where's your unit, Sam?"

Sam replied. "I'm under Major Cruz … " he stopped and shook his head. "I mean I was. Now that she's dead, I guess I don't know who I'm under. Maybe just Felipe."

Major Toby stalled the fork halfway to his mouth. "Major Cruz? I don't recognize that name."

"She was my English teacher. She became part of the resistance soon after the Japanese invaded. She was a great fighter."

Sudden recognition filled the major's face. "Ah, I think I know who you're talking about." He shook his head. "She's not dead." He grabbed his collar, fingering a small gold pin. "See this?" Sam leaned forward and studied the small golden pin. It was two snakes wrapping around a center pin and facing themselves at the top. There was a set of large wings coming off the top of the pin. "That means I'm a doctor. I was just in the operating room making sure Major Quinn didn't need any assistance. They got her breathing again and she's stabilizing. He dug the bullet out." He smiled at the wondrous look on Sam's face. "She's not out of the woods yet, but her chances are good."

THE NEWS that Major Cruz was still alive filled Sam with joy. He went back to the hospital but she was still in surgery. He wasn't able to see her. He wondered what he should do. He looked for the men who'd helped him bring her out of the jungle but couldn't find them. He wondered if they'd already gone back to the fighting. Now that he had a full belly, he decided it was time to get back himself.

He checked his M1 was loaded and ready. It had become like another part of his body the last few days. He found himself talking to it sometimes when he felt scared at night in the jungle. He patted its well-worn stock and slung it over his shoulder. "Time to get back to work, old friend."

He retraced his steps. The arduous task of hauling the major out on the stretcher had been a long, slow process. There were scars on the land where they'd had to slide the stretcher along the ground. It had taken two full days to get her out. He thought she'd surely die before they got her down but couldn't go any faster for fear of making her injuries worse. She lost a lot of blood and he could see splashes of it along the trail. Without the burden of the stretcher he moved much faster now.

Despite his speed, he didn't make it back to his comrades before the sun set and the jungle went black. He didn't relish spending the night alone. He ate a half loaf of bread the cook had given him and drank half his water. He found a soft spot of grass and matted it down. He slept fitfully, waking up every fifteen minutes to unknown jungle sounds. He gripped his carbine tightly and thought about all the night animals that could be stalking him.

When it was light enough to see, he continued his trek. He came across the rest of his comrades at mid-day. They'd moved deeper into the jungle from the spot the major had been shot.

He'd been challenged by the rear guard, who quickly recognized him and called out his name happily, like an old friend. It felt good to be back amongst his comrades.

He found Felipe at the center of the camp. When he saw him, he couldn't keep the smile from his face. Felipe smiled back. "Sam, you're back. How's the major?" Deep concern creased his forehead.

"She's alive. I thought she'd died, but I talked to a doctor who said she'd probably live. I tried to see her before I left but she was still in surgery." He shook his head and looked at the ground. "I thought she'd die on the trail. It was not easy getting her out of the jungle."

Felipe put his broad hand on his shoulder. "You did well to get her out, and you saved many others with your quick action at the ambush."

"Have there been anymore ambushes?"

Felipe shook his head. "No. That was a delaying force." He pointed into the jungle. "They're somewhere up ahead. We plan on pushing forward first thing in the morning. The news that Major Cruz is alive will energize the men. We were all worried."

SAM SLEPT BETTER HAVING the safety of his comrades around him. He woke early and stoked the small cooking fire. They ate K-rats the GIs had given them. They weren't as good as the mashed potatoes in the mess hall, but the K-rats tasted good. He didn't understand why the GIs complained about them so bitterly. To him, opening a bag filled with delicious food you barely had to prepare, was magical.

Without orders, the camp was struck and the men formed up. The Japanese had left an obvious path up the mountain. Sam wondered if his brother, Berto was leading them, and if so where he was leading them. As far as he knew, this was new territory. They'd never explored this raw jungle with their father. If he was leading them, he thought he must be leading them blind.

They moved carefully. The Japanese knew they were being followed and could easily spring another ambush. Felipe sent three point men, two to the flanks and one up front. They moved slowly, but steadily. Mid-morning the skies opened up and a deluge of rain turned the ground to liquid mud.

They were used to the torrential downpours but most lived in Cebu City and could find cover beneath their roofs. Being out in the elements was new to some of them. They were forced to stop. They hunkered beneath what little cover the overhanging trees could provide. Sam shivered and tried to keep his carbine dry by stuffing it under his shirt, but it was a useless gesture.

The rain finally stopped, but the ground was a soupy mess. They moved out and their progress was slow. Sam was concentrating on the next muddy step when he noticed the man in front stop and kneel. Sam pulled his carbine off his shoulder and kneeled. He searched the surrounding jungle, but only saw dripping wet leaves. The rain made the plants seem to glow vibrant green.

The point man made his way back, slipping and sliding down the slope. He went to Felipe and reported. Felipe relayed the message. Keeping his voice low, "There's a plateau ahead. Could be Japs." He looked at the point man. "Move up and have a look." The swarthy Filipino nodded and moved back the way he'd come. Felipe used a hand signal, and the men spread out.

Sam stayed crouched and moved off to the right. He found a thick tree and hunkered behind it, keeping his eyes peeled for any movement. The only sounds were the dripping of rainwater off leaves and the constant hum of jungle insects. He strained to hear the point-man moving forward but couldn't.

Twenty minutes passed before the point-man finally returned. He conferred for a long time with Felipe, gesturing and pointing uphill. Sam guessed he'd found the Japanese. He took a deep breath as he realized they'd probably be in combat soon. He gripped the carbine and checked and rechecked the safety. He could feel his heartbeat in his throat and he felt a wave of nausea overcome him suddenly. He swallowed and closed his eyes. *Get a hold of yourself.*

When he opened his eyes, he saw Felipe gesturing. A hand signal to move up slowly. More hand signals followed, but Sam had no idea what they meant. Panic rose in his throat. *What does he want me to do?* The nearest man was nine meters to his right. He was watching Felipe intently. He nodded, understanding the hand signals. *I'll just follow him,* Sam thought.

The soldier stood and moved forward cautiously. Sam moved from the cover of his tree and matched the soldier's footsteps. He felt better, finally moving. His body was tense and aching. Movement helped.

Sam found himself moving closer to the other soldier, trying to keep him in sight. He was only five meters from him when the soldier looked back and waved him off.

Sam nodded and moved off to the right. He let the soldier put distance between them. He'd keep an eye on him from the back. The ground was slick and he had to think about each step. The mud made squelching sounds whenever he lifted his foot. The muck seemed to be trying to keep him in place. He felt like he was walking in chewing gum.

The soldier stopped after thirty meters. He carefully went into a crouch, then onto his belly. Sam thought they must be close. He looked up the hill and nearly yelled out when he saw the dim silhouette of a Japanese soldier's helmet. It was camouflaged with shrubs and grasses. The only reason he saw it at all was the movement of his head. He was only fifteen meters away, sitting behind the ugly muzzle of a machine gun. Sam realized it looked like the same kind he'd seen in Cebu City on that first night.

Sam moved at a snail's pace into a prone position. He could feel himself sinking into the wet, muddy ground. He was thankful to be getting lower. *Mother earth will protect me.*

He could see the Filipino to his front putting his rifle to his shoulder. He was aiming away from the machine gunner. Sam noted the approximate location and brought his own weapon to his shoulder. He centered the sights on the helmet of the Japanese soldier and waited for some kind of signal.

His heart was beating so fast, he thought it would explode from his chest. *Calm down, calm down.* He put his finger on the trigger, just enough to feel the cool metal. He didn't want to shoot first and give away their position. He had no idea what the plan was but knew Felipe wouldn't want him to shoot until someone else did.

A full two minutes passed. He used the time to concentrate on his breathing. The helmet moved slightly as the Japanese soldier shifted. He saw a brown hand push the lip of the helmet back an inch. Now he could see the soldier's eyes. It seemed he was staring right at him. *Does he see me?* Sam imagined the machine gun barrel suddenly swinging and aiming straight at his forehead. He'd have to shoot then. He concentrated on the barrel. If it moved his way he'd depress the trigger no matter the consequences.

Sam flinched when he heard yelling from the right and left flanks, followed quickly with explosions and gunshots. His eyes fell off his sights for an instant and when he found them again the helmet he'd been aiming at was gone. His breath caught in his throat as he saw the machine gun barrel swinging to engage the flanks. He couldn't see the Japanese soldier anymore, but he had a good idea where his head would be.

He steadied his aim and pulled the trigger in quick succession. The carbine kicked lightly against his shoulder, it felt good. The barrel of the machine gun stopped and cocked upward. Sam stopped firing and looked over the top of the rifle, searching for his target, but he couldn't see if he'd hit anything.

He got to his knees for a better view. He still couldn't see the soldier but he could see others. A Japanese was behind the machine gun nest running with his head down. He weaved as he ran. Sam lined him up as best he could and fired, but the soldier didn't go down. The soldier saw him and dove headfirst into the machine gun nest. Sam sent more bullets his direction, but he doubted he hit anything.

The barrel of the machine gun suddenly came alive and swung toward him. His nightmare was coming true. He pulled the rifle tight to his shoulder, he'd only get one chance. He pulled the trigger. After the first shot, the pin thunked onto an empty chamber. Sam frantically pulled the trigger, but nothing happened. *Out of ammo!* The muzzle lined up on him and he could see the slanted eyes staring over the barrel, burning holes right through his soul.

Sam dropped and rolled to his left just as the machine gun opened up. He pushed himself backwards as the crack of bullets whizzed by and slammed into the spot he'd just left. The muddy ground erupted and sprayed him with chunky bits of wet slime. He covered his head and shoved his face into the mud, tasting it on his tongue. He was screaming.

The machine gun suddenly stopped, but Sam kept screaming. He heard yelling from the right and the Filipino soldier he'd followed got to his knees and hurled a grenade toward the machine gun nest. He ducked back down and waited for the explosion. There was firing all around him, but he heard the dull thump of the nearby grenade. He got control of himself and looked toward the Filipino who was getting to his feet with his Thompson at his shoulder. He fired toward the gun, and Sam could see the dim flames erupting from the muzzle. He watched the spent shell casings flying out in an uninterrupted line.

Sam shook his head and felt for his weapon, but it wasn't there. He panicked for an instant looking all around. He saw it half covered in mud a few feet to his right. In his haste, he'd dropped his prize possession. Embarrassment and shame filled him. He gritted his teeth and lunged for the carbine. He rolled to the right and went up onto one knee. He aimed and pulled the trigger, but nothing happened. He cursed his stupidity and went onto his back and dug into his pocket for another magazine. He quickly ejected the old and inserted the new. Mud dripped off the stock, but he put it to his shoulder and aimed up the hill. He couldn't see any targets but everyone around him was firing, so he joined in.

The Filipino with the Thompson dropped to his knees and pulled out his spent magazine. He caught Sam's attention and gave him a wide smile. Sam smiled back, hoping his blunder hadn't been noticed.

Suddenly the soldier's head snapped back and a red mist of blood sprayed the broad leaves behind him. The smile never faded as he dropped onto the forest floor, the back of his head missing. Sam shook his head trying to process what he'd just seen. Everything went into slow motion. The sounds quieted and all Sam could hear was the rushing of blood in his head. A sudden rage filled him and he gritted his teeth and screamed. The high-pitched sound was like a hyena laugh and all who heard it remembered it later.

Sam was on his feet and charging. The machine gun nest was right in front of him. The lone occupant was just inserting a new stick of bullets when Sam crested the lip of the hole. His carbine was at his hip. He unleashed ten shots at point blank range into the Japanese gunner and he fell back, gushing gore from multiple holes.

Sam leaped into the machine gun nest and slammed into the far wall. He noticed another dead soldier and realized he must've killed him when he first fired. The Japanese had a neat hole in the center of his forehead. There was a thin line of blood snaking down his face and dripping off his chin.

Sam pushed the dead soldier aside and poked his head up and saw multiple targets. His comrades were coming from the flanks and the Japanese were scrambling to adjust their fire. He heard yelling to his left and saw Filipinos advancing. He saw Felipe waving his arm, urging the men forward.

Sam rested his carbine on the lip of the back wall and found a target. A soldier was aiming down his long rifle and firing then ducking down to chamber another round. Sam kept his sights centered on the spot. The head popped back up and Sam squeezed the trigger three times. The helmet flew off and he saw the Japanese drop out of sight. He moved the rifle to the left and centered on another soldier. He fired and saw his bullets spray dirt and debris. The soldier ducked down. He didn't wait for him to appear again. Another soldier was sprinting across an open area. He had his rifle slung across his back and he was carrying boxes in each hand. They looked heavy. He was running left to right, so Sam swung his rifle to follow. He pulled the trigger and walked the bullets forward until he saw the soldier stumble and fall. Sam poured more fire into the spot, then ducked down.

He was breathing hard. He was about to pop up and find another target but decided he should check his magazine. He pulled it and was glad he did. He only had three shots left. He swapped out magazines and stood up again.

He saw a Filipino from the right side running into the open. His torso erupted with multiple wounds and he fell to the side. Sam felt a bullet snap past his head. He instinctively dropped and came up in a different spot. Another Japanese was running. He was crouched and weaving back and forth. Sam guessed which way he'd weave and fired. The soldier staggered and fell to his knees, like he was taking a break from a difficult sporting event. Sam centered his chest in his sights and fired twice. The soldier spun backwards, spouting a thin stream of dark blood.

Sam caught quick movement coming from the jungle line. His comrades were throwing grenades. He watched them arcing into the center of the plateau. He fired at a helmet sticking up. Then the grenades went off, sending dirt and debris flying into the air. He saw Filipinos emerge from both flanks. The soldiers to his left jumped up and ran forward too. Sam licked his lips and scrambled his way out of the safety of his hole. He immediately felt exposed and saw rifles swinging his direction.

He spotted a hole sixteen meters away and went for it. He dove headfirst and slid into the bottom of the muddy hole, as bullets snapped over his head. He heard a terrible yell right next to him and looked up to see a Japanese soldier stepping toward him with his bayonet lunging at his guts.

Sam reacted instantly. He rolled away and the bayonet sliced into the ground, narrowly missing him. Sam rolled into a crouch and brought his M1 up, but the Japanese wasn't alone. He felt a soldier slam into his back and pin his arms at his side. The Japanese to his front grinned cruelly and pulled his bayonet out of the ground. Sam struggled, but the soldier holding him was strong. He held him in a vise grip. The Japanese planted his feet and yelled. He reared back and Sam knew he was about to die. In desperation, Sam jumped and started frantically kicking. The Japanese lunged but Sam managed to kick the blade away. He felt the razor-sharp blade slice into his calf and he screamed.

The soldier yelled and lunged again, but before he could finish the job his chest erupted with spurting holes. He dropped his rifle and looked at his chest in confusion. Sam felt the arms holding him lose their power and drop away. He spun out of their grip and fell to the ground. The foxhole filled with more men. Felipe was beside him. "You okay?"

Sam felt the burning pain in his calf but tried to ignore it. He'd been saved. He looked up at Felipe's concerned eyes and Sam nearly burst into tears. But instead he simply gritted his teeth and nodded. "I'm okay."

Felipe pointed at his gushing calf. "Stay here, we'll finish these vermin."

The other Filipinos, his comrades, were at the lip pouring fire into the Japanese. Sam felt a surge of pride overcome him. He had to continue fighting beside his brothers. "I'm fine." He pulled his shirt off and began wrapping the wound with it. He winced but took the pain without crying out. Felipe yelled to someone nearby and soon Juan was crouched beside him, putting a proper wrap on the wound. Juan looked him in the eye, slapped his shoulder and handed him his rifle.

Sam nodded back and stood up. The pain flooded through his body and he winced involuntarily. He limped to the lip of the hole and threw himself beside his comrades. He fired five rounds toward a hole he'd seen a Japanese duck into.

Felipe yelled, "Move up!"

The soldiers surged from the hole and ran forward. Sam was slower, his wound throbbed, but he was close behind. The man to his right stumbled and fell. At first Sam thought he'd tripped and he reached to help him up, but when he touched his arm, he noticed a hole in his neck pumping arterial blood with each heartbeat. The man looked panicked as he clutched at his neck, then the light left his eyes and he slumped into the mud.

Sam felt the rage return. There was no more pain in his calf. He ran forward and was soon beside his advancing comrades. The main line of defenders was thirty meters ahead. He could see many helmeted heads behind rifle sights. He leveled his own and fired as he ran, weaving back and forth. A grunt off to his left caught his attention and he saw another comrade fall. Sam yelled and increased his speed. He was now the lead man. He thought he'd be shot any second. He fired until the firing pin slammed into an empty chamber. He was

only feet away from the lip of, what he now saw was a hastily dug
trench-line.

There was a rifle barrel directly in front of him. The terrified eyes of
an emaciated Japanese soldier stared up at him. The barrel raised, and
Sam kicked it to the side and jumped into the trench. The Japanese
soldiers immediately turned to attack him. Sam was crouched. He
gripped his carbine by the barrel, it was hot to the touch. He ignored
the burning and swung it like a baseball bat. He connected with the
nearest soldier's ribs and he grunted but continued moving toward
him. Sam sprang away at the same instant the loud crash of the Arisaka's bullet left the barrel at 2400ft/s. It slammed into the dirt wall. The
soldier beside the first was lining up on Sam's chest, but before he
could squeeze the trigger he fell to the bottom of the trench as a crazed
Filipino fighter landed on his back and clubbed him with the butt of
his rifle.

The first soldier was suddenly surrounded. He continued his thrust
toward Sam, determined to take him to the grave with him. Sam
brought his M1 up and deflected the bayoneted Arisaka upward. The
soldier's momentum, kept him coming. Sam stepped to the side and
the soldier slammed into the back wall. He quickly spun, sweeping his
deadly blade in an arc. Sam swung his M1 and caught the soldier's jaw
with a sickening 'smack.' The soldier's eyes lost focus and he staggered. Sam didn't hesitate. He swung again and landed another blow
against the dazed soldier's head. The side of his face caved in and
blood spurted from his ears and eyes. Sam watched the soldier die and
fall to the ground. He felt like he was watching it happen from out of
his body. Like he wasn't there at all but looking in through a window.

The world came rushing back and the sounds of men fighting and
dying was all around. Sam's arms suddenly felt heavy. His breathing
was coming in painful gasps. He fell to the ground not able to keep his
feet. He watched another Filipino, he thought it was Juan, fire his
carbine into a charging Japanese soldier. *Need to reload,* he told himself.
He fumbled to extract his empty magazine. His hands shook as he felt
for another. He finally pulled it from his pocket and was able to line it
up and insert it on the third try. *What is wrong with me?*

He pushed himself up, but he felt dizzy and the world started to collapse around him. Blackness was closing in. He felt he was looking at the world through a black straw. Blackness closed and he fell to the bottom of the bloody trench. He was stepped on many times, but he was beyond noticing.

~

THE NEXT THING SAM KNEW, he was looking up at an impossibly blue sky through the swaying leaves of the jungle canopy. The lush green leaves and vines against the stark blue background was beautiful and the sight made him think he was in heaven. The pain that suddenly lanced through his body when the men carrying him bumped a tree made him think he was in hell.

He shut his eyes tight and tried to understand the pain. The battle in the jungle came back in a flood of bloody memories and he rose up on his elbows and looked around frantically. He was staring at the rippling, sinewy muscles of a dark-skinned Filipino's back. He realized he was being carried on a stretcher. There was a concerned voice behind him. "Don't try to move. Just rest, Sam."

Sam arced his head back and saw the smiling face of Juan looking down at him. "What's happened? Are we retreating? Did we lose?"

Juan shook his head. He spoke to the Filipino at the front. "Let's take a break, Antonio." Antonio nodded and together they lowered the stretcher to the ground. Sam realized it wasn't a normal stretcher but one made from bamboo sticks and American GI ponchos. He tried to sit up further but the pain in his calf shot through him and took his breath away. He broke out in a cold sweat and immediately felt nauseous.

Juan spoke soothingly. "Don't try to move. Just remain still." Sam nodded and laid his head back. Juan called out. "Felipe. Sam's awake."

Sam wanted to see his old friend. He pushed himself up again and tried to ignore the pain. He gritted his teeth. "Help me sit up please." Juan shook his head but reached under Sam's shoulders and pulled him to an upright position. Sam bit his lip to stifle the cry threatening to burst from his throat. Juan propped a back-pack against his lower back and Sam leaned on it. "Thank you."

He heard someone approaching from behind and soon Felipe was crouched beside the stretcher looking at him with concern. "You gave us quite a scare. Thought you might have died back there."

Sam shrugged and looked at his calf. It was wrapped in a new bandage, borrowed from the GIs. "It's a bad cut, but I don't think it will kill me."

Juan interjected. "Any kind of wound can kill you out here. The real enemy's infection. That's why we need to get you back to town."

Sam nodded. "I'll be alright. It burns like fire, but ..." He shrugged again. "Nothing compared to some others."

Felipe gripped his shoulder. "There's something I need to tell you."

Sam saw the worried look and immediately wondered which one of his friends had died. "I can take it. What's happened?"

Felipe kept gripping his shoulder and looked at Juan then back at Sam. "It's about your brother. It's about Berto."

Sam's face went dark. "What? What about him?"

Felipe continued. "He was with the Jap force we fought ... "

Sam looked down, not sure how he should feel. "How did he die?"

Felipe shook his head. "He's not dead. He's alive. We captured him along with a few other Makapilis."

Sam's confusion turned to anger. "Did he fight? Did he kill any of us?"

Felipe shook his head. "No. He was near the rear, hunkered down in a hole. There were no weapons found nearby. He surrendered without a fight."

Sam didn't know how to feel. When he thought his brother was dead he had a feeling of loss sweep over him. Now that he knew he was alive, he felt his hatred return. He looked Felipe in the eye. "I'd like to see him."

Felipe nodded and pulled out his sidearm. He handed the 1911 .45 caliber pistol handle first to Sam. "Know how to use that?" Sam nodded and pulled the action making sure it was loaded. Felipe held his gaze for a few seconds before speaking. "He's your brother, but he betrayed your family and his own people. He's responsible for killing many of us by helping the Japanese. They would never have found their way through these jungles without his guidance. He will stand trial and no doubt, hang for his crimes." He indicated the pistol. "I'll give you the option of killing him, since he's done you the most harm."

Sam swallowed against a suddenly dry mouth. He felt the heft of the weapon. He returned Felipe's stare and nodded. "Bring him to me."

18

Corporal O'Connor didn't have time to think much about his scuffle with Platoon Sergeant Carver. Soon after joining Hotel Company as a corporal, the unit was sent from Bohol through the Tanon straight which separated Cebu Island from Negros Island.

The GIs of Hotel Company didn't know quite what to make of the new corporal in their midst.

Corporal Bucholz approached O'Connor as he sat on the floor of the troop ship staring at the metal wall. He sat beside him. "Looks like you been in the ring and got the bad end." O'Connor didn't acknowledge him. Bucholz thrust out his hand. "I'm John Bucholz. Lead in third squad. You're in my squad." O'Connor looked at the offered hand but didn't take it. Bucholz withdrew it and shook his head. "Hard case, huh?" Without looking at him, Bucholz lowered his voice. "I don't give a shit what happened back on Bohol. You got some beef with a Platoon Sergeant I hear, but it's none of my business. What *is* my business is this squad. We've been through a lot and were about to land on another hostile beach, with some sad sack hard case corporal. I hear they busted you from sergeant. I don't give a shit about any of that. Lieutenant Hopkins says I gotta have you in my squad, that's my tough shit. I don't care as long as you do as you're told when I tell you to do it. Despite your rank and your seniority, you're just another grunt in this unit." He let that sink in. "You got that, hard-case?"

O'Connor looked the corporal in the eye and nodded. "Yep."

Bucholz stood and looked down at O'Connor. "Good. We're two hours out. Captain Ludwig wants us to offload at night. Surprise any Japs that might be lingering. Don't make me come looking for you."

"You won't have any trouble from me, Corporal."

Two hours later O'Connor was on deck watching the sun sink into the shimmering sea. They were off the coast a mile and would be ferried to the beach when it got dark. Doing anything at night was tricky and it would give O'Connor a good idea how this Company worked. Even the most highly trained units had trouble pulling off night operations, particularly beach landings.

Three hours after the sun went down, the transport moved closer to the beach. The GIs were quiet, but O'Connor could sense their tension growing. He studied his own emotions. There was no fear, only a blackness that seemed to blanket him since learning of Celine's death. He'd always had apprehension, not necessarily fear, before operations, but now he felt nothing. He'd do what was required of him, nothing more or less. If he took a bullet, at least the indomitable pain of loss would end.

It was a moonlit night which helped the LCPV drivers find the beach. It seemed to glow like a beacon. O'Connor knew Navy swimmers had swum in, probably the night before, and checked the beach for hidden obstacles. Since the disaster at Tarawa, when the Marines got hung up on an unknown reef and were mowed down, the Navy always checked.

The landing went off without a hitch. The LCPVs ground onto the beach, dumped the GIs, then backed back out to sea without firing a shot. It was the first time in a long time O'Connor didn't have to be in control of anything or anyone but himself. He was still an NCO, but he had no teeth. The GIs treated him like he was just another GI. He blended in with his new squad. He liked the low stress of being a follower rather than a leader again.

The night maneuver took all his concentration. It was the first time in two weeks he hadn't thought about Major Cruz. He tucked her away in a dark corner of his mind. He realized he didn't much care what happened to himself, but he would do his best to keep the other GIs alive, despite their obvious dislike.

"Move to the tree-line." It was Corporal Bucholz waving them forward. O'Connor waited for the others to move and followed along. He watched the tree-line for anything out of the ordinary. If the Japs were there, they'd have an easy time spotting them silhouetted against the white sand. The moon blazed above them like a flashlight. He briefly thought what a beautiful night for a walk, if not for the war.

He was relieved to see the GIs knew what they were doing. They were veterans. They didn't bunch up and moved as quietly as they could. If he couldn't be with Able Company, at least he'd been put into an experienced group of soldiers.

They stopped when they got to the tree-line. O'Connor looked back the way they'd come. There was no sign of stragglers. They were stacked up along the edge of the jungle. He was impressed with their speed. He could just make out the dull, steady hum of the LCPVs returning to the troop ship. He thought he could make out their white wakes in the distance.

An order was given and the GIs stood and moved into the jungle. It was thick, but not impassible. They pushed in for ten minutes and penetrated one hundred yards. They didn't see any signs of the enemy.

Bucholz gathered them close. "We're spending the rest of the night here." He searched the group and pointed at O'Connor. "Hard-case, I want you twenty-five yards further inland. Set up an OP with Hendrickson." He held up two fingers. "Two-hour rotations."

O'Connor nodded and when he moved past, Bucholz glared at him, "Don't fuck this up." He ignored him and kept moving. He could hear Private Hendrickson following a couple yards behind.

He moved carefully, barely making a sound. When he thought he was the correct distance, he scanned the area for a good place to set up. The jungle was much darker than the beach, but slivers of moonlight penetrated here and there and he noticed a slight rise to his right. He waited until Private Hendrickson noticed him and signaled. Hendrickson nodded and covered him. O'Connor crouched on the hillock. He made sure it wasn't an anthill, or some other beasts lair and pulled out his entrenching tool. He scraped the top layer of rotting jungle detritus, then scraped the dirt away until he'd made a slight depression. It wasn't much and wouldn't protect them from incoming fire, but he didn't want to dig and make a bunch of noise.

Private Hendrickson slid in beside him and sat with his legs crossed. He propped his M1 Garand on his knee and scanned the area. O'Connor was on his belly but got to a sitting position beside Hendrickson. He whispered into his ear. "I'll watch the right, you take the left."

Hendrickson guffawed. "I'm not taking orders from you, Corporal."

O'Connor gritted his teeth and swallowed his anger. It went down like a jagged pill. "Fine, I'll cover right, you cover whatever the fuck you want." Hendrickson didn't respond. O'Connor couldn't help himself. "If you fall asleep out here, I'll cut your fucking throat myself." Hendrickson seethed but he knew he'd make too much noise if he responded the way he wanted to. O'Connor grinned. *This is gonna be a fun mission.*

IN THE MORNING O'Connor lifted his head from the mounded sand. He felt like shit. His body ached. *Feel like an old man.* There was no enemy activity during the night. There was the occasional distant rumble of artillery coming from the other side of the island, but it also could have been thunder. He looked toward the tall, lush mountains that formed the spine of the mountain. In the semi-darkness it looked dark green, almost black. He was glad they didn't have to haul their asses up there.

He and Hendrickson had been relieved from their OP sometime in the deep night. O'Connor did his best to find a comfortable piece of real estate to sleep on but settled for the mound of sand. At least it was dry.

He opened a can of K-Rats and had breakfast. He stood and stretched, feeling his muscles snap, pop and creak. The GIs around him were up. Some darted into the surrounding jungle to take shits. Dysentery, also known as raging diarrhea was always a concern out here, but he hadn't seen many cases during this operation. On Guadalcanal and again on Bougainville, Dysentery had swept through their ranks, putting more soldiers out of the fight than the Japanese did.

When it was full daylight the company moved back to the edge of the beach and got into a long, snaking single-file line. O'Connor slung his rifle and looked out to the shimmering strait. He could see the imposing outline of Cebu. The image made him think of Celine. *Wonder if they've buried her yet?* He decided if he lived through this war, he'd find her gravesite. He had some things he still wanted to tell her.

They made good progress through the morning. They crossed a few small creeks that flowed with clear water. They stopped at one and dipped their heads, cleaning off layers of dirt and sweat. O'Connor relished the coolness as it dripped down his back. He rubbed the grit from his neck and filled his steel helmet with water and dumped it over his head. *Gawd, that feels good.*

By midday they'd traveled about four miles. They could've gone faster, but they were given a week and a half to make the trek along the beach, so there was no reason to hurry. It seemed like a lot of time for an easy stroll. O'Connor wondered if the brass knew something he didn't.

They stopped when they came upon a more substantial river. Its briny water flowed deep and fast into the strait. O'Connor was immediately on edge. It looked like a perfect place for the japs to put up a defense and also natural habitat for crocodiles.

The company spread out along the banks, some moving into the jungle. Lieutenant Hopkins brought the NCOs together. O'Connor was effectively a private in everyone's eyes, but he joined them anyway. He ignored the hostile glances.

Lieutenant Hopkins looked like he probably played football before the war. He was average height, but his shoulders were wide and his legs stretched the seams of his pants. O'Connor guessed he was probably a fullback. He tilted his helmet back. "Captain Ludwig wants us to stop here for the day, maybe longer. We're gonna dig in and send patrols out." He pointed at the river. "There's word there's a village upstream with a bridge crossing. If nothing else the natives might know where the Japs are. Our platoon's taking the low position here on the beach. I want holes dug in an L shape, some facing the bay and the majority toward the river. We'll have to move into the jungle and link up with 2nd platoon. We don't want any gaps." He looked from man to man. "Any questions?"

Corporal Bucholz raised his hand. "We expecting trouble, sir?"

Hopkins shrugged his shoulders. "Nothing concrete. The captain's being careful and thorough." When there were no more questions, Hopkins nodded and said, "Get it done."

DIGGING in didn't take more than a few hours. The ground was soft and easy to dig decent foxholes. O'Connor made his big enough for two, but no one joined him. He was okay with that. He didn't need some pain in the ass to babysit. He'd be able to spread out and look at the stars all night. He'd sloped the hole and dug a trench in case it decided to rain, which he knew it probably would.

He'd just put the finishing touches on his hole and was about to test out it's comfort level and have a nap when Bucholz strode up to the edge of his hole. He had a shoulder width stance and looked down on O'Connor like he was looking into the bottom of a latrine. "The lieutenant wants a patrol. We're moving through our lines upstream. We're gonna find that village and see about crossing this river."

O'Connor squinted up at him, "So?"

Bucholz spit. "So, you're on that patrol, hard-case. Get your lazy ass out of that hole and snap to it."

O'Connor shook his head. *I should kill this son-of-a-bitch.* He got to his feet and hopped out of the hole. He stood to his full height and faced Bucholz. They stared into each other's eyes. Bucholz looked away first, seeing the eyes of a stone-cold killer. He pointed. "You're on point."

O'Connor spit and narrowly missed the corporal's boots. "Suits me fine."

IT FELT good to be on point again, leading a group of determined GIs. He knew they'd rather not have him in their unit, but when they were out here they relied on one another no matter who it was. It felt good to belong.

The jungle was thick but manageable. O'Connor led them along the river bank. The steady flow of the river helped center him and keep him focused. The old feeling of confidence returned. He was a woodsman at heart - a hunter.

He slowed when he started noticing signs of human activity. He moved cautiously until he saw a hut through the trees. He'd come to the expected village.

He crouched and parted the jungle to get a better look. It looked abandoned. He didn't see any local Filipinos, and the thatch structures looked run-down, as if they hadn't been cared for in a while. He heard the soldier behind him and he looked back to get his attention. He held up his fist and the GI passed the signal back and crouched with his rifle at the ready.

Corporal Bucholz moved forward and crouched beside O'Connor. Without a word O'Connor pointed at the village. Bucholz bobbed his head trying to get a better view. He signaled O'Connor forward for a better look.

O'Connor parted the bushes and moved through without making a sound. He had his carbine ready. He moved to the edge of the village and went prone. He was as still as a stone as he listened and took in everything he could. Something in the back of his head niggled at him. His intuition, his sixth sense was telling him something wasn't right. He'd learned not to ignore that niggling.

Slight movement off to the left caught his eye. He adjusted his head slightly, using his peripheral vision. There it was a again, in the far corner of the village. He focused on the spot and noticed something sticking out from a dark window. It looked like a tree branch, but something was different. Another movement behind the 'branch,' someone moving, adjusting themselves. *There you are, you son-of-a-bitch.*

He studied the rest of the village. They were well hidden, but he could pick out the telltale signs of an enemy presence. He carefully pushed himself back to Corporal Bucholz and whispered in his ear. "Japs in the far buildings. At least one Nambu in the far left hut."

Bucholz looked at him skeptically. "You sure?"

O'Connor struggled not to strangle him. "Course I'm sure."

Bucholz considered his position. "How many?"

O'Connor shrugged. "Doesn't matter. We should move back and have the Navy guns take care of it. Couple a rounds should do the trick."

Bucholz's face purpled and a large vein popped out on his forehead. "You're not in command anymore, *corporal.*"

Bucholz motioned the rest of the squad forward. When they were all there he whispered. "We've got a few Japs in the village, far left corner. We're gonna flush 'em out."

O'Connor shook his head. In a quiet, controlled voice he said, "At least get the rest of the platoon involved."

Bucholz shook his head. "We can handle it." He pointed at a crouched PFC. "Collins, move forward and confirm his report."

O'Connor seethed, but held his tongue. PFC Collins glanced at O'Connor then shuffled his way past. O'Connor watched him go. He didn't move well, making far too much noise. O'Connor checked his carbine and sunk lower. *The fireworks are gonna start any second.* He looked at Bucholz. "I'd get down if I was you." Bucholz didn't move but spit out a long stream of tobacco laced juice. O'Connor noticed other GIs moving away from the cluster and sinking lower.

The crack of a rifle made them all dive for cover. PFC Collins yelled out and more rifles cracked. Bullets lanced through the jungle, knocking leaves and branches down. O'Connor heard Collins returning fire. Despite his yell, he was still in the fight. He looked at Bucholz whose eyes were wide. "Orders. What are your orders?"

The machine gun opened up. Bullets slammed into palms and pulped their trunks, looking like men's insides. Bucholz yelled. "Fallback, fallback."

O'Connor's idea of laying low and not taking chances evaporated. "Bullshit, you've got a man out there."

Bucholz's panicked eyes darted around like a caged animal. "We'll be cut to shreds we gotta leave."

O'Connor ignored him. "I'm getting Collins back." Without waiting, he turned and fast crawled forward angling left. Soon he was out
of the line of fire.

The machine gun continued firing in controlled bursts, probing.
O'Connor didn't hear Collins firing anymore. He crouched behind a
palm tree and peeked his head around. He could see the Nambu's
barrel smoking, and occasionally spitting fire. More rifle barrels poked
out from the other huts firing randomly. One hut on this side of the
village looked like it had taken the brunt of the fire. He figured that
was where he'd find Collins.

Movement behind him caught his eye and he spun, but saw it was
GIs from the squad following him. O'Connor grinned and nodded at
them. Using hand signals, he pointed out the enemy positions. The
soldier nearest was mounting a grenade launcher attachment onto his
rifle. O'Connor got his attention and pointed at the hut with the
Nambu. The enemy fire had stopped. O'Connor assumed they were
scanning for targets.

The squad spread out around O'Connor. Once they were ready, he
pointed at the GI with the launcher. He held up three fingers and
counted down. When his hand was a fist, the soldier got into a crouch,
aimed and fired. At the same instant the rest of the squad opened up.
The grenade arced across the open space in the center of the village
and landed at the base of the hut, where it met the jungle floor. It
disappeared into the thatch for a second, then exploded.

O'Connor fired his carbine, spreading his bullets through the hut.
An instant later the hut started smoking. Soon flames licked from the
base and grew, moving upward. The machine gun was out of commis-
sion. He switched his fire to the other huts and fired until his magazine
was empty. The Japanese return fire intensified and bullets whizzed
and smacked into the ground all around.

O'Connor slammed in a new magazine. He yelled, "Flank left. We'll
roll 'em up. Covering fire." The GIs fire intensified and O'Connor
rolled out from the palm and sprinted to his left. Bullets followed close
behind, but he slid safely behind the thick trunk of a mangrove tree.

Three men had followed him. He yelled again, "Covering fire!" He
swung his carbine around the tree and fired into the huts. The angle

was such that he couldn't see the front of the huts. He fired into them from the side. Thatch was not effective cover from bullets. The nearest hut was burning brightly sending off sparks and billowing smoke. It was nearly completely engulfed. The rest of the squad slid in around him and brought their weapons up. He saw Bucholz slide in last.

O'Connor pointed at the GI with the launcher. "Put another one into the far hut." The GI rolled onto his back and pulled another grenade and pulled it into place. When he was ready, he nodded at O'Connor. "Covering fire." The GIs rose up and fired. The grenadier rolled to his feet, aimed, and fired. His shot was spot on. The grenade arced out and disappeared into the thatch and exploded. There was a flash, then smoke. A Japanese soldier ran from the building. He weaved back and forth but the GI's bullets found him and he dropped with multiple gunshot wounds.

O'Connor waved them forward. "Let's finish this." He came out from behind the tree and sprinted into the village space. He slid in behind a stack of wood. He crouched and fired into the nearest hut. The burning hut to his left was scorching the side of his face. He could see the charred muzzle of the Nambu. He wondered about the bodies that must be inside.

GIs followed him and streamed past. He kept firing, covering their advance. A bullet thunked into the wood he crouched behind, sending splintered chunks flying. He didn't see where it came from. He ducked and changed magazines. He had two more. He popped up and fired four shots then ducked again. This time there was no return fire. The other GIs were pouring bullets into the remaining huts.

O'Connor moved up and found cover beside a GI who'd just emptied his M1 Garand with a 'ping.' "You see 'em?"

The GI shook his head. "Nah, just hitting the huts." He expertly slipped a clip into place and readied himself to fire.

O'Connor aimed around the cover looking for return fire. The far hut was smoking where the grenade had exploded, but there was no more enemy fire. He went back behind cover. He slapped the shoulder of the GI and pointed. "That's the hut Collins was in." He pushed him. "Check it out, I'll cover you." The GI nodded and adjusted his crouch. O'Connor put his carbine up and said, "Go!" he fired into the nearest hut and the GI took off. He kicked the thatch door open and burst inside disappearing from O'Connor's view.

The rest of the GIs continued to move forward, firing intermittently. There was no return fire. The GI poked his head out of the hut. O'Connor looked at him hoping for good news, but the soldier looked grim and shook his head. He trotted back to O'Connor's side. "He's dead. Riddled with bullets."

O'Connor lowered his gaze, "Damn." O'Connor heard Bucholz yelling orders. O'Connor got to his feet. The village was theirs.

Corporal Bucholz was back at the hut with the Nambu. It was still burning, sending chunks of burning debris into the sky, threatening to ignite the other nearby huts. O'Connor didn't want to be inside the village if that happened. They'd be caught inside an inferno.

Bucholz was yelling for the GIs to form up on him. O'Connor stood and looked back at him. The GIs held their ground, looking to O'Connor. O'Connor nodded. "Let's get outta here before this whole place goes up. Collect PFC Collins and move to the river."

Two GIs went inside the hut and brought the shredded body of PFC Collins out. O'Connor asked, "Where's his weapon?"

The GI struggling with the feet answered, "It's in three different pieces. Shot to shit." O'Connor nodded and the Squad moved past the burning hut, giving it a wide berth.

They formed up around Bucholz. His face was beet-red. He'd noticed the men's hesitancy at his order to regroup on him. Collins's body was lowered to the ground in front of Bucholz. He paled. "Damn shame." O'Connor held his tongue. *He'd be alive if we'd let the Navy shell the place.* Bucholz pointed behind him at the river. "There's a bridge crossing just upstream. It's what we were sent to find. We'll hustle back to the company and report."

O'Connor heard the sound of many boots tromping through the jungle behind them. "Looks like the company's coming to us."

Lieutenant Hopkins burst into the village with his weapon ready. The jungle seemed to come alive with GIs, ready for a fight. Hopkins took in the scene as the soldiers spread out. Bucholz waved his hand. "Over here, sir."

Hopkins trotted over to the loitering GIs. He strode with purpose but pulled up short when he saw the bloody body. Collins's eyes were shut, but his face was a deathly gray and a deep cut on his cheek oozed. He slung his Thompson and shook his head. "What the hell happened here, Bucholz? I sent you out to recon, not get into a firefight."

Bucholz was quick to point at O'Connor. "O'Connor led the attack. Against my orders to pull back." O'Connor didn't say a word but stared at Bucholz. It was a cold stare, one that made Bucholz look away.

Hopkins leveled his eyes at O'Connor. "This true Corporal?"

O'Connor spit a stream of clear spit. "I led the attack, yes sir."

"Goddamit, you wanna tell me why you disobeyed Bucholz?"

O'Connor looked back at the squirming corporal. "I had my reasons."

Bucholz shook his head. "He's no good. That's why he was kicked out of his other company. He needs to be out of this unit, sir."

Private First-Class Fletcher watched the exchange. He shook his head. "Sir, that's not the way it happ ..."

He was cut off by Hopkins. "Did I ask you for your input, Private?" PFC Fletcher held his tongue but looked at the other men for help. Another was about to speak when firing erupted from the direction of the bridge.

O'Connor went to ground and pointed. "Japs coming across the bridge!"

Captain Ludwig was on the radio soon after the Japanese tried to cross the bridge. While he was calling in the guns the rest of the company spread out to either side of the bridge.

O'Connor was behind a stack of rotting wood. He could feel the wood splinter as it absorbed Japanese bullets. The concentration of fire told him there was a large force. He rolled to his right and chanced a look. Bullets whizzed by, but he was able to get a quick view of the bridge. It looked well-built and new. He thought it was probably built by, or at least designed by the Japanese. He pulled back as more bullets smacked into the dirt and sent spouts of soil into the air.

He looked behind him and saw the other GIs in his squad with their heads down. PFC Fletcher peered from beneath his helmet. O'Connor could barely see his eyes. "Stay down. Wait for the fire mission."

A GI closer to the bridge yelled, "Here they come!"

The suppressing fire subsided. O'Connor arched his neck and strained to see over the wood pile. He glimpsed khaki uniforms sprinting across the bridge. They flashed by the wooden struts.

O'Connor got to his knees and pulled his M1 up. He sighted on a figure running full tilt across the two-hundred-foot span. He led him and fired, but his bullets whacked into the heavy wood of a strut. It didn't take long before the soldier was in the open again. O'Connor touched the trigger and sent four more shots. The soldier staggered and dropped out of sight behind the next strut.

O'Connor dropped behind cover again and looked back at Fletcher. "They're coming across the bridge." Fletcher nodded and pulled himself into a crouch. O'Connor watched him sight over his carbine and fire. When Fletcher dropped down, O'Connor went up again. He saw a Japanese soldier halfway across the bridge, crouched with his Arisaka rifle at his shoulder. The Japanese fired and expertly worked the bolt. O'Connor aimed carefully and fired twice. This time there was no doubt. The soldier was flung backwards, leaving his rifle on the wooden railing. O'Connor dropped again and Fletcher went up.

The rest of the company was firing now, but the Japanese were making progress, leapfrogging over one another. A machine gun opened up from the far side of the span. O'Connor flinched at the sound, but the fire wasn't directed his way.

He popped up again and searched for the source. He glimpsed the telltale white smoke coming from the jungle near the other side of the bridge. He fired through the cover until his magazine was dry. He dropped down and reloaded.

O'Connor heard Bucholz yell. "Riverbank, riverbank!" O'Connor watched Fletcher shift his aim to the river. It flowed at the bottom of the canyon thirty feet down. It moved fast, but calm on its way to the ocean, completely aloof of the battle raging along its banks.

O'Connor stayed low, keeping the wood pile between himself and the fire coming from the bridge. He looked to the river and realized he'd was exposed from that direction.

He saw Japanese soldiers running through the jungle, some coming down to the riverbank. He aimed at a soldier bringing his rifle to his shoulder. He fired and watched his bullets slam into the crouched Japanese. The soldier staggered backward then toppled forward and splashed into the river. O'Connor put two more bullets into him and the body jolted, then slowly drifted downstream.

More soldiers were taking up positions on the riverbank and O'Connor knew he had to move or be sliced up. He yelled, "We've gotta move! We're exposed."

Japanese bullets whizzed past his ears. He kept firing into the jungle, moving his carbine from target to target, unsure if he was hitting anything. He heard the distinctive sound of a bullet hitting flesh and heard a grunt and the clatter of a dropped weapon. He didn't have time to see who was hit. He moved backwards, firing as he went.

When his magazine emptied he turned to sprint for cover, but the heavy whoosh of a passing locomotive overhead made him dive for cover. The jungle beyond the river erupted and the shock wave of a 5-inch shell rippled the river water and slammed into him, knocking the wind from his lungs. He stayed down as more big shells passed and slammed into the Japanese position.

The naval barrage lasted less than a minute, but it felt like a year. Each crushing impact swept over him and rattled his brain. When it ended he shook his head and listened as jungle debris rained down all around. It seemed like a quick, violent storm had passed through. He peered from beneath his dirt encrusted helmet. The river continued to flow, but it was covered with a thick layer of debris. He thought he could probably walk across it.

There was no movement from the far bank. There was only thick smoke and churned up soil. The machine gun was silent. He remembered the GI who'd been hit just before the barrage. He went into a crouch and looked for his squad. One by one heads emerged as they recovered from the close fire mission. He saw an inert form a couple yards away. The GI was on his back, staring into the bright sky.

O'Connor shook the dirt off and went to the soldier's side. He brushed the dirt off his still face. It was PFC Fletcher. He felt for a pulse, but knew it was useless. He barely knew him, but he knew enough. He was a good soldier and a good man. Yet another life wasted by the brutality of war.

More firing erupted from his side of the river. It was light at first but gaining intensity. O'Connor scanned the enemy bank but didn't see movement. He heard Captain Ludwig. "Move up! Move up! Take the bridge."

The GIs shook off the effects of the barrage like zombies rising from the grave. O'Connor's first instinct was to join the charge, but a deep tiredness overtook him and he stayed next to Fletcher's body. He stared at his unseeing eyes. There was no pain there. He looked completely at peace. O'Connor envied him. He heard yelling and tore his eyes from Fletcher's. The GIs were bounding across the bridge, firing intermittently towards the dense jungle.

Someone slapped his shoulder. "Come on soldier, move up!" It was Corporal Bucholz. O'Connor glared at him and the urge to shoot him was strong. The rest of the squad followed Bucholz. O'Connor staggered to his feet. He took one last look at Fletcher's graying face. He felt like an old man, but he trotted behind the rest of the squad.

19

Platoon Sergeant Carver didn't like how things had been left with Sergeant - now *Corporal* O'Connor. He'd fought beside him through every major engagement since the beaches at Guadalcanal, and now he was about to land on another island, but without him.

O'Connor had been shuffled off under guard right after the fight. It was the last Carver saw of him. That had been two weeks ago. He was told he'd been reassigned to Hotel Company which would be assaulting the island from the northeast, along with elements of the 40th Division. He heard they'd already landed and were driving down the beach to meet up with them in the southeastern corner. For all he knew, O'Connor could already be dead.

Carver and the 164th Regiment were landing at the south-east end, near Sibulan. They were to advance to contact with the help of the Filipino guides. Once the Japanese were engaged, the 40th would hit them from their flank. That was assuming they didn't run into any Japanese during their trek down the beach.

The boat ride from Tagliban Harbor to the landing zone, only took a couple hours. The sounds of naval gunfire rippled around the inlets, making it difficult to pin down exactly where it was coming from. It became immediately apparent when the troop ship crossed the tip of Cebu's western most coast line. Negros island was suddenly visible like a shining green snake. A big one. The U.S. Navy was shelling something far inland. So far, in fact, that Carver couldn't see the resulting explosions

The brass had told them they didn't expect a hostile landing, so the fire mission perplexed Carver. He nudged Lieutenant Swan. "What the hell they firing at, sir?"

Swan shrugged but pointed toward the towering mountains forming a spine through the center of the island. "The 182nd Division's been attacking from the northern side for nearly a month now. They've had it pretty rough from what I've heard. They've pushed the Japs back into the hills though. Probably a fire mission supporting them."

Carver nodded. "Nice to have 'em around, case we run into anything unusual."

"Most of the Japs are on the other side, but there's plenty on this side too. Division thinks there may be two thousand troops dug in those hills." He gestured to the low hills in front of the taller mountain range. They looked green and lush. Carver wondered how thick it would be. Cebu and Bohol hadn't been too bad. So far, the jungles weren't nearly as thick and rancid as Bougainville or Guadalcanal. "The local contingent of Filipino fighters tells us there's a few Japs still in Dumaguate, but we'll be landing in Sibulan a few miles north. We expect the Japs to run for the hills once they see us land."

"Why's that, sir?" Carver had been fighting the Japanese a long time and hadn't seen them run from a fight.

"It's what happened on the other side. The 182nd landed and the Japs faded into the jungle leaving behind all sorts of minefields and tank traps. It was effective. Our guys took a lot more casualties than if the Japs had stayed in one place and slugged it out. At this point, they know they can't stand and fight. Using guerrilla tactics, they can kill more of us, which is all they seem to care about."

Carver shook his head. "We can't seem to convince 'em they're beat." He looked out over the lush island with its white beaches. "A lot more of us are gonna die before this thing's over. If they're fighting like this here? Think what's gonna happen when we land on Japan.

Everyone able to wield anything evenly remotely dangerous will be gunning for us."

Lieutenant Swan slapped Carver's shoulder and leaned in close. "Shouldn't be telling you this," he looked around like he was searching for a spy. "The Americal Division's slated to be the leading force on that operation. Once were done here, we start resupplying and training for mainland Japan."

Carver looked at his feet and shook his head. The image of Lilly filled his thoughts, and a sadness flooded him. All thoughts of a life after this war shattered like a ship upon a craggy reef.

Lieutenant Swan was alarmed at his reaction. "Hey, don't sweat it, Sergeant." He beamed, "You and I are survivors."

Carver felt embarrassed. "Sorry, sir. Just tired I guess."

Swan nodded. "We'll be offloading within the hour. Have the men ready."

"Yes, sir."

～

"Get those men north of town and set up a perimeter," yelled Lieutenant Swan. Platoon Sergeant Carver directed Sergeant Levy to move the men through the town quickly.

As expected there was no enemy resistance. The landing had gone off perfectly. It had only taken two hours to get the entire Regiment offloaded. As on Bohol, they were met by the local Filipino resistance fighters. They'd assured them there were no Japanese in the area.

Captain Flannigan stood before the ranking Filipino officer and asked, "so, where are they?"

With a broad grin and broken English, he pointed south. "In Duagarte. They leave now."

Flannigan didn't like hearing that. "Let's move out and cut 'em off before they get to the hills." He looked around for Lt. Swan. "Swan! Where are you?"

Lieutenant Swan walked up to Flannigan with another captain in tow. Swan saluted and addressed Flannigan. "Sir, this is Captain Ludwig from Hotel Company, 40th Division. They've just arrived."

Captain Flannigan looked his counterpart over. He was filthy with mud and dust and smelled of jungle and cordite. "Looks like you've had a rough go of it, Captain."

Captain Ludwig squinted at the taller Flannigan. "We ran into the Japs on day one in a little village. They were defending a key bridge crossing. We finally took the bridge and have been in a running battle with the remnants of that unit ever since."

Flannigan frowned. "Casualties?"

Ludwig looked at his boots and nodded. "Lost twenty-two men. Most at the bridge."

Flannigan pointed south. "The Filipino resistance says there's Japs in Duagarte, but they're heading for the hills. Probably hooking up with the force you've been fighting."

Ludwig frowned. "It would be better if we kept that from happening. They're all but used up. If they connect, they'll be able to resupply."

Flannigan pointed past the village. "We could send soldiers up that valley, act like a stopping force." He waved the leader of the Filipinos forward. "Captain Garcia could lead us."

Ludwig nodded. "My men need to resupply, but we can be up there pretty quick."

Flannigan shook his head. "I've already got men moving in that direction. You should rest your men, get some hot chow." He looked him up and down and crinkled his nose, "Maybe bathe."

Ludwig squinted and scowled but was too tired to argue. "Combat's a dirty business, Captain."

PLATOON SERGEANT CARVER walked beside Lt. Swan. They'd left the cheering villagers behind and were weaving their way up a winding path beside a crystal-clear creek. On point was a cadre of hard looking Filipino fighters. "How far you figure we need to go?"

Lieutenant Swan shrugged. "Captain Ignacio has a spot in mind. Says it's a likely spot for the Japs to come through."

"Any idea how many Japs we're dealing with?"

"Nope. Only know they're battle weary."

Carver dropped back to check on the men. They'd been off the boat a day, but the heat, dust and strain of being in enemy territory made them look like they'd been at if for weeks. Despite their ragged look, he knew they were a deadly force of hardened veterans and he wouldn't want to be moving into harm's way with any other men. He thought about O'Connor. *Wonder how he's doing?* He thought of their fight. At first he'd been enraged by the blatant disrespect, but as the weeks passed he realized his old friend was lashing out at the situation, not him personally. He grinned, *son-of-a-bitch can sure throw a punch.* He touched his still tender nose.

A half-hour later Captain Ignacio halted the column. The canyon forked into another side canyon with a well-used trail. The jungle was thick and would force travelers toward the side-canyon trail. An idyllic little creek babbled over stones at the bottom of the canyon. Some GIs dipped their hands and rubbed the cool water over their necks and heads.

Carver assessed the area. He was at Lt. Swan's side again. "Good place to set up an ambush. The Japs have to come along the trail. They'll funnel right down on us."

Lieutenant Swan agreed. "We'll put second platoon on the uphill side and the Filipinos on the downhill side." He looked south. The jungle wasn't as thick behind them, like it had been thinned out before the war. Swan figured it was some kind of logging operation. "As long as they don't come from behind us."

Carver said. "We can put some security back there, sir."

Swan nodded. "Let's get it set up. Put the thirty-caliber machine guns on the flanks and one shooting straight down the path of the 'T.' I'll call in our coordinates, get some fire missions set up in case we need it."

The men set about digging in. The soft ground was easy to work with. The black, fertile dirt smelled loamy. The Filipinos didn't have entrenching tools but borrowed the GI's.

Within an hour the second platoon and the attached Filipinos were dug in. Now, all they had to do was wait. Carver was in a hole with Corporal Mathews. He had his M1 Garand propped on the side of the hole. They'd dug it deep and wide. There was plenty of room for both of them. They were on the side of the hill just up from the trail. The next hole to their right was the machine gun crew. They were a few meters up from the creek. They were well concealed, the deadly .30 caliber's barrel the only thing poking through the camouflage. If the Japs came down this path, they'd be torn apart.

Further up the hill, another .30 caliber aimed down the trail. They had a more limited view but would be able to engage anyone coming through the thick jungle. The third machine gun was set up on the other side of the trail amongst the Filipinos.

Carver looked through the jungle canopy. It was relatively thin and he could see through all the way to the sea. Great black clouds were forming across the bay and it looked like Cebu was about to get drenched. "Hope that shit stays over there."

Mathews looked where he was looking. "Doubt it. Hasn't rained in a whole day. We're definitely overdue." He slapped at his neck and his hand came away with a blood spot. "At least the mosquitos aren't as bad as Bougainville."

"Nothing was as bad as Bougainville. Far as I'm concerned the Japs can keep it."

~

THE DAY WANED and the GIs of second platoon tried to stay focused. The day turned dark as a black sheet of rain moved from Cebu to the bay. The GIs were directly in its path. There was no doubt they'd be caught in a deluge soon.

Lieutenant Swan ordered the men to break out their ponchos and dig outlet drains in their holes if they hadn't already. For most of the men, adding a way for the water to run out of their foxholes was as automatic as putting their boots on.

The bay disappeared, as the rain swept across and smacked into Negros. Soon after, the first fat drops started to fall on their ambush position. "Here it comes. Gonna be a doozy." Carver hunkered under his poncho but kept a slit open to keep an eye on the trail. Visibility dropped to a few feet as the sky seemed to open up like a faucet. The constant splatter on his poncho drowned out all sound. It felt like he was sitting beneath a particularly brutal waterfall.

The foxhole quickly deteriorated into a sloppy mess. The sides turned to goo and the bottom started to fill up despite the ditch they'd dug at the far end. Runoff from uphill sloshed over the lip and cascaded into the hole forming a minor waterfall.

Carver leaned close to Mathew's ear. "Creek's gonna rise." Mathews looked past sheets of rain and nodded. Carver continued. "I'm gonna move down and make sure the MG nest is far enough uphill. Flash flood could take 'em out."

Mathews nearly had to shout to be heard. "You won't get ten feet. You'll slide out of here like a hockey puck."

Carver nodded. "Yeah, I may not make it back to you." He secured his Thompson on his back and slapped Mathew's shoulder. He dug his hands into the muddy ground and lunged out of the hole. He immediately slipped and fell onto his chest. The slight downward angle was enough to send him sliding. He went a couple feet, gaining speed before he reached out and hooked a passing palm tree. He held tight and his body swung around until he faced back up the hill. The bright day from just a few minutes before was replaced with an unnatural darkness. He couldn't see more than a few feet in either direction. He strained to see Mathews, but it was as if he'd traveled miles in his brief slide.

He kicked his boots into the mushy ground, trying to get a purchase before he let go of the palm. The creek-bed was thirty yards from his hole, but it might as well have been in another universe.

He let go of the palm and his toehold held. He backed his way down the hill one step at a time. He felt like an ice climber on some bizarre watery descent. He finally made it to less steep ground and was able to stand. He searched the area but couldn't see anyone. He knew there was an entire platoon of men nearby, but he felt like he was on the moon.

He kept trudging down the hill and finally the sound of rushing water overtook the sound of the hammering rain. He crouched and squinted. He felt rivulets of cold water lancing down his body. Even the most robust rain gear wouldn't be enough to keep the rainwater out, and he wore an Army issue poncho. He took a few more careful steps toward the sound of rushing water. He called out, "Hello!" There was no point trying to keep quiet. If the Japs were nearby they'd be hunkered down for sure.

He took another step toward the edge of the creek and slipped. He fell onto his ass and immediately started sliding toward the creek he still couldn't see. *Shit, I'll be swept away and they'll never find my body.* He gained speed despite digging his hands and heels into the mud. Suddenly he hit an edge and dropped. He thought he'd hit the raging creek, but instead slammed into soft, protesting bodies.

The GI yelled, "What the hell's that?" He shook off the unknown visitor and Carver slipped to the bottom of the foxhole.

There was more yelling, but Carver's booming voice cut through. "It's me! It's Carver!"

He felt his voice was barely audible above the roar of the creek and the rain, but the nearest man heard him. "Carver? That you?"

Carver got to his feet. The bottom of the hole was filled shin-deep with water. He yelled into the soldier's ear. "We gotta get you outta here. The creek's gonna keep rising. You'll be swept away."

"We're twenty feet from the creek," He protested.

Carver shook his head, a motion no one could see. "I think it's right there and rising."

He tugged at the GI's shoulder but he resisted. "Lemme get the gun," he yelled. "Tommy, we're leaving," he yelled at the loader beside him.

Tommy yelled back. "What? Why?"

Carver yelled above the din. "Cause I said so. Now move out, now!" The rain subsided slightly in that moment and the visibility went from zero to a couple of yards. Carver's eyes went wide and he pointed. "Shit! Leave the gun, we gotta go now!"

The GIs looked up and saw the dark churning water of the creek. The placid, idyllic babbling brook they'd crossed with hardly a jump was now a massive, black cauldron, full of rolling debris. It was climbing toward them like an angry black devil and it was only feet away.

Carver jumped out of the hole and reached back to help the two

GIs out. He gripped the first man and pulled him over the side. He seemed to weigh a ton, but he got him out of the hole. The GI turned back to help his buddy, but Tommy was still trying to lift the .30 caliber off the mount. His efforts were thwarted by the slick ground. He couldn't get a good purchase and every time he tried to lift the gun, his boots went out from beneath him. "Forget the gun, Tommy. We gotta go, now!"

Tommy got back to his feet and looked up at his buddy. He lunged for the gun again, "Can't leave it here." He dug his feet in and pulled up. The machine gun came off the mount and he looked up grinning. "Got it. I told you -" He was interrupted when the creek surged and the mass of water and debris swept over the hole and slammed into his chest. He simply disappeared. One moment he was there, the next he was gone, replaced with an angry black mass of debris.

Carver held onto the GI's poncho as he tried to lunge for his friend. He held tight and screamed at him. "He's gone! We gotta move!"

The soldier wailed, "Tommy! Tommy, no!" Carver pulled him up the hill. He didn't look back but he felt the rising creek of half dirt, half water reaching to snatch him, like a hungry crocodile.

The soldier finally stopped struggling and shook Carver off. He made his own way, and they slogged up the hillside a few yards. For every step forward, they slipped half a step backwards, but they finally got far enough away from the raging creek, and stopped. Carver tucked into the base of a palm tree and the mud slid past him, feeding the creek. The gunner tucked tight and Carver could feel his body jolt as he sobbed for his friend. He pretended not to notice.

The rain lasted another twenty minutes but it subsided slightly and the creek didn't rise more. The daylight gradually returned and the rain suddenly stopped as abruptly as it started. The raging creek quickly lost its power. Carver watched as it dropped inch by inch then foot by foot. The sight was mesmerizing. It was still muddy, but the power that it possessed was gone. The foxhole they'd come from was gone, as if it had never existed, along with Tommy's body.

Carver looked up through the dripping jungle canopy. He could see blue sky. The day was waning into evening. It was as if the violence of the previous hour had never happened. The only evidence, the muddy ground and the line of black debris strewn along the high-water mark of the creek.

Carver reached out and squeezed the gunner's shoulder. "You okay?"

The soldier didn't respond at first. He looked up through red-rimmed, watery eyes. He wiped his nose on the back of his hand. He looked back to where the foxhole had been, then back at Carver. "Yeah, I'm okay."

Carver stood and surveyed the area. It looked nothing like it had. He couldn't see the foxholes and the platoon of GIs he knew were there. Then, one by one he saw heads popping up and looking around in dazed confusion. "I'm gonna go find Lieutenant Swan." The soldier nodded but didn't stand. He kept staring at the creek, like it would re-animate and climb up to kill him.

Private Haskins was the only casualty from the flash flood. Private First-Class Watts, the gunner, wanted to look for his body, but night was approaching and Lt. Swan wouldn't allow it. He barked out orders. "Get your foxholes back in shape and get those thirty cals back up. There's still a cadre of Japs out there somewhere."

As the light faded and darkness set in, Carver sat beside PFC Mathews again. Mathews whispered, "Think they'll come tonight?"

Carver shrugged. "They're probably desperate to link up and re-supply. From what I hear, they're low on everything, including food. If there's one time to move at night, this would be it."

Mathews stared into the jungle. A thin sheen of mist covered the ground. The darkness combined with the mist cut visibility to near zero. "If they do, they'll be right on top of us before we see 'em."

Carver nodded. "Long as we see 'em first we'll be fine. Try to get some shut-eye. I'll take the first watch."

Mathews nodded and slipped to the bottom of the muddy hole. The standing water was gone, but the sloppy mess it left behind seeped into his crotch. He removed his helmet and sat on it. It sank into the muck, but finally stopped when it was halfway covered. He dug into his pack and opened a can of C-Rats. He slurped up what passed for spaghetti and tried to get comfortable.

Carver heard his deep breathing moments later. He shook his head, wishing he could fall asleep that quickly. *He's like O'Connor, can sleep instantly.* The thought of O'Connor took his mind off the jungle. He knew O'Connor was linked with the 40th, the same unit that had been fighting a running battle with the Japanese he was set up to ambush. He'd gotten orders to set the ambush before he was able to check on his old friend. He worried briefly but decided there was no point to it. *He's been through worse than that.*

Two hours passed and the jungle was black. There was starlight sifting through the canopy, but Carver could only see a few feet ahead. The only way he'd know if the enemy was there, was if he heard them, or they stumbled into his hole. He checked his watch. He'd give Mathews another half hour. He could hear his soft snores from the blackness at his feet.

He adjusted his Thompson and shifted his feet. He felt the circulation return to his right leg. He hadn't realized he was standing awkwardly. The coolness and tingling felt good and took his mind off how tired he felt.

The jungle sounds suddenly quieted. He concentrated on the jungle. There was still a lot of insect noise, but some part had quieted. It was subtle, but his veteran's ears noticed it immediately. He gripped his Thompson tighter and strained to see into the gloom. He concentrated on his peripheral vision. The soft babble of the now tame creek sounded loud as he concentrated. Then he heard a splash. Not large, more like a footfall. Like someone was crossing or walking along the side and misstepped. He held his breath and listened. There it was again.

He kicked PFC Mathews and felt him instantly jolt and tense. Without a word, Mathews got to his feet and was near Carver's left shoulder. Carver whispered, "Something's coming down the creek."

Mathews shifted his M1 and strained to hear. All grogginess disappeared, replaced with alertness. Another sound, this time the barely audible snap of a branch. In slow motion, Mathews put his rifle to his shoulder, aiming over the sights.

They both nearly jumped out of their skin when the bark of a rifle erupted below them and lit the night with a muzzle flash. Carver had no targets but he aimed in the direction he'd heard the noise and fired off five rounds. Mathews joined in sending his own .30 caliber bullets into the night.

There was yelling coming from the darkness, then there were muzzle flashes in the jungle. Carver's night vision vanished when he fired his Thompson, but he saw multiple muzzle flashes coming from the jungle to his front. He shifted his aim from the creek to the new targets and walked a ten-round burst into the night. Mathews also shifted and emptied the rest of his clip. It pinged and he dropped down to reload. "Reloading!" he yelled.

Carver felt the buzz of a bullet passing close and he ducked down. The two remaining .30 caliber machine guns opened up and for a few seconds the enemy fire was drowned out. Carver popped back up and waited for another flash, but there wasn't any. He swung his Thompson back and forth, breathing hard. He wanted to fire at the spot he'd seen the flash, but the Japanese soldier may be waiting for that. Mathews finished reloading and popped up again, ready to engage. "Don't shoot unless you've got a target." He could hear Mathews breathing hard and moving his rifle side to side, but he held his fire.

The .30 caliber machine guns lowered their firing cadence to five round bursts, ending when the tracer round lanced into the night. There was no return fire. Carver listened for retreating troops, but his ears were ringing. He heard Lt. Swan yell, "Cease fire," and the guns stopped. "Anyone hit?" There was no response. *Thank God,* Carver thought. "Stay in your holes, they may be sneaking in closer."

Carver dropped down and whispered, "Reloading." He ejected the magazine and inserted a new one, putting the half-spent mag back in his pocket. Carver rose back up. Together, they watched for anything out of the ordinary. Ten long minutes passed. There was the occasional shot from other sectors. *Nervous soldiers seeing ghosts in the night,* Carver thought.

He could feel Mathews tense suddenly. At the same instant he heard the soft thump of something landing nearby. He reacted instantly. He dropped down and pulled Mathews along with him. He screamed, "Grenade!" at the same instant it exploded.

More explosions thumped along the line. Debris rained down on Carver's foxhole. There was screaming coming from GIs. Carver gritted his teeth. "Get ready!" Carver and Mathews were inches away. Carver waited another five seconds then yelled, "Now!" As one unit, Carver and Mathews stood up.

Carver immediately saw movement charging toward their hole. He didn't have time to aim. He leveled his sub-machine gun and blazed away, holding the trigger down and sweeping the area. The flame from his muzzle lit up the agonized faces of multiple Japanese soldiers.

Mathews fired repeatedly until his clip pinged. He didn't have time to reload, the surviving Japanese were charging and would be upon them in a moment.

He reversed his grip and held the barrel end of the M1. He could feel the heat of the barrel but ignored it. A Japanese was lunging toward his heart with his bayonet mounted Arisaka. Mathews swung the M1 and knocked the lunge away. The soldier tripped into the hole. Mathews ducked and had just enough time to move under the forward part of the foxhole. The Japanese soldier slammed into the back wall. The muddy hole was suddenly crowded and Mathew's had trouble turning around to engage the enemy. He dropped his rifle and pulled his K-bar knife from the scabbard on his waist. He jabbed and felt the blade slice and glance off the soldier's forearm. The Japanese screamed in agony. With speed he didn't know he had, Mathews lunged the blade over and over into the soft flesh, not caring where he hit, as long as it was flesh.

Sticky blood gushed over his hand. The Japanese dropped to the floor. Mathews heard the final click of Carver's Thompson. Mathews felt exposed. His back was facing the enemy. He tried to spin, but his feet tangled in the dying soldier's legs and he fell on top of him. In the darkness he could see Carver's silhouette blotting out the stars. He was yelling something, but Mathews couldn't understand it through the ringing in his ears. Then Carver leaped and was out of the hole. The sudden space, allowed Mathews to untangle and stand.

He scrambled out of the hole. Carver was struggling with another soldier. They were grunting and screaming at one another. A dark shape from the left appeared and Mathews saw the glinting of a bayonet. The Japanese was running at Carver's back. He'd skewer him if Mathews didn't act. He still gripped his bloody knife. He lunged forward like a free safety hitting an exposed receiver. He wrapped his arms around the soldier, slamming his knife into his back. It was a solid hit and they went flying into the night.

When they hit the ground, Mathews released his grip and rolled to his feet. The knife was gone, still planted in the soldier's back. He couldn't see his victim, but another shape appeared out of the darkness. The enemy was running to finish the job on Carver, who was still locked up with the other soldier.

Mathews felt like his lungs were on fire. He couldn't catch his breath, but he didn't have time to recover. He launched at the passing soldier and ran into him broadside. The soldier screamed in surprise. Mathews straddled his chest, but he didn't have a weapon. He reared back his right fist and slammed it into the soldier's face. He felt teeth break, but the pain in his own hand made him yell. The soldier was dazed. Mathews balled his left fist and slammed it into the soldier's nose. It collapsed with a crunch and blood spurted from beneath his fist. In the darkness, he could barely make out the soldier's features. He remembered his helmet. He pushed it forward off his head and in one motion slammed it down into the soldier's face. The three-pound steel pot clanged and stunned the Japanese. Mathews plunged it down again and again until the soldier stopped moving.

He sat atop the soldier, his chest heaving, trying to catch his breath. He could see the dim outline of a soldier where Carver had been, but he couldn't tell if it was his sergeant or the Japanese. The figure stepped his direction. Mathews tried to move off the dead Japanese, but he couldn't seem to get his body to work. The dark soldier continued striding toward him. If it wasn't Carver, Mathews didn't think he had the energy to fight.

A gruff voice cut through his growing panic. "That you Mathews?" Muzzle flashes continued lighting up the jungle, but the intensity had died down. Carver knelt down. "You okay?"

Mathews nodded and in a shaky voice he barely recognized said, "Yeah - yeah I'm alright."

Carver pulled him off the motionless body. "Let's get back to the hole. Doubt the Japs are finished with us yet." Mathews tried to stand but his legs didn't want to cooperate and he had to lean heavily on Carver. "You hit?"

Mathews shook his head. "Don't think so. Can't seem to catch my breath."

"Well get your shit squared away, soldier. Come on." He dragged him to the edge of the hole. He kicked the body of a dead Japanese soldier that was perched on the edge and started to lower Mathews into the muddy foxhole.

Mathews shook him off. "No, there's a dead Jap at the bottom. I'm not going in there."

There was a sudden increase in firing. The .30 caliber, which had been silent the last few minutes came alive again and sent lancing death tracers into the jungle. Carver crouched. "You got a weapon? My Thompson's around here somewhere, but I can't find it."

Mathews shook his head. "My rifle must be in the bottom with the dead jap. Left my knife in someone's backside over there." Carver nodded and hopped into the hole. Mathews could hear the soft thump as he landed on the man he'd killed.

"Here's your M1." In the darkness he could see Carver holding it up to him. "Muddy as shit." Mathews reached for it and felt it's familiar weight. He had to prop it on the ground. "Cover the jungle while I clear this hole out."

Mathews nodded and wiped the sludge from the stock and barrel. He felt in his pocket and found a loaded clip. He carefully inserted it and shuffled his feet until he faced the jungle. He wondered if he had the energy to aim and fire. He gritted his teeth and shook his head. He resolved not to give up. He felt a rejuvenating surge and positioned himself better. He searched the darkness for targets.

There was still fighting in the creek-bed, but there didn't seem to be any Japs up where they were. He hoped the others were holding the line, or they wouldn't last through the night. He could hear Carver struggling to push the dead weight of the soldier out of the hole. He grunted and cussed but finally got the body over the lip and rolled him down the hill. Carver spoke between heaving breaths, "I've got his rifle. See if he's got any ammo."

Mathews took one last look into the jungle. He put his rifle down and turned to the body. He didn't relish what he had to do. He was about to put his hands into the man's pockets when there was a loud commotion from the jungle directly behind him. He knew in an instant it was a charging Japanese. Instinct set in and he dove to his right, reaching for the M1 as he did. He rolled twice then came up onto his knees.

The sharp crack of a rifle followed immediately by another shot split the night. The blast from the two rifles lit up the grisly scene momentarily. Mathews got a flash of a charging soldier and the bloody body on the ground. The Japanese went down, slamming headfirst into the body. The angle was wrong. He couldn't fire for fear of hitting Carver. More movement from the jungle. He swung his M1 and fired. The rifle nearly jumped out of his grip, but he readjusted and fired again. The target went down and he pointed the barrel toward the jungle. He pulled the trigger until it pinged. He reached for another clip, but his ammo pouch was still at the bottom of the hole. His pockets were empty.

Another loud crack from the direction of the hole spurred him into action. He got to his feet and yelled, "Coming in from your right, don't shoot." He didn't wait to hear a response. He crossed the ten feet to where he'd seen Carver shoot. Suddenly the ground was gone beneath his feet and he fell into the hole. He slammed into Carver on the way down and landed in the bloody muck at the bottom. Carver swung the long Arisaka rifle and rested it on his forehead. "Don't shoot, it's me."

Carver barked, "Dammit! I almost shot you." He pointed the rifle back out toward the jungle. "Get your ass up."

Mathews struggled to find a grip in the muddy sides and finally got to his feet. "Are there more?"

Carver didn't take his eyes off the jungle. "Don't know. Can't see shit. Be ready."

"Shit. I've gotta find my ammo." He dropped back down and started feeling the muddy bottom. It didn't take long before he felt the half-buried ammo pouch. He pulled and it slurped out of the sludge. He reached inside and found another clip. He pushed it into place and rejoined Carver at the lip of the hole. "Ammo's dirty, but hopefully functional."

They stood shoulder to shoulder searching for more Japanese. After five minutes the firing from the creek died down to the occasional shot. There was no movement. Drifting white smoke snaked around them in the stagnant air. Carver spit. "Think we stopped 'em ... for now."

20

Corporal O'Connor and the men of Hotel Company were exhausted. They'd been in a running fight for nearly two weeks. All O'Connor wanted to do was sack out for a week. He'd found the hastily erected mess hall and found an out of the way corner and eaten a meal that didn't come from a can. He savored every bite of the meatloaf and fresh bread. *Those Navy boys sure know how to cook.*

The rain started soon after he finished eating. He was walking in the street. The cascade of water instantly turned the streets to muddy, impassable little creeks. He sprinted to find shelter, eschewing the military tents for something more substantial. He burst through the front door of a sturdy looking house. The surprised faces of a family of Filipinos met him. Their faces changed from fear to smiles when they saw it was an American GI. They called him in and gave him a cloth to dry off with. He was ushered in and they sat him at their table where they'd just sat down to eat.

O'Connor was already full, but he took off his steel pot and sat with them. The food was delicious, some kind of sweet meat. Despite having just eaten a full dinner, he stuffed himself with more. The rain hammered outside. The din on the roof sounded like artillery, but inside it was warm and dry.

He thought about his old unit. He knew they were out in the jungle, lying in wait for the Japanese he'd been fighting along the beach. He looked outside. The gray sheets of rain looked like a massive waterfall. *Those boys are catching hell right about now.* There was nothing he could do about it, so he tucked into the dessert. He had no idea what it was, but it tasted amazing, some kind of mushy fruit.

The rain finally stopped. Outside the streets looked like rivers. *A real gully washer.* He realized it was a phrase his father used. He let his mind drift to thoughts of home. He pictured the little cabin in the woods, the wide, well-worn path that split, one leading to the well, the other to the two-hole outhouse. He remembered hating having to trudge through the wet and sometimes the snow, to take a shit. It seemed like hell to him then, but now like heaven.

He hadn't thought of home for a long time. It was an unattainable goal to return there. He'd never survive long enough to make it back. The war seemed to be winding down, it would have to end soon. He shook his head and looked east. Night was closing around the world quickly. He thought of Japan and the thousands upon thousands of soldiers still willing to fight and die to keep him from setting foot on their homeland. He shook his head and wiped the thought of survival and home away. *Worst part of the fighting's still ahead.*

O'CONNOR WOKE from his slumber and instinctively clutched his rifle. He sat up from the bed the Filipinos had insisted he use. It was a wood and thatch bed, the best in the house. He swung his feet to the floor and started putting on his boots. Something was happening outside. He could hear American voices yelling. It was a call to form up.

He was dressed and ready under a minute. He went to the door and looked back into the dimly lit house. The man of the house, Juan, was up and staring back at him. O'Connor thanked him for his hospitality and stepped into the night. The air was heavy with the stench of wet decay. A thin layer of fog drifted along the street. He shivered, despite the warm mugginess.

GIs were jogging toward the center of town. O'Connor recognized one and yelled. "What's going on, Duncan?"

Private Duncan turned when he heard his name. He squinted and recognized him. "Damned if I know, Corporal. Sergeant Flanders told us to meet in the town center."

O'Connor looked toward the hills and wondered if something was happening with his old unit. He adjusted his belt and trotted after Duncan.

Once they were loosely formed up, Lieutenant Hopkins addressed them. He looked like he'd been woken up too. "A platoon from Able Company's found our group of Japs and are in a fight for their lives. They've called for reinforcements and we're it."

There was grumbling all around and O'Connor heard Duncan mutter, "Can't them damn 164th boys take care of themselves?" O'Connor gritted his teeth, but kept his mouth shut.

Hopkins continued. "Make sure you've got plenty of ammo and food, we don't know if we'll be coming back here any time soon." He pointed at a group of soldiers hanging near the back. "Bring the four-inch mortars and all the .30 caliber Brownings we can find. There's still a Jap force to the south of us. We want all the firepower we can get in case they hit our flanks." He looked at his watch. "We leave in thirty minutes."

An hour later O'Connor was in the middle of the single file line snaking through the jungle. It was pitch black out and every step his boots sank into mud. They were being led by a group of Filipinos that seemed to know where they were going.

O'Connor heard the distant sounds of fighting. It ebbed and flowed like the tides, sometimes constant and steady then barely a shot. It was impossible to know how far away the fighting was. Sound was an odd thing in the jungle. It seemed to sometimes absorb and other times pipe it through like a gramophone.

They didn't try to stay quiet. The ground was slick, and each passing GI made it worse. By the time a halt was called, O'Connor was covered in a thick layer of mud from his boots to his crotch. The line of GIs stopped and weapons pointed into the dark gloom.

The sounds of fighting was definitely closer now. The word passed back that Lt. Hopkins was sending out the Filipinos and a couple GIs to link up with the platoon. O'Connor didn't envy them. Hooking up with a force in contact with the enemy at night was a great way to get shot by friendly fire.

Thirty minutes passed and O'Connor had to adjust his position. He was slowly sinking into the muck. He thought he might need to be hauled out with a winch.

Finally, there was movement in the line. He got to his feet and felt the blood rush back into his limbs. He had to use every ounce of strength to break free. The mud finally relented with a squelching sound. There was cursing up and down the line as each GI had to pull himself from the sticky goo, but finally they were moving again.

The battered platoon was happy to see them. O'Connor realized it was the 2nd platoon, his old unit. It was easy to stay anonymous in the darkness. He took up position with his new squad. They were the southernmost unit, protecting the rear and the heavy mortar crews.

Sergeant Flanders spoke to Corporal Bucholz. "No sense setting up the mortars before seeing what's above us." O'Connor thought it was pretty obvious the jungle canopy would negate the usefulness of the mortars but he hadn't brought it up. He wasn't in a command position anymore, just another rifleman. He'd helped dig the area out where the mortars would go, but knew his effort was being wasted.

Now he laid on the wet ground, facing south. It was the dead of night and he couldn't see more than a few feet. He wanted to search out Platoon Sergeant Carver, but figured it was an excellent way to get killed. He'd find him once it got light if he was still alive.

He remembered how they parted; dragged kicking and screaming after exchanging fisticuffs. The time away and the long two week running fight, made the incident seem like an age ago. He'd been enraged, but he realized he wasn't really upset with his old friend. He was mad at the situation. He was mad at the world for taking his woman out of his life forever, while Carver's was still safe and sound in the rear, wiping wounded soldier's noses. He'd reacted badly, he knew that and he figured Carver understood. As he felt himself sinking slowly into the mud again, he decided he'd apologize.

A soldier slid in beside him and squinted through the night. "Who's that?"

O'Connor recognized Corporal Bucholz. He sneered, "It's O'Connor."

Bucholz reared back like he'd smelled something rotten. "Anything to report?"

O'Connor murmured, "Nope."

"I just spoke with Sergeant Flanders. Lieutenant Hopkins thinks they'll hit us again tonight. The platoon from the 164th got beat up pretty bad. Even lost a guy to a flash flood. They held though, but the Japs probably don't know they've been reinforced, so Hopkins thinks they'll make a final push." He scowled at O'Connor even though he knew he couldn't see him in the dark. "You'll be nice and safe back here."

O'Connor wanted to reach out and strangle him. He leaned in close and whispered. "You know Bucholz, I could snap your neck right now, haul you out to the jungle and everyone would think you were killed by Japs." Bucholz pulled away like he'd spit poison. He spluttered and tried to speak, but O'Connor gripped his arm and squeezed. Bucholz tried to pull away from the vice-like grip but couldn't. O'Connor hissed. "Leave me the fuck alone, Corporal."

Bucholz searched to see if anyone was close enough to have heard the insubordinate words, but O'Connor was too smart for that. Bucholz blanched. He'd seen O'Connor fighting for his life all week and despite his dislike, respected his soldiering skills. He cursed under his breath. O'Connor relaxed his grip and Bucholz pulled his arm free. He slinked off into the night. O'Connor watched him go and decided he'd have to keep an eye on him. *Don't want a bullet in the back.*

O'CONNOR FOUGHT TO STAY AWAKE. His eyes were heavy. He bit his lip, drawing blood. The sharp pain focused his senses and kept him awake. He hadn't heard or seen anything out of the ordinary. The mortar crews would shift positions occasionally, keeping the circulation moving, but other than that, it was deathly quiet. The creek babbled soothingly somewhere in the dark and he wondered if it was the same creek that had killed the GI he'd heard about. *Yet another way for the jungle to kill a man.*

He looked at his watch. He could barely make out the luminescent dials, but he thought it said 0430. It would be getting light in another hour or so. He welcomed the dawn, he didn't like not knowing his surroundings.

He shifted his position and felt blood return to his legs. He moved his foot back and forth and the pins and needles coursed up and down his leg. He reached for his back-pack, propped a few feet away. He remembered a candy bar stuffed into the side pocket. He'd just pulled it free and was about to peel open the paper when there was sudden gunfire to the north. He startled and dropped the candy bar in the mud. He cursed and picked it up and shoved it into his pants pocket.

He looked behind him and saw the flashes of rifles and machine guns through the jungle. The shooting was sporadic at first but intensified. The .30 caliber Brownings opened up and he wondered if they were his units or Carver's.

He pushed himself to his knees and brought his M1 to a ready position. He saw the face of the nearest soldier light up with a muzzle flash. It was Private Duncan. He was turning toward the shooting. O'Connor called to him. "Keep watching the rear. You'll know if the Japs break through." O'Connor couldn't see him but heard him shift back to guarding the rear.

There was yelling and firing and the occasional detonation of what he thought must be grenades. *Japs are close enough for grenades.* He heard the mortar crew next to him start to assemble their pieces. He heard them thunk in the heavy base plate and attach the tube. He looked above and noticed the dawn was lightening the sky. He could see heavy branches above. *No way they can fire through that.* He turned his attention back to the rear. *They'll figure it out. I'm just a rifleman.* He could hear Bucholz yelling something, and realized he was urging the mortar crews to set up. The sergeant in charge yelled back and shut him up. O'Connor let out a long sigh and concentrated on the jungle.

The fire fight lasted seven minutes, but it seemed longer. Without looking behind, O'Connor thought it sounded like the Japs had bitten off more than they could chew. The firing of the bolt action Arisakas and their yells when they charged, stopped. He thought they must be killed or retreating. The dawn was coming. It would be light enough to see in another ten minutes. He wondered if they'd pursue the Japs and finish them off.

His train of thought was abruptly cut off when he saw movement coming through the jungle. He froze and focused. *Did I see that, or was it my imagination?* He saw it again. He brought his M1 to his shoulder.

Private Duncan saw him and whispered. "What? What's going on?"

O'Connor's stare and his steady aim, was all the answer Duncan needed. He pulled his M1 to his shoulder and sighted down the barrel. He still didn't see anything, but he'd learned to trust O'Connor's instincts.

O'Connor tracked the soldier sneaking through the jungle. He was covered in uprooted bushes and branches and blended well with his surroundings, but once O'Connor spotted him, he couldn't hide. O'Connor's heart rate increased and he licked his dry lips. The soldier was only twenty yards away, moving from cover to cover with skill. From the corner of his eye, O'Connor saw more movement, more soldiers. He kept his sights on the lead man. He'd let him get a few yards closer. He hoped the rest of his squad was on their toes, or it would be a quick, one-sided fight.

The Japanese soldier veered his way. He was fifteen yards away and coming straight for him. Through the dimly lit misty jungle, he looked like a bush that had come alive.

O'Connor put pressure on the trigger. The rifle bucked in his hand. He fired three rounds and saw the soldier's chest turn red and he dropped out of sight. He quickly shifted to the next man. He'd stopped at the sudden shot. It was the last mistake he made. O'Connor shot him in the belly and he went down screaming.

There was yelling from the line of Japanese and suddenly they were up and charging. O'Connor tracked the nearest soldier and sent a volley at him. He went down. O'Connor felt a bullet smack the ground beside him. He rolled to his right and came onto his elbows and found another target. The soldier was screaming and running headlong through the jungle. O'Connor fired the rest of his magazine into him and he finally came to rest only feet in front of him.

O'Connor rolled to his back and reached into his ammo pouch for another mag. He heard rippling fire coming from his squad. If they could hold off the first wave, it would be enough time for the rest of the platoon to shift positions and support them. If they didn't, they'd roll right over them and the heavy weapons units.

The Browning .30 caliber off to the right opened up and ripped a swath of death through the jungle. O'Connor reloaded and got onto one knee with his left foot forward. There were targets everywhere. He braced the carbine on his shoulder and fired three rounds into each charging soldier. They were yelling and weaving and firing, throwing off his aim, but he hit more than he missed.

He saw a group of three sprinting up the middle, straight at the mortar crew. He yelled a warning, but his voice was drowned out by the firing. He was sighting on the group, but they were getting too close to the line and he worried about hitting GIs. He pulled off and fired on another target behind the three men. His target dropped. He thought the mortar crew would be overrun, but at the last instant one of them rose up with his Thompson at his waist and hosed the three Japanese down. They toppled like bowling pins when the heavy slugs hit them.

More shapes to his immediate front caught his attention and he swung his rifle back. They were close, too close. He shot the nearest soldier and saw his surprised eyes as three rounds lanced through his chest and shoulder. He spun and dropped, clutching at his spurting chest. O'Connor leaped sideways just as the second man came bursting through the final cover. As he darted past him, O'Connor put the barrel on his neck and fired. Blood sprayed and the soldier went flat, like he'd been pinned by a giant's hand. The third soldier was behind him. O'Connor knew he was in trouble. He dropped to the ground as the soldier fired and the bullet grazed his helmet, ripping it off his head.

The searing pain startled him, but he had no time to dwell on it.

The Japanese soldier was chambering another round. From a sitting position O'Connor brought his carbine up and fired from the hip. He pulled the trigger as fast as he could and the bullets walked up the soldier's body.

O'Connor got to his feet. He saw dim shapes all around him, grappling and fighting hand to hand. Private Duncan was swinging his M1 Garand like a baseball bat. O'Connor saw him connect with the side of a Japanese soldier's head. He crumpled like a rag doll, his teeth little white specks spinning in the low light. There were two more.

O'Connor yelled and lunged to help the private, but another screaming soldier slammed into him and took him to the ground. The Japanese landed on him and he felt the wind get knocked from his lungs. He gasped for air as the Japanese rolled off him and sprang to his feet like a gymnast. O'Connor was on his back. He watched as the Japanese soldier brought his rifle up and the barrel centered on his chest. *This is it!* He waited for the bullet, but suddenly the soldier's head exploded in gore and O'Connor felt bits of his skull and brain smattering his face. The body dropped sideways, staying stiff as it fell. In its place a GI stepped forward and reached his hand out for him. He recognized the gruff voice. "You hit?"

He tried to speak, but he still couldn't catch his breath. He gasped, "C - C - Carver?"

Platoon Sergeant Carver grinned, but suddenly pulled his Thompson to his shoulder and fired off a quick burst. O'Connor could clearly see his old friend's face light up in the muzzle flash. His teeth were gritted and he looked like a devil, but it was the happiest sight O'Connor could remember seeing. Carver dropped his smoking barrel and looked down at him again. "Get your sorry ass into the fight, Corporal!"

O'Connor felt the breath return to his lungs and he pushed his aching body off the ground. His carbine laid in the mud beside him and he reached down and swapped out magazines. "I'm with you, Sergeant." He stepped beside Carver and brought his M1 to his shoulder. There were even more targets but they weren't as close. *Must be the second wave.* He dropped to a knee and fired methodically into the charging mass. More fire poured into the Japanese as more GIs moved to the rear, filling the gap. The .30 caliber to the right was still hammering away and he noticed it was having deadly affect. He yelled. "We need an MG over here."

Carver dropped beside him and between bursts said, "They're setting up now. Give 'em covering fire." More GIs sank beside them and added their rifles to the fight. The Japanese stopped charging and found cover. The volume of incoming fire increased and O'Connor and Carver dove to a downed palm tree. Carver held his helmet as bullets smacked into the tree and whizzed just inches over their heads. He touched his own head and pointed at O'Connor. "You're hit."

O'Connor touched his head and looked at his hand. It was sticky with blood. He remembered getting hit only minutes before, but it seemed like he was remembering it in a fog, like it happened years ago, to somebody else. He shook his head. "I'm fine."

Carver reached over and touched the wound. With his thick, gnarled fingers, he peeled the slit back and shook his head. "Looks deep."

O'Connor pulled away from the sudden pain. It cleared his head. "Dammit! That hurts!"

Carver just grinned. "Got any pineapples?" O'Connor felt his belt for a grenade but came up empty. He shook his head. Carver said, "I've got one." He yelled to the other soldiers cowering behind cover, trying to make themselves a part of the rotting jungle floor. "When the shooting stops they're gonna come at us hard. Get grenades ready."

He heard Lieutenant Swan yelling orders. "Get that MG up and running. They're coming!"

O'Connor felt like he was home again. He suddenly remembered Private Duncan. The last he saw he was taking on two Japs by himself. He looked to the spot. All he could see were twisted bodies.

The firing tapered and there was a shrill whistle from the jungle. "Here they come!" yelled Swan. O'Connor looked his way and saw the lieutenant helping the MG crew set up. He opened a can of ammunition and handed it to the loader. Geysers of dirt fountained beside him with near misses. He wanted to yell for him to get down but knew he wouldn't hear him and probably wouldn't listen if he did. A feeling of affection washed over him as he watched Swan. *He's turned into a leader.*

Beside him, Carver pushed himself onto his knees and reared back to throw the grenade. He yelled, "Grenade," as it left his hand. Other GIs rose up and tossed their own grenades. Carver dropped back down. He yelled, "There's a shit ton of 'em coming." Seconds later the grenades went off and as one, the GIs got to firing positions and opened up.

The MG on the right sent out lethal bursts as they found the range, mowing down soldiers as they sprinted. They were everywhere. When one was cut down another two took their place. The sound was deafening as the two platoons tore into the onslaught.

They were all veterans and despite the overwhelming force charging them, they didn't panic, but took careful aim, making each shot count. Despite the accurate fire, the Japanese were making progress. Carver's pin slammed on an empty chamber and he dropped down, yelling, "Reloading!"

Beside him O'Connor fired over and over. His barrel was red hot. "There's too many of 'em." He looked over at Lt. Swan. He was screaming into the radio, calling in close artillery support no doubt.

He slammed the radio handset down and O'Connor heard him yell. "I can't get through!"

O'Connor gulped. They were on their own. He fired until his magazine emptied. Carver was up and firing as O'Connor reloaded. The machine gun finally opened up, adding to the carnage. The gunner was holding the trigger down and swinging the barrel side to side.

Swan punched his shoulder and yelled, "Short bursts! You'll burn the barrel up!" He had to scream into the gunner's ear, but he finally nodded and took more careful aim and reduced his rate of fire to five to ten-round bursts.

The intensity of fire stalled as more and more GIs were forced to reload. The Machine gun on the right flank was cutting down Japanese soldiers at a steady pace, stalling the following soldier's advance. They stumbled and fell on their own dead and dying.

The Machine gun to the left suddenly stopped firing and O'Connor heard the loader scream. "We've got a jam!"

Lieutenant Swan yelled, "Get it fixed!" He rose up and fired his Thompson into three Japanese that suddenly burst from the close jungle.

O'Connor dropped a soldier only feet away. He poked Carver and yelled. "I'm moving to Swan, he needs help."

Carver didn't stop firing but grunted back. "Go!" he fired a three-round burst into the chest of an advancing soldier.

O'Connor rolled to his left staying behind cover. When he got to the end of the downed palm, he got to his feet and sprinted the last few yards. He felt the heat from near misses and dove to the ground. He slid into the side of Lt. Swan. Swan startled and started to swing his Thompson but saw who it was. "What the hell are you doing here?"

He rose up and fired and answered between shots. "Looks like you could use some help." The thick jungle was close here, but he could see shapes dashing toward them. He took careful aim and fired. When he was out, he dropped down and fished in his ammo pouch. "Only got two more mags." He glanced at the machine gun crew. The gunner had a metal rod jammed into the breach, trying to pry out the bent round. "Hurry up with that gun!"

Lieutenant Swan suddenly rose to his feet and screamed like a banshee. O'Connor saw his gritted teeth and the fire from his muzzle lit up his face, giving him a hellish look. O'Connor finished loading and rose up too. He was met with a Japanese soldier hurling himself at him. O'Connor had just enough time to move to the side and the soldier flew past. O'Connor followed him with his barrel and fired into his back. The first shot hit high on his shoulder, the second shot blew out his spine.

Swan fired from the hip and caught the nearest soldier in the gut, but not before he fired his submachine gun. Three bullets slammed into Swan's side and he spun backwards.

O'Connor saw him go down and yelled, "No!" He jumped out of cover and fired at the soldier who'd shot, then spun and fired into the seemingly endless mass of Japanese. He felt a bullet slice past his ear. The quick pain and the sight of Swan going down enraged him. He ran toward the enemy and fired until he was out of ammo. He didn't have time to reload.

A short, skinny soldier was running at him with death in his eyes. O'Connor lunged his barrel into his gut as hard as he could. The sickening pressure release as the barrel forced its way into the soldier's body made O'Connor drop the M1. The Japanese screamed and looked at him as if he'd cheated. O'Connor whipped out his K-bar knife and slashed down on the soldier's face. He cut his cheek to the bone and the Japanese fell to the ground clutching the wound.

O'Connor stepped over him and slashed at the next soldier who was running past, charging the MG nest. O'Connor's knife sliced into his shoulder as he passed and he howled but kept his forward momentum. Another Japanese was directly in front of him. He was bringing his rifle up to shoot O'Connor in the chest. O'Connor sprang and got inside the rifle's arc. He slammed the K-bar into the soldier's gut and twisted it back out. With his free hand he punched the soldier in the face and bits of tooth and gristle flew from his mouth. O'Connor felt his hand break, but there was no pain. He was in a fury.

Another soldier ran past him and he lunged but missed. O'Connor went down on his stomach and landed on the bloody back of a dead soldier. He rolled to his back in time to see a Japanese soldier lunging his bayonet toward him. There was no time to react. The blade came at him and he wondered what the cold metal would feel like. At the last instant there was a roar of fire and the Japanese soldier was simply no longer there. The only thing left was his rifle sticking out of O'Connor's side, pinning him to the dead soldier beneath him.

The pain lanced through his body and seemed to freeze his blood. He became light headed and tried to stay conscious, but the pain was wafting through him in waves and he struggled to keep the world in focus. He looked at the wound. The bayonet was stuck to the hilt. He thought it looked like some grotesque limb he'd suddenly grown. The world felt cold and his vision closed around him.

21

P latoon Sergeant Carver sat beside Corporal O'Connor's bedside like he'd done everyday for the past two weeks. O'Connor's condition had improved, but there were a few days early on when the doctors weren't sure if he'd survive. The bayonet had nicked his kidney and he'd almost bled to death. He'd been rushed back to Sibulan and stabilized. After a long surgery to stem the bleeding and repair the artery, he'd been shipped back to Cebu City which now had a more permanent field hospital.

Carver had sat with him as he suffered through infection and fever. He'd listened to his mumblings and rantings as he seemed to relive the entire war. His body burned with infection, but now seemed to be stabilizing. The doctors thought he should be waking up soon and Carver wanted to be the first person he saw.

It was 1 AM when Carver was jolted from an uneasy sleep by the words, "Where am I?"

Carver leaned forward and could see O'Connor's shining eyes in the darkness. The puckered slash along his scalp from the near miss was still visible. They'd shaved his head so they could stitch the wound shut, and the bald spot shone. He reached out and touched O'Connor's hand. O'Connor pulled back like he'd been hit with an electric shock. "Easy does it. It's me, Carver. You're safe in a hospital. Take it easy."

O'Connor went up on an elbow and winced at the pain. Carver pushed him back down. "Let me get the light." He reached back and flicked on the desk lamp. The soft glow made O'Connor blink and hold up his hand. "You've been out awhile."

O'Connor kept his eyes shut. "How long?"

"We pulled you out of the jungle two weeks ago. You've had surgery and had to fight a nasty infection, but the docs seem to think you're gonna make it."

O'Connor opened his eyes and stared at Carver. "Did. Did Swan make it? I remember him getting hit."

Carver dropped his gaze to the floor and shook his head. "There was nothing we could do. You broke the back of the attack with your crazy charge. The Japs fought like they always do, but you turned the tide. By the time we beat them back, Swan was already dead."

O'Connor shut his eyes hard. The line of his mouth a white slit. He muttered, "Dammit."

"The men took it hard. He was a fine officer. He fought the Japs off long enough to get the MG up and running again. That, along with your heroics made the difference."

O'Connor shook his head. "Heroics?" he rubbed his eyes remembering the confused look of the young Japanese soldier he'd thrust his rifle into. "It wasn't heroic."

Carver nodded. "I know. I know what it was. It was war." He looked at O'Connor. "I'm so sick of this fucking war," he growled.

O'Connor looked at his Platoon Sergeant and friend. "How's Lilly?"

The name seemed to snap Carver from his revelry. His eyes lit up at her name, but he shook his head and quickly stifled the feeling. "She's fine as far as I know. Haven't heard from her in a while. The mail hasn't been coming on a regular basis. Something to do with supply."

O'Connor winced as a shot of pain rode through his body. "If she's half as lovestruck as you are, I'm sure she's still interested."

Carver looked across the room and out the window to the green jungle. "Sometimes I think I should tell her to find someone else. Someone who's not liable to die in the next few months."

"That's bullshit. You both knew what you were getting into." Carver nodded and O'Connor adjusted his pillow. "Where they sending us next you think?"

Carver shook his head. "The Japs are finished in the Philippines. We're staying here on Cebu for the foreseeable future." O'Connor raised his eyebrow waiting for the other shoe to drop. Carver smiled. "Can't fool you." He looked O'Connor in the eye. "The 164th is slated to be the first wave on the shores of Japan. We're invading the home island."

O'Connor nodded his head. "I should be healed up just in time for that show." He looked across the room. There were GIs wrapped in white gauze, some with legs and arms suspended, healing broken bones. "That'll make everything we've done up to this point look like a damned picnic," he whispered. Carver nodded and O'Connor's gaze softened. "I'll do everything I can to be ready."

A MONTH LATER, O'Connor still felt sore, but he'd been out of the hospital for a week and was back on his feet. The doctor told him to take it easy, but O'Connor needed to get off his back. He needed to start getting strong. He had to be ready for the final invasion. He had to be ready to die beside the soldier's who'd been a part of his life for the past three years. He'd started with short walks around the base, then longer walks, then finally, jogs. He never ventured outside the compound. He didn't know why at first, but realized he was afraid of seeing things that would bring back memories of Celine.

A part of him desperately wanted to go find her grave, but that would mean finding the Filipinos who'd fought with her. He didn't want to reopen a wound which had so recently been scabbed over. He didn't want to relive losing her, so he stayed in the compound and slowly worked himself back to fighting shape.

He was sitting on the bunk when the doctor came in and sat beside him. O'Connor didn't much like doctors, but this one had saved his life so he cut him a break. "It's time for you to rejoin your unit, soldier." O'Connor nodded, and the doctor continued. "You've recovered remarkably well. Your tenacity to get better is a tribute to yourself and the Army."

O'Connor stood and saluted the Captain. The doctor saluted him back, then extended his hand. O'Connor took it and they shook. "In this job, I've put a lot of soldiers back together then sent them right back out to die. I wish I could send you home, but this coming push is too vital. They need every man."

O'Connor shook his head slightly. "I wouldn't allow it, sir." He grinned. "Even if you ordered it, I would've disobeyed and rejoined my unit." The doctor dropped his hand and gave him a questioning look. "I'm supposed to die over here. I've no doubt of that now. We're invading Japan. Every Jap kid, old man, woman and girl will have it in for us. You heard about the suicides on Iwo and Okinawa?" The Captain looked at his boots and nodded. "Killing themselves rather than being captured? They're out of their minds. Japan will be a blood bath. We're supposed to be the first wave. Hell, we probably won't make it off the beach."

The Captain stiffened. "That's not a great attitude, soldier."

O'Connor shrugged. "I'll fight. I always do, just not expecting to come out the other side in one piece."

THE NEWS TRAVELED through the compound like a wild-fire in the Santa Anna Winds. The war in Europe was over. The news caught up to Platoon Sergeant Carver while he was watching new recruits forming up for a morning session of physical training.

Raw recruits had been flowing onto Cebu for a month now, shoring up the GI losses from enemy fire, jungle disease and rot. The battle for Okinawa was still raging. The Japanese continued to fight for every inch of ground, despite being outnumbered, outgunned, and malnourished. Despite their tenacity, there was little doubt of the outcome.

He heard the news from an ecstatic new sergeant, named Hutchinson. "Did you hear the news, Platoon Sergeant? The war's over. May 7th's gonna be a day to remember."

For an instant Carver saw a glimmer of hope poke through his death shroud. "What're you talking about, Sergeant?"

"The Germans surrendered. The war in Europe's over. Hitler's dead."

The light extinguished. "The Japs didn't surrender."

Hutchinson's smile faded. "Well, no. But they'll have to now. I mean it's them against the world. They can't win."

Carver turned his back on the sergeant. "You've got a lot to learn about the Japs, Sergeant." He tried to protest, but Carver cut him off. "Get your squad on their feet." He pointed to the distant hill to the north. "You've got one hour to get your men to the top of that hill and back. You'll have to double time to make it."

The sergeant's color drained. "But shouldn't we celebrate our victory? Don't the men deserve a party or something?"

Carver clenched his jaw and looked at his watch. "Time's-a-wasting."

THE MEN of the Americal Division were training hard for the invasion. Cebu Island became a bustling hive of activity. GIs from other divisions were spread throughout the island. Tent cities were springing up, seemingly overnight.

The 164th Regiment was up to full strength and Carver was happy to have *Sergeant* O'Connor back. O'Connor's heroics on southeastern Negros had caught the attention of a general in the 40th Division. He'd inquired and found out about his recent transfer and demotion. He was appalled to find that a soldier who'd earned the Silver Star Medal on Guadalcanal would be treated so poorly. He immediately reinstated him to Sergeant and transferred him back to his long-time unit. A letter of reprimand was put into Captain Flannigan's file, forever nullifying his hope for higher rank.

With the war in Europe over, the focus was to defeat Japan. The attention of the entire world was focused on the Pacific Theater in a way never seen before. Suddenly they could have anything they wanted whenever they wanted it. They had new weapons, new uniforms, new boots, whatever they asked for, they got.

For the veterans, all the hubbub didn't mean much. They'd still have to assault the beaches and fight tooth and nail for every inch of Japanese soil. So, they trained hard.

O'Connor's wound ached most days, particularly during the mock assaults when he low crawled up the beach under mock enemy fire. The pain and the training helped to focus his mind, and for a while he didn't think about Major Celine Cruz. He still hadn't ventured from the American compound. He wanted to visit Celine's family or at the very least, visit her final resting place, but he couldn't find the courage to face it.

On August 6th, 1945 the first atomic bomb was dropped on Hiroshima Japan. Three days later, a second was dropped on Nagasaki. Both cities were wiped off the map along with hundreds of thousands of Japanese citizens.

For the men of the 164th, news filtered down that something big had happened, but there were no specifics and the training continued.

On August 15th, 1945 the 164th Regiment was formed up looking sharp in the morning heat. Platoon Sergeant Carver stood at attention along with the rest of the men. Captain Stark, alongside Colonel Mathieson called the men to attention and they snapped into tight formation with straight backs and rifles.

Colonel Mathieson stepped forward and bellowed. "Men. I have the honor to deliver to you the greatest news any commander of fighting men can deliver. Today, the Japanese have finally seen the light and have agreed to surrender." He stood staring at the men, who stared back. The only sound was the light breeze shifting the American flag hanging limp on the flagpole. The moment passed and the men stole glances sideways at each other. The colonel raised his voice. "The war's over!"

Like an inadequate levy holding back rising rain water, the first break was small, a low murmuring, then the floodwaters took over and the men, like the water were dancing and screaming. Sergeant Carver couldn't seem to process the information. He stood stock still. A passing private whose grin was ear to ear slapped him on the shoulder. The jolt, shook him from his revelry. His mind kept repeating the phrase he'd just heard, *the war's over, the war's over.*

He looked to Sergeant O'Connor who was staring at him from across the yard. Between them, men danced and backslapped. O'Connor smiled, his sideways hick smile and waded through the men, accepting handshakes and backslaps. He finally arrived beside Carver. O'Connor extended his hand and Carver stared at it for a moment then reached out and shook. No words came, but the look they shared was full of the hellish journey they'd traveled together from the very beginning.

Carver's eyes went dark and without having to tell his old friend what he was thinking, O'Connor knew. "Did you send the letter?" Carver gave an imperceptible nod. The pain in his eyes was obvious. "Send her another one."

Carver shook his head. "Can't believe the war's over. It's like a dream." He released O'Connor's hand and strode through the celebrating GIs. He found Colonel Mathieson and strode up to him. He was with a cluster of officers and they were laughing and back-slapping too. Carver noticed O'Connor following behind. Carver snapped to attention and saluted.

Colonel Mathieson finally noticed him and returned a half-hearted salute. "Congratulations, Platoon Sergeant. You made it!"

"So, it's true? The Japs really surrendered?"

Mathieson grinned and nodded. "Nothing's been signed yet, they're still working that stuff out, but they've issued a cease fire order to their commanders. Of course, it could be days before some get the word, but it's really happening. I expect they'll make it official in the next couple of weeks."

Carver nodded and turned back to O'Connor. "I'll be damned."

22

A week later, Carver sat on a wooden ammunition crate under the shade of a palm tree. Beside him was a stack of letters. He closed his eyes thinking of Lilly. He thought of her big hands holding the pencil that wrote the words, wishing he could feel their warmth. He thought of the hammock in the jungle they'd shared on those hot steamy nights as they explored each other's bodies. The passion and joy he'd felt seemed out of reach now.

The mail finally got through and he had a stack from her. He cherished each letter. He'd written her back and told her he'd understand if she wanted to find someone not living in a combat zone. He hadn't heard from her since. It had only been a couple of weeks and he knew the mail delivery system was spotty at best, but he couldn't help worrying that maybe she'd taken it to heart.

With the war over he should be the happiest man in the world. He should be celebrating like the others, getting drunk every night and dancing into the wee hours of the morning, but he couldn't shake the worry. The past four years had been filled with horror and loss. It was finally over and he felt worse than ever. His heart ached. He realized he needed Lilly like he needed oxygen.

The buzz of another C-47 transport plane made him look to the horizon. The transport traffic had slowed since the Japanese surrender, but there were still three or four flights a day bringing food and other necessities. Some carried passengers. He watched the dull green plane grow as it neared. He saw the undercarriage open and watched the wheels lock into place.

He thought about leaving his spot. He might get corralled into helping offload it if some asshole officer saw him loafing. He leaned back and decided to stay and watch it land. There were a few airfield personnel scattered about. They'd ignored the sullen Platoon Sergeant who always seemed to show up and sit under the palms at the side of the airstrip.

Carver watched the transport make a perfect, three-point landing. A puff of dust on the wheels and it was rolling toward the taxiway. It pivoted and taxied almost directly at him, then turned broadside. He thought he better leave, it looked like they'd offload the cargo to his spot. He held the stack of letters. He stood and carefully stuffed them into his pants pocket. He stretched his legs and wondered where he should go for the rest of the day. It was hot, perhaps a swim in the bay.

The C-47's engines shut down and the big props came to reluctant stops. The sounds of the wind through the palms returned. The side door opened and he saw silhouettes moving against the darkness. *Personnel.* The ladder extended and he watched as the first person, a man dressed in new green Army fatigues, walked on stiff legs to the second step then turned and extended a hand as if to help another passenger. *A woman,* he thought.

He watched as the figure stepped from the darkness and took the man's hand. She had to duck, but once she was on the first step she squinted, shielded her eyes and looked around.

Carver knew her instantly and he couldn't believe his eyes. *Lilly!* She wore a long Army issue skirt and had a lieutenant's hat sitting askew on her full head of lustrous brown hair. Without knowing what he was doing, he moved toward her, spellbound. He never took his eyes off her.

She didn't see him but finished walking down the steps with her hand in the other officer's. When she was on the ground she pulled her hand and the officer reluctantly released her.

When Carver was halfway to her, he panicked, *what am I doing?* He stopped but couldn't make himself look away. She was so beautiful, shimmering in the midday sun like an angel. She finally saw him standing there gawking and for an instant they both froze not knowing what to do. She put her hand to her mouth and ran to him. He was frozen in place. She extended her arms and threw herself into his arms. "Doug, oh Doug, it's really you."

He wrapped her up and lifted her off the ground. It felt like a dream he never wanted to wake from. "Lilly, oh Lilly. My God it's really you." He swung her around and she gripped him like her life depended on it.

He finally put her down and she pushed back and gripped his face between her hands. Streaks of tears moistened her cheeks and he wiped them away. He smelled her scent, her sweet smell and it intoxicated him. He suddenly remembered protocol and looked around for the other officer. He was walking away quickly. "Might've got you in trouble."

She flung her head back and her hat fell into the dirt. Her thick auburn hair cascaded over her shoulders. She smiled up at him. "I don't care about any of that. I love you Doug Carver!"

The words righted all the wrongs. The war, the killing, the loss, all vanished and was replaced with his soul overflowing with love for the woman in his arms. "I love you too, Lilly James."

Sam Santos sat alone in the early morning darkness of his inherited home. The ramshackle hut he'd grown up in always seemed bright and full of life, but now he saw it for what it was, dank and lonely. The normal smells of food percolating on the wood fired oven mixed with the scent of flowers which he could never find, was missing. He stared into the soft glow of the yellow flames and wondered where his sister was. He looked to the only room off the main living area. It was a dark cavern. He expected to see his sister's bright smile at any instant as she emerged with disheveled hair crossing her face and getting caught in her mouth. He sighed and felt his loneliness deepen.

There was a soft knock at the door. He realized he'd been hearing it for quite some time. He shook himself from his thoughts of better days and went to the door. He opened it slowly and saw a boy standing patiently. "Hello, Anthony."

Anthony smiled. He'd been a resistance fighter during the occupation. He'd fought alongside Sam despite his young age. Sam flashed on memories of Anthony firing his M1 rifle which seemed far too big and heavy for his frail frame. He'd been terrified to fight, but like many others, rose to the call when he was needed.

Seeing him now in his doorway, Sam realized how impossibly young he was. Sam was a teenager, but Anthony should still be playing in the dirt with wooden soldiers, not toting a rifle and playing for real. "It's time to go, Mr. Santos." His voice was that of a child.

Sam nodded. "I'm ready. Lead the way."

They walked through the streets. The morning light was brightening the town, promising another hot and humid day. As they neared the town's center more and more Filipinos joined them, until soon there was a parade of citizens. The feeling was somber as they trudged to the heart of the city. Sam greeted those he knew with nods and brief hellos. No one came too close, leaving him space as if he were somehow contagious. *It'll soon be over.*

The town's center had been cleaned up months before. The wide open space was now mostly filled with a large, new structure. Sam hadn't seen it yet. He stopped and looked up at the towering scaffolding. It was stoutly made with gleaming wood planks. He wondered how long it would stand. What would they use the wood for once it had served its purpose? *Will the wood be haunted?*

He moved through the crowd, people parting and looking down as he passed. He stood at the front, looking up at the structure. *Do I want to see this? No! But I must.* He scanned the crowd and saw Felipe staring back at him. He was standing at the base of the structure. Sam hadn't seen him since they'd come out of the jungle. Felipe hadn't spoken a word to him. Sam understood that he was disappointed in him, but now his gaze looked more sinister, as if he was staring at the enemy. Sam looked away.

The crowd got quiet when the Mayor of the city, Domingo Constantine walked up the stairs and stood on the platform and gazed out over them. He raised his hands as if to quell the applause that wasn't there. "Citizens of Cebu City. Today we bring to justice those found guilty of treason. These men have caused pain and suffering to their fellow Filipinos that is even more cruel than the Japanese occupiers themselves, because they were our friends and neighbors. Our brothers, fathers, cousins, uncles and grandparents. They chose to help the occupiers instead of standing with their own. When the darkness descended on our island, they chose to abandon us. They should not be pitied but hated. They deserve death."

Silence. If his speech was intended to rile the crowd, it had the opposite effect. There was a murmur and a rustle as the crowd parted off to the right, forming a corridor. Sam saw his brother, Berto leading the ragtag group. Their hands were tied behind their backs and they shuffled, dragging chains that gouged into their ankles. They got halfway through the line of citizens before the first obscenity was heard, followed by another and another, then someone lashed out with a thin strip of bamboo and whacked the side of Berto's arm. Berto flinched as bright blood seeped from the gash, but he kept his head down, shuffling faster. Soon there were rocks and rotten food flying. They were spit on and punched. When they finally made it to the base of the scaffolding they were covered in blood and dirt.

Sam marveled at the change in his brother. He'd been proud, the first to fight when he felt wronged, but now he stared at his feet, not able to lift a finger in his own defense. Sam imagined the prisoners hadn't been treated well since their capture.

Felipe marched the first five in the group, up the steps. Berto was first in line. He stopped at the far end of the scaffolding and stood beneath the rope that hung just above his head. Sam watched him intently, not knowing if he wanted him to look up or not. He felt conflicted. Part of him wanted to beat him until he was dead, the other wanted to forgive him and be a family again. The shivering, bleeding person about to be hung was all the family he had left.

Berto didn't look up until Felipe's assistant reached up and pulled the slack from the rope and wrapped the noose around his neck. His eyes scanned the crowd. Sam was frozen in place as he watched his brother searching the crowd. His eyes finally found Sam. Sam stared back.

The last time he saw him was in the jungle. Sam had a pistol then but chose not to kill his only brother. Now, months later, Berto looked emaciated and weak, but his eyes still burned. Sam straightened his back and forced himself not to look away. It was as if the crowd disappeared and only Sam and Berto were there, staring. Sam didn't know how long it lasted, it seemed like a life-time.

Finally, Berto looked away, back down to his feet. The mayor was on the pedestal talking about treachery and justice, but Sam didn't hear him. He was still staring at his brother. A part of him wanted to run up the ramp and free him, but he knew that was impossible. His brother was doomed to die by hanging and there was nothing he could do to stop it.

The mayor finally stopped speaking and the crowd went silent. When Felipe's assistant offered Berto the cover for his head, Berto shook his head. He brought his eyes up again and found Sam still staring. Berto's eyes softened. He seemed to plead forgiveness.

Sam grit his teeth. *Does he deserve forgiveness? He killed Lola and doomed Yelina to a fate worse than death.* But he was still his brother. Just before Felipe pulled the lever which opened the floor and sent Berto to his death, Sam softened his gaze and gave a slight nod. As Berto dropped, seemingly in slow motion, his eyes conveyed sorrow. Sam closed his eyes when the rope went tight and snapped Berto's neck. He quickly turned and left, not wanting to see his brother swinging, convulsing and shitting.

~

THE NEWS of Platoon Sergeant Carver's woman arriving made O'Connor happy for his old friend. He'd watched him the past few weeks slipping into a dark depression. He was glad to see him renewed. He wasn't an easy man to find, however. Carver and Lilly were inseparable. The only time he saw him without her was when she was on duty in the base hospital, or he had to attend to some piece of company business.

Seeing Carver's happiness deepened his own sense of loss. He could feel himself falling into a dark place. He tried to ignore the pain eating away at his insides. He tried to convince himself that what he had with Celine Cruz wasn't what he thought. After all, they'd only been together once, and as magical as that night had been, it wasn't the basis for a lifetime. He told himself all those things, yet he still couldn't erase her from his mind. He had to do something to break the hold she had on him.

He hadn't left the base since he was wounded for fear of seeing things and people that would remind him of her, but he decided it was time to face it. Perhaps the experience of standing over her grave would somehow help him get over his grief.

He left the compound in the morning before the brutal heat. He walked through the streets of Cebu City. There were few Filipino citizens around. He wondered why. The only evidence of the war, were the occasional bombed out building or passing Jeep or troop transport.

He wandered the streets for an hour, not talking to anyone. The streets remained strangely empty. He started to search for signs indicating a cemetery. He saw a lone Filipino walking down the center of the street, staring down as if deep in thought. O'Connor thought he looked familiar. He stopped and watched him. As he got closer, recognition dawned. "Sam? Sam, is that you?" The Filipino stopped and looked up at him. His eyes were red as if he'd been crying. O'Connor's face turned concerned. "What's wrong? What's happened?"

Sam shook his head. "Justice. I should be happy." He shook his head, "But he was my brother." He told O'Connor about the hanging.

O'Connor put his hand on his shoulder. "No one should be happy to watch their brother die. No matter what they did to deserve it."

Sam nodded and wiped his eyes. He studied O'Connor. "Where have you been? I've not seen you. I assumed you were killed or wounded."

"I was wounded." He pulled up his shirt and showed his puckered pink scar on his side. "I've stayed in the compound recovering. This is my first time venturing out. Lucky to bump into you." Sam nodded and smiled. O'Connor remembered that smile, it was good to see. "Say, I was wondering if you know anything about Celine ... I mean Major

Cruz." His voice cracked but he recovered. "I'd like to pay my respects. Maybe lay some flowers by her grave. It would mean a lot to me."

Sam looked confused. "Her grave?" He shook his head. "She's not dead. She's alive!" Emotions flooded his senses. Anger that Sam would tease him, then confusion, then a flash of fear, then hope. His face flushed deep red and he felt his fingers tingling. He couldn't find words. Sam's grin went even wider and he gripped O'Connor's arm. "Come on, I'll take you to her!"

O'Connor ran behind Sam as he wove through the city. They were nearly sprinting when they pulled up in front of a ramshackle building. They were both breathing hard. Sam spoke between gasps. "She's inside teaching."

O'Connor felt like he was outside his body as he strode to the doorway. He peered inside and saw it was a one room schoolhouse.

He stood in the door-frame willing his eyes to adjust to the low light. When he could finally see, he saw a group of Filipino children staring at him. Their tiny brown faces filled with wonder at the tall American. A book slammed on the ground from the front of the room, making O'Connor flinch. He focused on the diminutive form of the teacher who'd dropped the textbook. She stared at him as if she'd seen a ghost. A yelp escaped her lips, then she ran to him and leaped into his arms and their lips locked onto each other. The children started hooting and laughing, but O'Connor could only hear the rushing of blood coursing through his ears.

AFTERWORD

Thank you for reading the 164th Regiment Series. It's been a pleasure learning and writing about these valiant soldiers. They were one the first Army units to go on the offensive against the Japanese. Their heroism and truly astonishing ability to power through awful circumstances leaves me in awe.

The 164th series has come to a natural end but that doesn't mean the end to more gritty combat novels.

Join my WWII readers list to receive news on upcoming books and new releases. Signing up is free and you'll never be spammed.

Chrisglatte.com

ALSO BY CHRIS GLATTE

Tark's Ticks Series

Tark's Ticks

Tark's Ticks: Valor's Ghost

Tark's Ticks Gauntlet

Short Stories

Hellcat Down

Island Hop

Made in the USA
Monee, IL
17 July 2023

39224681R00138